Slope of

LOVE

The Remingtons, Book Four

Love in Bloom Series

Melissa Foster

ISBN-13: 978-0-9910468-7-4
ISBN-10: 0991046870

SLOPE OF LOVE

Cover Design: Natasha Brown

WORLD LITERARY PRESS
PRINTED IN THE UNITED STATES OF AMERICA

A Note to Readers

I have had so much fun writing the Love in Bloom series, and *Slope of Love* was no exception. Every once in a while, a character surprises me, and Rush Remington is one of those characters. His friendship with Jayla Stone made me long to be near my best friend. (Luckily, my best friend is always with me—I married him.) I hope you enjoy getting to know Rush and Jayla as much as I enjoyed writing their story.

Slope of Love is the fourth book of The Remingtons and the thirteenth book in the Love in Bloom series. While it may be read as a stand-alone novel, for even more enjoyment, you may want to read the rest of the Love in Bloom novels.

Melissa Foster

For Stephen and Sandra Foster

PRAISE FOR MELISSA FOSTER

"Contemporary romance at its hottest. Each Braden sibling left me craving the next. Sensual, sexy, and satisfying, the Braden series is a captivating blend of the dance between lust, love, and life."
—*Bestselling author Keri Nola, LMHC*
(on The Bradens)

"[LOVERS AT HEART] Foster's tale of stubborn yet persistent love takes us on a heartbreaking and soul-searing journey."
—*Reader's Favorite*

"Smart, uplifting, and beautifully layered. I couldn't put it down!"
—*National bestselling author Jane Porter*
(on SISTERS IN LOVE)

"Steamy love scenes, emotionally charged drama, and a family-driven story make this the perfect story for any romance reader."
—*Midwest Book Review (on SISTERS IN BLOOM)*

"HAVE NO SHAME is a powerful testimony to love and the progressive, logical evolution of social consciousness, with an outcome that readers will find engrossing, unexpected, and ultimately eye-opening."
—*Midwest Book Review*

Chapter One

THE MUSCLE ON the side of Rush Remington's jaw bunched as he glanced out the window at the snow that had been falling since the plane touched down in Colorado. Rush didn't need much to be happy—a snowy slope, a set of skis, a daily dose or two of protein powder, and a little time with his best friend. The ski team equipment had been shipped separately and had already arrived at the Colorado Ski Center, where he and a few other Olympic ski team members were teaching ski workshops this week. Rush pulled two duffel bags from beneath his seat. One was packed tight with protein powder, movies, and gummy bears—his best friend's go-to snack—the other stuffed to the hilt with his clothes.

He dug his vibrating cell phone from his pocket—another text from Jayla. He and Jayla Stone had been best friends for more than fifteen years, and this was supposed to be *their* week to hang out. He eyed the reporters waiting by the entrance of the lodge before stealing a look toward the back of the van, where Jayla sat beside Marcus White, pretending to rummage through her purse for something. Rush knew that she was really avoiding making eye contact with him because of Marcus. The only thing in that damn purse was a man's wallet—because *women's wallets are too bulky*—her keys, personal products (wrapped in tissues and hidden in a zippered pouch because *they're embarrassing*), and probably a few empty bags of gummy bears.

He read the text from Jayla. *Cute reporter. Blonde. Red coat.*

At six foot two, with a shock of dark brown hair, an ever-present tan, perfect teeth, and an insatiable appetite for exercise, the media—and women—loved Rush, but today he was in no mood to smile for the camera.

He laughed under his breath and shook his head. A year ago he'd have scoped out the hot blonde, scored by midnight, then forgotten her name by the next morning when he and Jayla met for breakfast. She'd have teased him about adding a notch to his belt or some other random shit, and then they'd have hit the slopes. A year ago he was a totally different guy.

He texted her back. *If she's not made of powder, I'm not interested. Just wanna ski.*

In a week, the competitive ski season would be over, and Rush could have all the women he wanted without worrying about them messing with his head and, in turn, screwing with his ability to win. But getting laid by some random woman wasn't anywhere on Rush's agenda. Rush had planned on revealing to Jayla that he finally realized he was truly, madly, and infuriatingly in love with her. Now his plan was shot to hell, and he had no interest in doing anything other than making it through the week and coming out on top of the North Face Competition, the last race of the season.

He didn't have to look at Jayla to know that her eyebrows were drawn together and she was reaching for that empty bag of gummy bears, hoping to find just one more to calm her nerves. Or to know that Marcus fucking White was eyeing every move she made.

Rush followed the other members of the ski team who had volunteered to teach the ski workshops off of the van. Cliff Bail and Patrick Staller looked like they had just walked out of *Skier* magazine with their strong physiques and dirty-blond, sun-streaked hair. They checked out the female reporters as they headed for the resort with Kia Lyle and Teri Martin on their heels. Rush hung back, hoping the reporters would get their fill of interviews with his teammates and give him a break. He inhaled the crisp, cold mountain air, kicked the blanket of fresh snow with the toe of his boot, and surveyed the grounds of the place that he'd call home for the next week. The majestic three-story stone and cedar lodge was set against the backdrop of snowcapped mountains. Curvy slopes carved wide white paths through the trees, snaking from the mountain peaks to the valleys below, and it took his breath away.

Reporters and cameramen were on him seconds later, shoving microphones in his face and snapping photos.

"Rush, do you have anything you'd like to say to

your fans?"

Rush answered the male reporter without breaking stride on his way into the lobby, with a serious look in his eyes and a practiced media-worthy smile. "I appreciate their support, and they can count on me to be ready for the next Olympics."

He wondered if they'd even caught his last words as Jayla stepped from the van and every camera turned in her direction. Since winning two Olympic gold medals, Jayla had been hounded by the press even more than he had. Nothing beat a hot female Olympic medalist. Having been friends with her for years, he was thrilled for her success, though he couldn't ignore the ego slap at being cast aside by the press. He didn't blame them really. Jayla was America's sweetheart, the new face of Dove, and the best damn role model young girls could ask for.

The Olympic ski team had been sponsored by leading ski manufacturers and clothing manufacturers. After winning his Olympic golds, Rush had secured several of his own sponsors, ranging from sunscreen manufacturers to energy drink manufacturers, and since winning her Olympic gold medal for the downhill event, Jayla had also received sponsorships from hair care and beauty product manufacturers.

"Dude, you a statue? Let's go." Marcus pushed past Rush, carrying a leather bag thrown over his shoulder.

America's sweetheart and the new girlfriend of this asshole.

"Three bags. Over there," Marcus snapped at the twenty-something bellboy who looked like he'd just come from a day at the beach, with his long sun-streaked bangs covering his eyes and tanned face.

Rush gritted his teeth to keep from giving him a two-fisted lesson in manners. *Asshole.* He and Marcus had trained together for the last three years. At the Olympics two years earlier, Marcus failed to qualify to compete in the medal rounds while Rush had gone on to become one of the few men to win Olympic medals in all five disciplines: gold in the slalom and giant slalom, and silver in the Super-G, downhill, and combined. Marcus had been a prick before Rush won, and he'd turned into a prick extraordinaire ever since. And for the last three weeks, he'd monopolized every second of Jayla's time—a harsh reminder that Rush had waited too long already, and he needed to tell Jayla how he felt about her before she and Marcus got in any deeper.

Rush watched him barge through the glass doors with his chin held high. He'd like to knock that pointy chin into tomorrow.

Marcus shouldn't even be there. He hadn't volunteered like Rush and a few of the other team members had to help his buddy Blake Carter's wife, Danica, teach a ski workshop for kids from her youth center, No Limitz. Community outreach was important for Rush's and his teammates' images, but Rush hadn't volunteered for that reason. Blake was his buddy, and he liked to promote the sport to youth. Hell, if it were up to Rush, he'd teach kids to ski the minute they could walk.

Rush held the door open as the volunteers from the women's ski team filed through, listening as Jayla tried to disengage from the press.

"Any messages for your fans?" The red-coated reporter shoved a microphone in her face.

Since winning her gold, Jayla had been all over television and radio commercials as well as print ads for Dove and a few of her other sponsors, and young girls from all over had emailed her in support, many thanking her for inspiring them. Jayla wasn't the type to get an inflated ego. Prior to Marcus consuming Jayla's personal life, Rush had been by her side when she personally answered many of those emails, and her genuine gratitude had reeled his heart in even more. Then again, gratitude and sincerity were integral parts of Jayla's sweet nature.

"Yes. I appreciate their support. I love hearing from them, and I hope to make them proud next weekend."

"Any plans for the next Olympics?" a different female reporter asked.

The next Olympics might be two years away, but Rush, Jayla, and the rest of the team practiced as if it were right around the corner.

"Train and win." Jayla slung a bag over her shoulder and waved as she walked away. A reporter hurried beside her, and Jayla slowed just long enough to say a gracious thank you before catching up to Rush.

"Thanks, Rush," she said as she came through the door.

Rush leaned in close and tried to mask the storm brewing in his gut. "Thought you were coming alone."

She narrowed her eyes. "So did I."

He'd seen her flinch when she lifted her bag, and

since she'd had two previous shoulder injuries, Rush did what he'd always done. He reached for her bag.

She glared at him. "I'm fine."

He held up his hands in surrender.

Most women were needy, clingy, and while Rush was all too happy to spend a few hours getting his groove on and pleasuring them, he wasn't the type to listen to bitching and moaning and to answer questions like, *Do these jeans make me look fat?* He'd learned this lesson early in life, when he'd answered honestly on more than one occasion. *No, the lard in that cake you just downed makes you look fat.* Jayla wasn't like most women. She was intense, competitive, strong. Those were just a few of the many qualities he loved about her. She was a freaking bulldog when she wanted to be, and she was also stubborn as a goddamn mule.

Rush tried to ignore the clutch in his chest as she flipped her long brown hair over her shoulder and flashed a smile at Marcus. He and Jayla had met at ski camp as teenagers, and they'd quickly become as close as two friends could be. He trusted Jayla with his dirtiest secrets, and he knew her deepest fears. He was surprised that after all these years she still put up with him and that he hadn't fucked up their friendship, especially now that he realized—or rather, *accepted*— what a womanizing douche he'd been for all those years, something he'd never tried to hide from her. He had his eldest brother, Jack, and a comment from Jayla to thank for that little eye-opening nugget of truth. Although they'd shared the details of their personal lives, they'd never judged each other, and for the first time ever, he was having a hard time keeping his mouth shut. In order to make it through this messed-up week, he pushed aside thoughts of Jayla and Marcus and focused on the upcoming North Face Competition, the last race of the season.

"Ow!"

Rush turned and caught a glimpse of Jayla rubbing her arm. He clenched his jaw and narrowed his eyes, locking a heated stare on Marcus. He could hardly believe she'd gone out with him once, much less that they were still together after three weeks. It made no sense at all. Marcus was a total controlling prick, and Jayla was...He wouldn't allow himself to think of the litany of qualities he loved about her or how long it had taken him to finally open his eyes and realize just how much he loved them.

Jayla was facing the opposite direction, and without walking over, he'd have no way of knowing if Marcus had hurt her or if she was bitching about breaking a nail. Then again, Jayla didn't give a shit about her nails. Never had.

Marcus slung his arm around Jayla's shoulder and turned away with a smirk. Rush didn't miss the way Jayla's body went rigid beneath his touch.

Not my problem.

Chapter Two

JAYLA RUBBED THE back of her arm where Marcus had squeezed too hard. He'd done that a lot lately. Squeezed too hard, demanded too much. Everything about Marcus was intense, from his brooding dark eyes to the way he stewed over every move he made on the slopes. Jayla had never met a man who stayed up nights mulling over what he could or should have done differently, down to the millisecond. It was that intensity that had first drawn her to him—and it was that intensity that had driven her to the decision to break up with him. Now she was seriously reconsidering her decision to volunteer this week. Marcus wasn't supposed to be there. He was supposedly *too busy to help a bunch of nobody kids.* In fact, volunteering had been Jayla's brilliant plan to decompress before her last competition. A few days without Marcus—and with Rush—would have allowed her to actually relax and would provide the space she needed to go through with the breakup and rehab her aching shoulder in private.

"Sometimes I don't realize my own strength," Marcus said in that sexy, apologetic voice that made her heart soften. Well, that and his insanely handsome face and rock-hard body, which made most women's brains turn to mush—as hers had in a moment of stupidity. She'd always been careful about the men she dated. They were in training when Marcus had asked her out, and she'd thought it would be a good distraction from her sore shoulder and the stress of competition. If she was honest with herself, she would admit that maybe...just maybe...she'd accepted the date to make Rush a little jealous, which was asinine at best.

He's only here to get me settled in. She glanced at his luggage, which sure looked like he planned on staying for the week. Her stomach clenched. She'd known she needed to end things with Marcus two weeks ago, but between training, competing, and Marcus's flash temper, she hadn't wanted to deal with the aftermath of the breakup. She was a queen at masking her emotions, but the pain in her shoulder was slowly testing that ability. She knew that what the doctor had told her after her last injury was true. They'd been able to rehab her through the first rotator cuff injury and the second shoulder injury, a small labral tear, but with two shoulder injuries in just under two years, another labral tear could mean her competitive skiing days were over.

She had bigger problems to deal with than breaking up with Marcus.

She glanced at Rush, hoping he hadn't heard them and that he hadn't seen her flinch at the twinge in her shoulder when she'd lifted her bag. He stood at the registration desk, his back to them. She'd never kept secrets from Rush, but after she'd seen his reaction to her first two injuries, she wasn't about to tell him about the latest one. She hadn't even told the coach. They'd both be on her case to see the doctor, which would probably mean being told—*officially*—that she could not compete. There was no way in hell she was going down that sorry path. In another week, Rush would be back to his womanizing ways and focusing on making up for this year's celibacy—which she found strange for him anyway. A quick bang with no strings attached had always been his way to ease the pressure of competition. But swearing off women completely during competition? That was *not* typical Rush Remington style. In another week she would have three months to spend rehabbing her shoulder in peace...and counting down the days until she saw him again.

Rush turned, and his electric-blue eyes caught on hers. Her breath hitched, and her pulse sped up at the jolt of attraction that she'd always felt toward him but knew better than to act on. God, she hated the way her body reacted to him. *That's what I get for falling in love at thirteen with a guy who runs from commitment like the word itself carries leprosy.* The right side of his lips cocked into a sexy half smile before he turned his attention to Teri and Kia.

"Look at Teri and Kia," Marcus said with a snort, shaking his head. "They're like fan girls when Rush is around."

Her chest tightened. Marcus was always dissing

Rush, and though Rush was a player, he had never purposefully hurt Jayla, which was more than she could say for Marcus.

She watched Rush lean against the wall, and although his back was to her, she knew his eyes were at half-mast in a casual, I-know-you-want-me gaze. *Ugh!* She had all of Rush's looks memorized. Not that she was proud of that fact, or would ever admit it to anyone except herself.

"Earth to Jayla." Marcus waved his hand at her. "Eyes on *him* again?"

She'd fantasized about being one of the women who shared Rush's bed, what it might feel like to have his big hands on her body, his chest pressed against hers, and then—thankfully—sanity would find her again. The last thing she needed was to be a notch in Rush Remington's belt and risk ruining their friendship. Being his friend was safer, easier. She got the best parts of him.

Well, almost...

She shifted her gaze to Marcus and exhaled. Why was it that when it came to Marcus she was a wallflower and when it came to everyone else in her life she was anything but?

"No."

"Let's hope not. I'll go get you checked in," Marcus said and headed for the registration desk.

She watched Marcus lean on the registration desk and pictured his eyes wandering over the attractive blond receptionist's perky breasts. The blonde smiled and fiddled with her necklace. She was sure Marcus thought she didn't know about his wandering eye or the way he flirted with anyone in a skirt. Or jeans. Or snow pants. She turned away just as Rush, Teri, and Kia disappeared out the back door that led to the private cabins they'd booked. A spear of jealousy shot through her. She'd give just about anything to be with them.

Her cell phone vibrated in her pocket and she read the text as Marcus crossed the lobby toward her. Her heart stilled when she saw Rush's name on the screen and quickly read the text. *Sneak out later? Like camp?*

She laughed beneath her breath and texted back. *Can't.*

She'd been *can'ting* for weeks because of Marcus. She should have taken her sister Jennifer's advice and dumped him right away—or she should have called her other sister, Mia, and had her force her to do it. *Hindsight might be twenty-twenty, but it feels like shit.*

"Okay, you're all set." Marcus held up a key.

She reached for it, and he flicked his wrist, burying the key in his palm. She had to end this—upcoming race or not—before she kneed him in the groin and told him exactly what she thought of his controlling ways.

She sighed, thinking about Marcus and Rush—and Rush's revolving bedroom door. She'd gone out with Marcus looking for something more. A real relationship, and maybe even to finally try to get past her feelings for Rush. She was starting to believe that her girlfriends were right. Maybe she should consider doing what they did. A few free drinks, a night of pleasure, and never look back. That's the last thing she wanted to do. *Maybe all men really are assholes.* She felt her heart squeeze. *Even Rush Remington.*

CAN'T. RUSH WAS so sick of Jayla saying or texting *can't* that he could puke. He flopped onto the king-sized bed in his luxurious cabin and crossed his hands behind his head. Blake Carter's cousin, Treat Braden, owned the resort, and true to his reputation, it was nicer than most of the resorts Rush had stayed in recent months. The spacious cabin had cathedral ceilings with exposed wooden beams in the living room, kitchen, and the bedroom suite. The living room had a propane fireplace, oversized sofa, comfortable reading chair, and a big-screen television. He let his mind drift to Jayla. He wondered if she was calculating how much practice time she could fit in, as they used to do in her pre-Marcus days, or if she was thinking of him.

His chest clenched at the situation. Goddamn, sweet, funny Jayla with her beautiful brown eyes, long brown hair, and those kissable, cupid lips. The thought of her lips touching Marcus's made his gut twist. He and Jayla were securely entrenched in the friend zone. Until about a year ago, when something his brother Jack had said and one of Jayla's comments about his revolving bedroom door had finally opened his eyes, he'd thought that was right where they belonged. He was wrong. Damn wrong.

His muscles tensed as he thought of her and Marcus. He sprang from the bed. That was one bit of trouble he didn't need to get involved in. He grabbed his parka and headed out the door.

Kia and Teri were on their way up to the resort.

Kia's thick red hair fell in loose waves past her shoulders, while Teri wore her dark hair up in a ponytail. They made no secret of wanting a piece of Rush—singularly or together—but beyond the fact that Rush wasn't physically attracted to either of them, he'd never believed in dipping his ski in the team snow.

Until he realized he was in love with Jayla.

"Hey, Rush," they said in unison.

"Going up to the meeting?" Kia asked as she chewed on a piece of gum like a cow.

"Looks that way." He heard yelling coming from one of the cabins.

"*Ugh!* Marcus and Jayla," Teri said as they all turned in the direction of the shouting.

He stopped cold. He could count on one hand how many times he'd heard Jayla raise her voice over the past fifteen years, and one of the five times was currently taking place.

"That guy's such an ass," Teri added. "I have no idea why she's with him."

"She won't be for long. She's just waiting out the competition. She's a better person than me. I'd have broken up with him right when I realized he was a jerk. But you know Jayla. Nothing comes between her and winning. Anyway, she'll break up with him right after the race Saturday. That way she won't be dealing with a jerk *and* a breakup." Kia shook her head.

"You think?" Rush ran his hand through his hair, trying to ignore the urge to head straight down to Jayla's cabin and wring Marcus's neck.

"I know," Kia said.

Good. Maybe that's what she was doing now. He pulled out his phone and texted Jayla—*Need me?*—as they headed into the lodge for the meeting with the coach and the Carters.

The conference room was lined with windows on two sides, with a spectacular view of the slopes. He and the others settled into the fancy leather chairs that surrounded a large glass table. With mahogany trim around the windows and doors and oak floors with mahogany inlaid in diamond design, the room reeked of class.

Patrick sat down beside him. "Dude, how about those cabins? Pretty nice, huh?" He was tall, muscular, and loved women too much. He was always getting into trouble by sleeping with some local guy's girlfriend in the towns where they competed. Rush liked him despite his bed hopping ways—maybe even because of it. At least initially, until Rush realized his own views had changed. Patrick was a guy's guy, a straight shooter, and the first to admit his weakness to women.

"Awesome," Rush said.

"You see the babe at the front desk?" Patrick pulled off his knit cap, and his short black hair stood on end.

"Didn't notice." It was bullshit, but thinking of the receptionist brought his mind back to Jayla and the cry of pain he'd heard in the lobby. Now he wondered where the hell she was. She was usually early for meetings. Not that he should care. She was all wrapped up in Marcus. Let him worry about her. *Yeah, like that's gonna happen.* He cared. He cared a whole hell of a lot. If that asshole hurt her...He had no idea how she could or would ever let that happen. *She wouldn't.* He took momentary comfort in that fact, reminding himself again that Jayla wasn't his. He had no business stepping into her relationship. She was a twenty-eight-year-old woman with more balls than most guys he knew. She could handle this.

Patrick whistled. "Damn. She was stacked."

Rush caught sight of Jayla outside the door talking to Marcus in a harsh whisper. When Marcus's hand reached for her, she flinched and took a step backward.

Well, fuck me. Rush rose to his feet as Marcus stepped closer to Jayla. In the next breath, Jayla turned, her eyes locked on the floor as she came into the room with Coach Cunningham and Chad, the assistant coach, right behind her. Rush sent Marcus a threatening stare before sitting back down, as if every muscle in his body hadn't been corded tight as a jaguar ready to attack.

Jayla sat across the table from Rush, between Kia and Teri. Kia and Teri leaned in close, whispering to Jayla, and goddamn if her eyes weren't damp.

Not my problem. He called bullshit on himself again. Jayla would always be his...*problem.* He pulled out his cell to make sure he hadn't missed a message from Jayla. *Guess she didn't need me after all.*

"Listen up." Coach Sean Cunningham was the strictest, most cutthroat coach in competitive skiing. Even pushing sixty, he was six feet of barrel-chested bulk, with more brown than gray hair, a thick neck, and even thicker arms. Chad stood off to the side. He was short, stocky, and although he tried to keep a rigid exterior to match Coach Cunningham's, his friendly brown eyes and boyish face betrayed his efforts.

Coach Cunningham took charge with a dead-serious, commanding tone. "You'll be teaching by day, training in the evenings, and although there's no curfew for this week of teaching"—he set his steady, slate-blue stare on Patrick, then moved it from one player to the next around the table—"you know the rules. You show up hungover, you can't practice, or I see *one* deficit, we go to curfew. Got it?"

"Yes, Coach," they answered in practiced unison.

He set his eyes on Jayla. Rush sat up straighter, his full attention on Jayla's lack of eye contact. She knew better than not to meet the coach's eyes, which could mean only one thing. Whatever was going on with Marcus had messed with her head too much for her to react. That was the danger zone. If Marcus messed with her head, he'd mess with her focus, and in turn, her ability to win her competition.

And that was why he couldn't ignore whatever the hell was going on with her.

"One deficit, and all hell breaks loose." The coach let the words hang in the air. All eyes slid to Jayla.

Deficit? Rush knew she would do anything to continue competing. Including covering up lingering pain. Athletes lived in a state of denial when it came to injuries. Coaches, too. They'd rather pretend that the best couldn't be stopped, and admitting otherwise weakened their faith in the team and their strength overall. Rush knew athletes were a strange breed— himself included. It wasn't going to change anytime soon. And after the way the coach was staring at Jayla's shoulder, he was sure she was covering up more than just a relationship gone sour.

After the tension in the room grew thick, which Rush was certain was Coach Cunningham's intent, the coach continued. "You have free rein today and tomorrow; then you're mine in the afternoons. Now, please give your full attention to Danica and Blake Carter. Danica coordinated these workshops. She runs No Limitz, the community center in Allure, the next town over, and Blake owns AcroSki, a local ski shop that's sponsoring the classes."

"Thanks so much, Coach Cunningham, and thanks to each of you for volunteering to teach," Danica began. Dark corkscrew curls sprang wildly in every direction, giving her thick mass of hair a windblown look, but Rush knew that was how she always looked. He'd met her husband, Blake, a few years earlier, when he was in town for a competition. He'd gone into Blake's ski shop and the two had talked for hours and had since become good friends, which was why when Blake told Rush about Danica's ski clinic, Rush presented it to the team.

Danica continued. "We've put these classes together as a way to try to give kids—teenagers in particular—something more to focus on than trouble. Not that these kids are troublemakers, but I think it's easier for teenagers to stay out of trouble if they have interests beyond the opposite sex." She paused and flashed a friendly smile. "We've got three classes scheduled for each of you every day. You'll be paired up. Two instructors per class, as I'm sure your coach has already mentioned, and I can't tell you how much we appreciate this. You'll be teaching kids between the ages of six and fifteen. They're beginners, and some of the teenagers are...well, teenagers." She shrugged. "We've all been there."

Blake was well over six feet tall with jet-black hair and friendly eyes. He picked up a piece of paper and added, "We've paired a male and female instructor for each course."

Patrick elbowed Rush. "Sorry, dude, but I'd much rather teach with a chick than you anyway. Maybe I'll get lucky."

Rush glanced at his female teammates. Kia and Teri would flirt with him the whole time, and that would drive him crazy, but if he worked with Jayla, he'd be sidetracked by his love for her and what a shit Marcus was to her, and that would drive him a different type of crazy.

"Rush, you'll be teaching with Jayla. Patrick, you're with Kia, and Cliff and Teri, you'll be teaching together." Blake gave them their schedules and thanked them again before ending the meeting.

Great. He eyed Jayla, who still hadn't lifted her eyes from her lap or texted him back. He had no idea how he'd navigate teaching with Jayla. There was no way he could keep his mouth shut about Marcus. It was hard enough to stop himself from climbing across the table and taking her into his arms.

Rush waited for the others to leave so he could talk to Blake and Danica alone.

"Rush, great to see you." Blake opened his arms to Rush. Rush's eldest brother, Jack, was engaged to

Blake's cousin, Savannah Braden. They'd soon be family.

"There's nothing hotter than two burly men hugging it out." Danica laughed as Rush disengaged from Blake and kissed her cheek.

"Look at you. You're not even showing yet."

"That's one of the great things about being tall." Danica patted her stomach. "Three months along isn't that far anyway. Thanks for bringing your team into this, Rush. We really appreciate it."

"Sure, no problem." He ran his hand through his hair, a nervous habit he'd had for as long as he could remember. "Listen, is there any flexibility in the teaching roster?"

Blake and Danica exchanged a look.

Blake patted Rush's shoulder. "Sorry, Rush. Your coach specifically asked that we put you with Jayla. I guess she's got a boyfriend issue, and he wanted her looked after."

"What the...? And that's my problem...why exactly?" He crossed his arms, his biceps flexing as he pondered the situation. "Sorry. This isn't your issue."

"Do you have a problem with Jayla?" Danica asked.

Rush knew that prior to opening No Limitz, Danica had been a therapist, and he was in no mood to be evaluated. "No. It's fine. Sorry I brought it up."

"Are you sure?" Danica asked. "Because if there's history between you two, we don't want to put either of you in an uncomfortable position that might compromise the efficacy of the program for the kids."

History? Rush was hoping for a future. *Yeah there's history, all right, but not the type you're talking about.*

I'd never treat Jayla the way I used to treat women. "No, it's nothing like that. It's fine. Really." He wasn't about to piss off the coach, and the more he thought about the coach's decision, the more concerned he became about Jayla, Marcus, and her focus when training. The women's coach wasn't there this week, and Coach Cunningham had taken over training for both groups. With only six of them, it wasn't a hardship, but their coach usually kept his nose out of their personal affairs—unless they impacted their performance in competitions. Rush knew that Jayla must have blown a practice or the coach saw something in her relationship with Marcus that he couldn't ignore.

"Well, at least it says something about what the coach thinks of you," Blake said. "But then again, we all know you're the best skier out there. Even if I can kick your ass in acroskiing."

"Yeah, well, some of us like to be fancy, and some of us just go for speed," Rush teased.

"Okay, boys, let's not beat our chests too loudly. Thanks again, Rush. So, we'll see you at eight tomorrow morning?" Danica reached for Blake's hand. "Honey, I'm just gonna run to the bathroom."

After Danica left the room, Blake narrowed his eyes at Rush. "Is there something between you and Jayla? Should I go up against your coach to change the teaching schedules?"

"No, man. We're cool. Thanks anyway." The more he thought about it, the more he realized that he didn't want Cliff or Patrick anywhere near Jayla. Even though he didn't have any real concerns about Cliff, he knew Patrick would try to take advantage of her vulnerability. Even thinking about Jayla and vulnerable in the same sentence blew his mind. The Jayla he knew was anything but vulnerable. But after seeing her this afternoon—really seeing her—he wondered what else he'd missed.

Chapter Three

NEED ME? WHAT does that even mean? Jayla had read the text two ways. First with a hopeful heart, which wished for an innuendo for something more, and then with her painfully accurate best-friend eyes. *Do you need me to come kick the shit out of Marcus?* She didn't need to be taken care of. Not by Rush. Especially not by Rush.

She paced the tile floor of the bright, well-appointed ladies' room. It was the only place she could go to think where Marcus wouldn't barge in. In just three weeks he'd snaked into every crevice of her life—and not in a good way. There was a time when she thought she wanted a guy who would fawn over her, but while Marcus started out as attentive, he quickly became controlling. And by the time she realized what had happened, she was knee deep in the last weeks of competition and couldn't afford the distraction of a breakup. But seeing Rush in the lobby had jolted her out of the competition stupor she'd fallen into, and with only one competition left, it was time to finally break things off with Marcus. She was ashamed that she'd let competing come before breaking up with a guy who didn't deserve one date with her, much less three weeks of them.

She'd tried to hold firm to her decision to end things with Marcus, and she'd broached the subject before the meeting, but he'd gone off on a tangent about her looking at Rush in the lobby, and she'd dropped it so she wouldn't be late for the meeting. The last thing she needed was to piss off the coach, too.

Her muscles were so tight that her shoulder pulsed with a dull ache. She wondered if her life could get any more complicated. She'd have to be on top of her game while working with Rush. One flinch and he'd pick up on it. She could only hope that he'd be too wrapped up in his own training and the teaching to take notice.

She dug Tylenol and Motrin from her pocket and popped them in her mouth, then cupped her hands beneath the sink and swallowed them with a handful of water. She stared in the mirror. Where was the woman she'd worked so hard to become? The proud woman who paid her own way through ski camps and training, proving herself and securing enough sponsors to train at the level she needed in order to try out for the Olympic team. She had bags under her eyes. The emptiness she felt showed in her skin, and if she was honest with herself, she heard it in her voice, too. *Face of Dove? Not even close.* During training and competitions, she and Rush usually trained all day and hung together in the evenings at least a few times each week. But Rush was a bone of contention between her and Marcus. And Rush had kept his distance the last three weeks. She didn't blame him, but she missed him to her core.

"Why did I ever accept a date with Marcus in the first place?" she said to her reflection. A toilet flushed and she covered her mouth. *Shit.* She'd been so troubled that she hadn't even thought to check the stalls.

Danica came out of the stall in the back of the bathroom and smiled as she walked to the sink to wash her hands. "I asked myself that question a few times before I found my husband."

Jayla forced a smile, though she really wanted to run out of the bathroom and hide her head in the snow.

Danica eyed her in the mirror as she dried her hands. "You're Jayla, right? You'll be teaching with Rush?"

"Mm-hm." She thought about the invisibility cloak she and Rush often joked about, and she wished she had one right about now.

"Well, not that you asked, but any man who makes you wonder why you are dating him isn't worth another thought." Danica looked Jayla up and down. "Especially for someone as pretty and talented as you are. I say, dump him if you're still with him, and if you're not..." She shrugged. "Get rid of the memory of him as fast as you can. Burn whatever reminds you of him and cleanse yourself of it." She looked at her watch. "Oh, Gosh. I gotta run." She opened the door, then turned back to Jayla. "Listen, if you ever want to talk, I'm a pretty good listener."

"Thanks." She watched the door close behind Danica. *Now she thinks I'm a loser, too.* She checked to see that the rest of the stalls were empty; then she turned back to the mirror, pointed at her reflection, and spoke with the decisiveness of her sister Mia.

"You're done with this shit. Pull up your big girl panties and lose the asshole." She flung the bathroom doors open and walked out—colliding directly into Rush. Her hands slid down his chest as she clawed for purchase to keep her balance. He caught her in his powerful arms as she keeled to the side and winced in pain before she could check her emotions and hide her reaction to the pain.

"Hey." It wasn't an accusation, it was more of a, *Hey, are you okay?* without the need for the last three words.

"Sorry. Sorry." She looked into the blue eyes she'd used to pull her through too many lonely nights.

"Are you okay? You were flying like someone was chasing you."

I was chasing myself. "I'm just...in a hurry."

"I texted you."

"Sorry. Coach had me sidetracked." It wasn't really a lie. "I'm good. Really."

He narrowed his eyes. "Is that how we're playing this?" He looked down at her hands, still clinging to his chest.

Oh God. What am I doing? She pulled her hands away. "Sorry. I...I gotta go."

His concerned eyes locked on her. "Jayla, take a deep breath. You're panting."

I can't remember how to breathe.

"It's me, remember? I know I haven't been around much lately, but...Are you okay?"

No. "Mm-hmm."

"Are you sure? Because I'm here. Right now, and I've got nowhere else to be if you want to go somewhere and talk." Rush was a foot taller than her, and when she didn't respond—*couldn't respond*—he bent down and leaned in close. A breath away. "I've kept my mouth shut, but damn it, Jay. That guy's like cancer. He's sucking the life right out of you. You're stronger than this. Smarter."

Her knees weakened, and she steeled herself against falling into his arms. "Nice of you to notice."

"What does that mean?"

I don't know, but it sounded tough. Rush had always believed in Jayla, and he'd looked out for her and really cared about her doing what was best for her, above and beyond anyone else's needs. Now all those reasons she loved him as a friend were trying to break her ability to keep her feelings for him hidden.

He searched her eyes, and she wanted to tell him she was going to dump Marcus. That had been exactly where she was headed when they'd collided, but something else was tugging at her nerves. Anger? Annoyance? Maybe. At herself. For being turned on by another man who would only hurt her in the long run.

"I don't need to be told what to do," she said in a harsher tone than she intended.

The muscle in his jaw jumped. "I never thought you did. But now? I'm worried about you."

She took a step back. "I can deal with this. I stay out of your love life. How about staying out of mine?"

The hurt that flashed in his eyes caused years of memories to pummel her heart. They'd been from opposite worlds when they'd met at the tender and confusing ages of thirteen and seventeen. She, from a family who couldn't afford ski camp, and he, from a family who could have bought every camp west of Kentucky. Rush was running from an overbearing father. Trying to blaze his own path, prove that he was worthy in his own right, even at seventeen. She'd dreamed about Rush summer after summer, counting down the days until winter break when she'd see him again. Emails and texts were great, but they could never replace seeing his eyes crinkle at the corners when he laughed, or the weight of his arm draped over her shoulder like they were joined at the hip, even though they'd never even shared a kiss and he'd never treated her as more than his best friend.

Rush ran his hand through his hair, drawing her attention back to the present. Her eyes sailed over the rough stubble on his cheeks, his broad shoulders and muscular chest. He wasn't just a guy anymore. He was a man, and she knew just what kind of man he was, making it easier for her to walk away.

RUSH COULDN'T GET the feel of Jayla's curves against him, or the look in her eyes, out of his head. She wasn't herself. The spark in her eyes was shadowed by worry, stress, and something he couldn't really read. Where the hell had his head been over the last few weeks? He crossed the cabin floor and sank into the couch. He'd been so focused on the upcoming competition and on telling Jayla how he felt about her that he hadn't paid enough attention to the whole Jayla-Marcus thing. He'd thought it was a fling. That she'd go on a date or two and then she'd be...What? His? Hell, he had no idea what he thought, or what he'd expected, but he hadn't expected Marcus to be there this weekend.

Maybe it really was none of his business. He felt so removed from her life right now that it bugged the shit out of him. And on top of it all, she was hiding an injury. He hadn't missed the way she'd gripped his shirt tighter with her left hand than her right. *Her goddamn shoulder.* They needed to talk like they used to. To spend a few hours just hashing out what was going on in his heart and in her head. It had been weeks since they'd stayed up late and strategized about training, or caught up on what was going on with their families. Hell, it had been weeks since they laughed or teased each other about stupid shit that they'd never allow anyone else to get away with. He missed Jayla, and he missed their friendship.

He was too frustrated to remain still. He needed to get out and ski. It was after ten, but he could still squeeze in an hour on the slopes if he hurried. He grabbed his coat and headed outside, stopping on the front porch to zip his parka. The cold air stung his cheeks, but it was the loud voices coming from Jayla's cabin that called his attention.

Walk away.

She's doesn't want my help.

His phone vibrated with a text and he pulled it out, hoping it was Jayla, and glad for any distraction, since his legs seemed unable to do what his mind told him to.

The text was from Patrick. *We're at the bar in the lodge. You coming?* He could use a drink...or five. Hell, he could use any reason not to get involved with Jayla and Marcus, but as his fingers hovered over the phone, his conscience took over. He cared too much about Jayla to walk away.

"Fuck." He sat down on one of the chairs on the porch and responded to the text. *Not tonight. Thanks anyway.*

Patrick's response came through a few minutes later. *Whatever. You're missing out. Tons of ski bunnies.*

Rush could make it through a complete training season without another ski bunny, but knowing that his coach was concerned enough about Jayla to make him work with her, and seeing that damn look in her eyes, there wasn't a chance in hell he'd make it through the next ten minutes without knowing she was okay. He pulled his ski hat down low and shoved his hands deep into his pockets, then debated what to do.

He didn't have much time to think. The door to Jayla's cabin flew open and Marcus stomped down the porch steps and headed toward the resort. Rush jumped to his feet and crossed the deep snow to Jayla's cabin, muscles flexed, eyes locked on Marcus as he faded into the dark. His heart hammered against his ribs as he climbed the steps to the porch and found the door ajar, the cabin dark. *Shit.* The last thing he wanted to do was embarrass her, but if that asshole hurt her...

"Jayla?" Anger and worry drove him through the door. "Jayla? It's me."

He scanned the small living room. Signs of Jayla were everywhere. Her coat and scarf were tossed on the back of a chair, her boots sat by the front door, and there was an open bottle of Hawaiian Punch on the counter. Another of Jayla's guilty pleasures. He went through the open bedroom door. Empty.

"Jay?" In three determined steps, he was staring at the empty bathroom. He spun around, and that's when he noticed the slightly open door on the far wall and Jayla sitting on the rear steps, her arms crossed over her legs, her head resting on them. He whipped the door open. "Jayla."

"What?" she snapped. She turned to face him with a serious scowl. Her brows were knitted together, and her lips were pressed tight. She was trembling beneath her sweatshirt and jeans.

Before he'd realized how much he loved Jayla, he wouldn't have hesitated to sit beside her and take her in his arms, but now Rush was momentarily taken aback. He wasn't adept at balancing feelings of love with feelings of friendship. Hell, he wasn't adept at balancing feelings of love in any regard. Jayla was the first and only woman he'd ever fallen in love with—and he didn't want to mess up their friendship or the chance at something more. "I...um...I heard you guys fighting and saw Marcus stomp off."

She turned away. "So?"

"So, I was worried that something happened to you." *And why are you being such a bitch?*

"Yeah? Well, I'm a big girl. I've been just fine for the past three weeks, haven't I?"

The anger in her voice stung, and he guessed he

deserved it. "Okay, then." He turned to leave, but couldn't take a single step away. Instead he joined her on the steps.

"What are you doing?" She moved over, and he could tell by her determined shift that it was not to make space *for* him, but to create space between them.

That stung more than her anger.

"Sitting." He should leave. Get up and go meet Patrick, or go back to his cabin and watch a movie. He should do anything other than sit near his friend who had no idea how much he loved her. She smelled so damn good that he moved another inch away from her, to keep himself from reaching out when she clearly didn't want him to. This earned him a narrow-eyed stare from Jayla.

"You think I'm a loser for being with him for so long."

"I...? Hey, I'm here, aren't I?" Rush had thought he'd experienced Jayla's entire range of moods over the years, and he probably had. But now, with her emotions so raw and his heart aching to make her better, it all felt new. Venomous. Personal.

"And I'm supposed to be what? Impressed by that?" She looked away.

It should have been easy for him to reach for her, but while his heart drove his arm toward her, his mind hesitated, causing his reach to seem tethered and awkward. Jayla leaned away.

"Really?" He held his palms up in question.

She glared.

"What is wrong with you? I didn't yell at you. Marcus did."

Her jaw was set so tight he thought her teeth would crack.

"You should never have been with him in the first place. You deserve a man who will cherish you."

She narrowed her beautiful eyes. "Like you're a relationship expert? What do you know about cherishing women? You treat them like they're disposable. Use, forget, replace, repeat."

The truth of her words cut him to his core. He leaned his elbows on his knees and buried a fist in his palm. "Shit, Jayla. You're right, and I'm sorry for who I was, but I never treated you that way, and it just about killed me today to see that look in your eyes."

Jayla pushed to her feet and glanced down at him with a defeated look in her eyes he didn't recognize. "Yeah? Well, don't feel bad for me. I'm just fine."

She walked inside the cabin, leaving him there to feel like a complete ass.

And a little like a stranger.

Which he hated more than feeling like an ass.

Chapter Four

JAYLA AWOKE WITH a roaring headache and deep, searing pain in her shoulder. She'd spent half the night worrying that Marcus would come back and the other half of the night fading in and out of sleep and thinking about Rush. It didn't help that she'd somehow ended up sleeping on her right side. Marcus's bags were still on the floor, which meant he'd be back at some point. She felt nauseous thinking about how angry Marcus had gotten, and the nausea was chased by self-loathing for being stupid enough to think she could ever have not been distracted by his incessant jealousy over Rush and his controlling behavior. She knew she was a fool for even going out with someone who didn't like Rush. Rush was part of her life. He was her best friend—*and I love him*. She'd allowed Marcus to come between them, and she hated herself for it. As ashamed as she'd felt for ignoring his aggressiveness and the rest of the nightmare that was Marcus White for the past two weeks, she'd drawn a firm line with both him and in her own mind, and she already felt stronger, despite the headache and the pain in her shoulder.

She'd listened for Rush to leave last night, and she must have fallen asleep, because she couldn't remember hearing a sound. *Goddamn Rush.* Last night she'd wanted to climb into his arms and tell him how much of an idiot she'd been not to draw the line sooner with Marcus, just like she would have done any other time. But last night, the way Rush had looked at her felt different. She'd tried to write it off as wishful thinking in her fantasy-filled mind. She'd even tried to write it off as a look of pity, but Jayla knew the difference between pity and desire, and the realization shocked her. Then embarrassed her—and then it pissed her off, because how could he risk their friendship with a look like that after she managed to resist looking at him in that way for so long? He'd never looked at her like that before, and as badly as she wanted Rush to notice her as more than his best friend, with all she was going through, this was not the time for him to start. If only she had an Off button for her girlie parts. She didn't trust herself. It was dangerous to lean on him now and easier to be angry with him.

The season was coming to a close, and soon their conversations would move from competition and training to the latest woman Rush was dating. He'd ask about the guys she was dating—which half the time she'd made up because her life was so boring in comparison. And they'd joke about his revolving bedmates.

Same stuff, different year.

Women loved Rush. Even his name was cool. Jayla had always hoped that somewhere in the flourish of their success, he'd eventually see her the way she saw him, and he'd change his womanizing ways once and for all. *For me. For us.* But she'd been wrong. And she realized that even though they never stuck their two cents into each other's dating lives, she'd sort of expected him to step in with Marcus—and it was that change in her thinking that made her worry about how she was seeing him. He was her best friend, not her sentry.

After she showered and dressed, she did a set of the shoulder rehab exercises she'd gotten from her physical therapist after her last injury; then she stood in the kitchen drinking coffee and devising a plan to rid herself of Marcus and all the weak-girl crap she'd fallen into. She'd have Marcus's bags mailed back to him and then she'd text him and tell him not to bother coming back. A knock at the door sent a shock of worry through her.

Marcus.

She didn't want to argue anymore. She hated arguing with anyone, and with Marcus it was a total waste of her time. She was done with him.

She set down the coffee mug and stared at the door. *Shit.*

Another knock drew a loud, frustrated exhalation. She threw a thermal shirt over her T-shirt and grabbed her coat, shoved her feet into her boots, and headed out the back door. If it was Marcus, she was not going to be trapped inside arguing with him. At least outside she could walk away. She heard three more loud knocks as she rounded the side of the cabin and peered onto the porch.

Rush stood in his heavy boots, one hand on his hip. He ran his hands through his hair with an adorable, slightly worried furrowing of his brow. He was too damn easy to like with his Levi's hugging his perfect ass and at least two days' growth on that handsome face of his. Jesus, she'd been such a bitch to him the night before, and here he was again. Typical Rush. Her crush exploded into some sort of lust and made her heart go a little crazy. She was usually so good at keeping her feelings for him contained. *What is wrong with me?* Rush was the one man she shouldn't be lusting over.

Like she was right now.

She closed her eyes and fisted her hands, willing herself to stop thinking of him like that. *He's my best friend, and I love our friendship. I need our friendship. And I need a womanizing boyfriend like I need another shoulder injury.* Besides, she was swearing off men. She'd thought about it all morning, and if Rush could swear off women during this competition season, she could swear off men.

Maybe forever.

She opened her eyes, and Rush was still there, standing on her porch, all hot and adorable, and—*Stop it!*

He lifted his hand to knock again and glanced in her direction. The left side of his mouth was doing that nervous twitchy thing.

"Hey. I just wanted to make sure you didn't have any trouble last night." He crossed the porch toward her. "I stuck around for an hour or so, but..."

Jayla took a step back. "You did? Well, aren't you chivalrous. I'm fine." *Oh God, get out of bitch mode.*

He stepped off the porch and sent her stomach fluttering.

"You sure? You look a little shaken up."

"I'm good."

"Okay. Want to grab some breakfast?" His thick navy parka brought out the blue in his eyes.

Stop thinking about his eyes, and stop being a nervous, crush-lusting ass.

"I'm good. Thanks." She needed to walk away. She'd managed to keep them in a friendship box for so long, and now, after everything that happened with Marcus, the armor she relied on to keep her feelings for Rush in check must have cracked. She was vulnerable—and he was hard to resist. He came closer. *Too close.* He placed his hand on her shoulder and she stiffened as a pain sliced through beneath his hand.

His eyes were filled with concern. "Listen, I'm sorry for whatever you went through with Marcus. If you want me to kick his ass, it'd be my pleasure."

The smell of his minty breath coalesced with his aftershave and brought back a rush of memories: *lying beneath the stars in the snow, shivering so hard their lips turned blue, both refusing to get up before the other. Holding hands as they skied without poles. Tumbling on top of him when she sneezed and made them both lose their footing.* She could still feel the ache of wanting him to kiss her as if she were thrown back in time. Even then she knew that wanting more would mean risking his friendship, and Rush had always been the one person she could count on over the weeks of training. Her family supported her love of skiing, but Rush *got* it. He understood her drive, the passion it took to succeed, and the desire to be the best. He also understood her. When she was sad, or mad, or happy, or just plain needed to be silly. He *got* her better than anyone ever had. *Or maybe ever would. Shit. Stop it.*

She took a few steps toward the back door, felt his hand fall away—and wished he would put it back. "That's okay. I've got to...Um. I'll see you on the slopes." She disappeared around the rear of the cabin and threw her back against the wall, breathing hard with her eyes clenched shut. *What was I thinking?* If she was strong enough to end things with Marcus, surely she could continue to keep her distance from Rush, as she'd managed to for so many years.

Maybe.

"What are you doing?"

Jayla froze. She opened one eye. "Um...hoping my invisibility cloak is working."

Rush laughed and leaned in close. "I'm not sure who you are, but I miss my best friend, and I wish you'd send her back. I'm not liking this bitchy, awkward version of her as much."

"She's..." *Mortified.* "A little confused right now."

His eyes widened a little. "About?"

"I don't know. She didn't return my texts when I asked." *Oh my God, I'm such a loser.*

He smirked. "Mine either." Rush leaned one hand on the wall beside her head. "Jesus, you smell good." The surprise in his voice mirrored the surprise in

Jayla's mind.

Since when do you notice how I smell?

He narrowed his eyes and drew back, putting space between them. "If you find her, tell her to snap out of it, and tell her I have these." He pulled a bag of gummy bears from his pocket.

Of course you do.

Chapter Five

THERE WERE A million reasons he shouldn't have gone back to her cabin earlier that morning, but by the time he'd gotten there, he'd known he had no choice. He *needed* to be there. He needed to make sure Jayla was really okay. Hearing her argue with Marcus had sent a bullet through his heart, and when she'd been angry with him and left him on the back porch, it was like an arrow had chased that bullet's path. But what he'd seen in her eyes that morning—the way she looked at him with wanting eyes, eyes he'd dreamed about for the last few months, looking up at him from beneath his naked body—he was pretty sure anger was the furthest thing from her mind. It confused the hell out of him. He'd wanted to see that look in her eyes for so long that it tore at his heart, but he knew she was in no place to hear what he so desperately wanted to reveal.

Now that Marcus was out of the picture, Rush shouldn't have any concerns about teaching with Jayla. She was a good instructor, and she was the only woman he could spend time with day in and day out and enjoy every minute of it. But as he watched her show a teenage boy how to hold the poles properly, smiling in a way that he hadn't seen her smile in weeks, he couldn't think of a single other place he would rather be. That alone was reason enough for him not to be there. Jayla didn't need his feelings confusing things as she got back on track—and he wasn't sure he could hold them in much longer. The moon-eyed boy followed every direction she gave, and when she tilted her head to the side just a little and touched his shoulder, he realized he was staring and tore his eyes away.

"You going to stand there, or are you going to teach?" They were the first words Jayla had said to him since they began the afternoon workshop. They were teaching a group of fifteen-year-olds and had already gone over balance, straight runs, and introduced them to the snowplow turn. The snowplow turn was also called a wedge, an elementary turn where the tips of the skis are closer than the tails. They'd practiced it until they were bored of it, and now the kids were ready for their first run down the bunny hill.

Rush hadn't realized he'd zoned out. "Is your group ready?"

She looked at the group and smiled. "We're more than ready."

This brought a round of cheers from the kids.

For the next hour, Rush and Jayla spent much of their time helping the students get off their butts and back on their skis. Suzie Baker, one of the students, had big blue eyes, straight blond hair, and was dressed for a ski fashion show in pink ski pants, with a matching jacket and hat. She wore thickly applied makeup, and she'd attached herself to Rush like Velcro. He tried to get Jayla's attention, hoping she might peel the girl from his side since Suzie had progressed from staring to licking her pouty teenage lips in a way no teenager should, but Jayla was doing everything within her power *not* to look at him, and it bugged the shit out of him.

He raked his eyes down the curve of Jayla's hips, remembering when she'd been a smart, funny, lanky teenager. They'd spent so many nights talking about everything and nothing at all, and he'd come to realize that all of the time they'd spent together over the years building trust and securing their friendship had been so much more. They'd been building a foundation as solid as the mountains they skied. Jayla had grown into a beautiful, confident woman, and over the last year, Rush had finally matured enough to recognize that foundation for what it was, and he'd mentally moved Jayla from the friend zone to the lovable, cherishable woman zone. Where she stood alone, for no other woman could ever measure up.

They taught three classes, and by the end of the afternoon, the sky was sheet white and threatening snow.

"That wasn't so bad, was it?" Rush stood beside Jayla, watching the kids join their parents.

She kept her eyes locked on the kids. "Nope."

"You have a knack for it."

She pulled off her hat and shook her hair free.

He felt a rush of heat pulse through him and turned away. As he'd changed and matured over the past year and come to realize just how much he loved Jayla and how much she meant to him, his body had begun reacting sexually to her, and sometimes, even with those loving feelings stirring around inside him, it *still* took him by surprise. He decided to put himself through a little test. Maybe the heat was from Suzie Baker's mom, who was checking him out, lagging behind instead of taking Suzie into the lodge. He purposely set his eyes on the tall blonde with legs that went on forever. In the past, a woman like that would have given him a jolt of competitive let's-see-if-I-can-bang-you lust.

Nope. Not a spark.

He slid his eyes to Jayla again with her no-thank-you attitude and tight ski pants, and his body went hot. The desire that heated his blood was unmistakably driven by Jayla, and this time, it didn't surprise him at all. Jayla wasn't just pretty; she was sweet and caring, smart and confident without being snotty or overbearing. She cared about others more than she cared about herself, and while Rush knew that Jayla could use all of those things to hook any man she wanted, he also knew that she respected herself enough not to. Rush had learned from her in that regard. As he watched her now, Rush knew beyond a shadow of a doubt that Jayla was the only woman he wanted. The only woman he'd ever want.

She glanced up, and their eyes caught.

He couldn't tear his away.

She did what he wasn't strong enough to. "Later,

gator." She stuck her pole in the ground to push forward.

"Wait. Wanna hit the slopes for a few hours?"

"I've got some things to take care of." She took off before he could respond.

In all the years he'd been competitively skiing, Rush hadn't been in a real relationship. A quick stress-relieving romp was enough for him, and because none of the women he'd slept with had meant anything to him, it was easy for Rush to separate the bedroom thoughts from his training grounds focus. Now, with Jayla, everything was different. It shouldn't bother him in the least that Jayla had other stuff to do.

But it did.

A lot.

He headed for the trail that wrapped around the mountain, hoping to ski the desire out of his body and the frustration from his mind.

JAYLA COULDN'T ESCAPE fast enough. It had been painful enough trying to ignore how sweet Rush had been with those kids for hours on end. He was patient and kind, and her mind had started to wander down a new and even more dangerous path. She wondered what Rush would be like as a father. Troublesome thoughts. And then there was Suzie practically throwing herself at him right there on the slopes.

Rush had that effect on nearly every female on the planet, but when Suzie's mother eyed him like he was there for the taking, all she could envision was a mother-daughter wrestling match. Not that he'd ever touch a teenage girl, but Jayla's mind wasn't exactly wrapped in sanity at the moment. It was drowning in lust, and she didn't do lust well. There was no way in hell she was going to be sucked into the sexual vortex that was Rush Remington. They were friends. She had to nip this shit in the bud before it ruined their friendship and drove her mad in the process.

She went down to her cabin to collect Marcus's bags and bring them up to the resort to have them mailed out when she noticed the cabin door was wide open. She stopped cold. Her pulse kicked up and she looked around to see if anyone else was around. She was alone. *Of course.*

She debated going back to the lounge or finding Rush and asking him to go with her to the cabin, but she'd slipped into weak-girl mode with Marcus and she'd be damned if she'd ever do that again. She took a deep breath and headed for the porch. Marcus stood in the middle of the living room with his bags over his shoulder and an angry look on his face.

"I came to get my shit." He wore the same clothes and irate scowl as the night before.

Jayla stood just inside the open door and shoved her hands in her pockets to keep him from seeing them tremble. "How'd you get in?"

He held up the key before tossing it onto the couch. He walked toward her and she stepped aside to let him pass, but he stopped beside her. It wasn't the look in his eyes that she noticed; it was the dark energy that he exuded, so different from Rush's positive, warm aura. *What the hell did I ever see in you?* It pissed her off just thinking about it. She clenched her teeth and took another step back.

"Look. I'm sorry for all the shit that happened. I shouldn't have yelled at you, and I shouldn't have grabbed your arm in the lobby. I'm just—"

"Save it, Marcus. I'm done with all of your excuses. I put the competition ahead of myself. I stayed with you way too long to avoid being distracted over a breakup while we were competing, and I'll never do that again." She clenched her teeth again, this time to keep them from chattering.

"Jayla—"

"Leave, Marcus." She held her breath as he walked out the door. *How could I ever have thought that you were a reasonable distraction from my feelings for Rush?*

He stopped before descending the porch steps and looked back over his shoulder, a deep V between his brows. "It's just as well. It was Rush you were after, not me."

She breathed fast and hard, biting back the retort that vied to fly from her tongue. *I have never been after Rush Remington!*

Okay, maybe she hadn't been *after* Rush, but clearly she had never gotten over the feelings she carried for him, and the way he looked at her made her wonder if he finally felt something, too.

An hour later, she was still a little shaken by her run-in with Marcus. She'd showered and just finished another round of shoulder exercises and popped a few Tylenol and Motrin—which was the equivalent of using Scotch tape to seal a gunshot wound—when she received a text from Rush.

Night ski?

She craved the comfort of her best friend. Surely, she could ignore whatever feelings had been creeping forward. Of course she could. They'd lived a lifetime without even so much as a kiss. Why was she wigging out now? She thought of Rush showing up last night and realized that maybe she was *too* comfortable around him. Was there such a thing? She'd never thought so, but now she worried that she might chew him out again for no reason—or jump his bones.

She chose the safe route and texted back, *Tired, but thanks anyway.*

An hour and a half later, there were three hard knocks on the door. She froze, then remembered that Rush had knocked the same way earlier that morning. She pulled the door open a little, peeked out, and found Rush fumbling with a stack of DVDs, microwave popcorn, and his big, stupid slippers.

"You're supposed to be skiing," she said.

"I did. I've gone three weeks without my best friend." He pushed past her and set everything down on the counter. "Probably my fault, but you know." He shrugged.

"Tunnel vision during competition. Yeah. I know."

"Now that Marcus is gone, the tunnel has widened." He made himself at home, opened the cabinets, fished out two wineglasses, and set them on the counter.

"You know why you've never had a long-term girlfriend?" She leaned on the counter and fiddled with his keys. He still used the little ski keychain she'd given him about a hundred years ago. For the first time in weeks, she felt like she was back on solid ground.

"Because I never wanted one?" He arched a brow.

"No. Because you won't get rid of those stupid slippers, and you drink water from wineglasses. Real women like to be wined and dined."

"Maybe real women do, but best friends don't need me to pretend. Besides, if I were tied up with some needy woman, I wouldn't be able to come over and watch you wallow in your Marcus-less life. I figured you needed a little rehab."

Worried he was talking about her shoulder, she said hopefully, "Movie rehab?"

"What have you always told me?" He shrugged off his coat and hung it on the back of a chair.

"That your ego is too big?" She flipped through the DVDs and held up one of them. "*Eyes Wide Shut?* Really?" She rolled her eyes.

"I packed a bunch of movies since this was supposed to be our week to hang out. Thanks for getting rid of you know who."

"Don't even bring up that ass."

He shrugged. "Fine by me. I didn't know what mood you'd be in, so I made sure to bring your favorite and your most hated movie. And..." He put the popcorn in the microwave, then pulled two enormous bags of gummy bears from his coat pocket.

Jayla reached for the candy. "You really are the best." *And I've been such a bitch and avoiding you. How could I ever avoid you? Why did I? Ugh. I'm such an idiot. I can't even think straight.*

Rush held the bag out of reach. "You women are all alike. You only want me for my candy."

You couldn't be farther from the truth. "I have a feeling the candy I want you for and the candy your ski hos wants you for are very different." She moved in close and placed her thumb to the ticklish spot just inside his jeans pocket—the one that she'd learned about when they were kids and he'd tackled her in a tickle fight—then she squeezed.

"Hey." His arm came down and she snagged the bag.

And just like that they'd fallen back into their comfort zone. That was one of the things Jayla loved most about their friendship—it was never more than a breath away. She suppressed the butterflies in her stomach and smoothed the kink in her crush-lust armor, settling it right back into place.

"Works every time." Jayla glanced in the living room and realized she'd left the red rubber therapy band she used for her shoulder exercises on the doorknob to the bedroom. With the bag of candy in her fist, she grabbed the band, tossed it onto the bed, and closed the door.

Rush opened two bottles of Vitamin Water and poured them into the wineglasses. "What do you always say to me at the beginning of training season?"

"Please keep it to yourself." She grabbed a glass and stuck *Spaceballs* into the DVD player.

"What? It's great advice. There'll always be another one right around the corner."

He held her gaze and her heart squeezed. She'd completely misread him. He must not have been feeling anything more for her if he was suggesting that she date other guys. She flopped on the couch and tried to act like her hope hadn't deflated.

"That's great advice for a guy who thinks sex is like fine wine and he should taste as much as he can. It's not good advice for a girl who has just sworn off men forever."

Rush slipped his feet into his fuzzy, quilted slippers, which made him look like he was wearing two rabbits on his big feet. He carried the popcorn over and sat beside her. Rush put his arm around Jayla, and she tucked her feet up beneath her.

"Forever, huh?"

She cuddled in beside him as she'd done so many times before. Natural. Easy. Comfortable. Her pulse sped up a little despite the armor she'd slipped back into, and she took a deep breath. *Friends. We're friends. That's good enough. It has to be.*

"Maybe."

"I hear if you don't use certain body parts, they fall off." He tickled her ribs with the tease.

She laced her fingers with his as the movie started. She'd missed their friendship these last few weeks. She'd missed *them*. She'd missed him. "That's only for guys. Besides, who says I won't use them? I'm just swearing off men."

"They say batteries are a girl's best friend."

"I'm beginning to think that whoever *they* are, they just might be right."

Rush pulled a blanket from the back of the couch and tucked it around her legs. "You might be right. We can be assholes."

"Yeah, you can. But you did bring my favorite movie, and you get a free asshole pass for that."

He held his phone up in front of them. "Smile."

"Rush..." She covered her face. They had taken hundreds of random photos over the years, and in most of them Jayla was in some sort of disarray and Rush was beaming like a fool. He'd initiated the idea of an album, and he'd carried the idea forward throughout the years more than she had. She wondered now, as she was pressed against his body, if the album could possibly mean as much to him as it did to her—despite her discomfort of being the focus of photographs.

"Come on. Good times, bad times, you know how this goes, and you know I'll take it anyway. We'll add it to our album. Please?"

She stuck out her tongue and he clicked the picture.

As she soaked up the comfort of his friendship, she knew she had been right all those years to keep her feelings for him silent. She couldn't risk their friendship by trying to be something more with the one person who not only understood her as a person, but really got her passion for skiing, her drive and determination, the one person who helped her push herself to be more than she ever knew she could. She trusted Rush in a way that she didn't even trust her family, who she knew loved her and who supported her on a different level. They were there for her like a safety net. They'd catch her when she fell. Whereas Rush would never wait until she fell. He would become her legs, her strength, her skis, the very legs she stood upon. He'd hold her, breathe for her, find her balance for her, and when she made it down the mountain safely, he'd haul her right back up to the top of the mountain and push her to do it again—all by herself.

Because he knew she could.

Even if she didn't have to.

Chapter Six

RUSH WOKE UP at four in the morning after he and Jayla had watched *Spaceballs*, *Star Wars*, and finally *Tomb Raider*, because Rush knew that Jayla would rather die than watch a sappy movie where the female lead was too weak to take care of herself. He straightened up the living room and went to the bedroom to grab a heavier blanket for her. Even though she'd been there only a few hours, the bedroom was already Jaylaized. Three pairs of ski pants hung over the closet door, two pairs of boots and a pair of sneakers lay on the closet floor, and a picture of her family was displayed proudly on the dresser.

He picked up the photograph and smiled. She came from a large family, just like he did, and he'd met them many times. Her younger brother Jared looked up to her, and her older siblings looked out for her. *Sort of.* They weren't as close as Rush's family, getting together as often or trying to make it to most events as a group, but they loved one another, and if Jayla ever really needed them, they'd step up to the plate. But Jayla was too independent to need that kind of support, so Jace, Mia, and Jennifer lived their busy lives and kept in touch through emails, occasional phone calls, and holiday gatherings. Occasionally, one or two of them would make it to one of her competitions, and Rush had always felt a twinge of sadness for Jayla when his entire family would show up to support him. She never seemed to mind. His family had known her for so long that they treated her like she was one of them.

Rush glanced at the photo again, remembering a few times when Jayla had mentioned Jace being overprotective, but that seemed to ease after she was out of high school. His eyes lingered on Jen. Jen was a lot like the person Rush used to be. She liked men, and she liked sex. Rush had never seen anything wrong with that, but now the idea of Jen having any influence on Jayla took on a whole new feel, and he had to work hard at pushing the jealousy away.

He set the frame back on the dresser and moved toward the bed, hoping that he was mistaken about what he saw. He picked up the long rubber therapy band and gritted his teeth. "Damn it, Jayla." He set it on the nightstand and grabbed the blanket from the bed.

Forty minutes later, he sat on the edge of the bed in his own cabin with his head in his hands. He'd showered and changed, had a protein shake, and couldn't stop thinking about the Thera-Band. He'd seen Jayla flinch when she'd lifted that damn bag. He'd hoped he was wrong and that the coach had been more worried about her focus than an injury, but the band could mean only one thing—that the injury was bad enough for her to *need* to hide it. He headed up to the gym in the resort with a sinking feeling in the pit of his stomach. It didn't make him feel any better that when he'd tested the waters by mentioning other guys were waiting *around the corner,* she gave no indication of the interest in him he thought he'd picked up on earlier.

He and Jayla, like most professional athletes, lived with the fear of incurring an injury bad enough to end their career. Snow was their blood, and competing was their oxygen. How many times had they played out the what-ifs together? *What if you could never ski again? What if you could never compete again?* What happened to ex-athletes?

The gym was empty, which was a good thing, because Rush wasn't in the mood to talk. After stretching, he worked his biceps, pumping the heaviest weights he could, fighting against Jayla's answers to their what-ifs. He didn't want to let them in, and he was powerless to stop them. *It wouldn't matter. I'd die from withdrawals.* He knew it went deeper than the innate need to ski. Washed-up skiers didn't get big advertising contracts like other ex-professional athletes did. At least he had a degree he could fall back on, though he couldn't even imagine ever needing to. Jayla hadn't gone to college. She worked two jobs in the summers and poured all of her money into her skiing career, hiring the right coaches, buying the right gear, training at the best camps. Her parents supported her efforts, but they didn't have the financial means to fund her or her siblings' educations. He knew Jayla was good with finances, and she probably saved almost every penny her sponsors had paid. He also knew that when skiing was all a person had ever wanted to do, going without could feel like a catastrophic free fall. If that happened to Jayla, he'd make damn sure that he was there to catch her.

He moved to the leg press and loaded up the weights, competing against the worries racing through his mind. What if Jayla lost her ability to compete? How would she handle it? What would happen when America no longer saw her as the strong, talented, smart, beautiful woman he knew she would always be, regardless of if she was a competitive skier or not, and started to see her as a washed-up Olympic champion going through an identity crisis? Because life as she knew it would change if she couldn't compete. And that scared the hell out of him, which meant it probably petrified her.

Which is exactly why you're keeping your injury from me.

Chapter Seven

THEY WERE HALFWAY through the third class of the day when Jayla noticed Coach Cunningham standing by the lift watching her. She ran through her motions for the past ten minutes and couldn't remember flinching or rubbing her shoulder. No, she was sure she hadn't, despite the intermittent twinges of pain. She'd been so focused on the kids that she'd been able to almost ignore the ache. She tried to distract herself from the coach's scrutiny and cast her eyes away from where he stood, catching a glimpse of Rush talking to Suzie Baker's mother. *Not exactly the distraction I'd been hoping for.* Kelly Baker had been vying for his attention all morning with stupid questions that could have waited until the class was over.

Rush glanced over and rolled his eyes. Even though it stung knowing that he'd probably take the woman's phone number, she loved that she and Rush could make light of the way women chased him. The sharing of those intimacies that were usually reserved for same-gender friends reiterated their trust in each other. She loved that they didn't hide things from each other, or pretend they were something they weren't. *Except my injury, but that's different.* She took a second to convince herself of that and then pushed it aside and went back to the scene between Rush and the blonde unfolding before her. Soon he'd lean on his ski pole with a seductive look in his eyes and turn back to the class, but not before lingering on the blonde's eyes just long enough that the woman's pulse would kick up—and Jayla's heart would ache.

Why do I do this to myself?

She couldn't help but watch a minute longer. Rush's eyes now darted away from the blonde, like he was looking for an escape. Jayla's pulse kicked up at the thought, though she was sure it was just him playing hard to get or some other type of ploy.

He walked away and didn't look back. In fact, Ms. Baker was staring after him with an angry look on her face. Rush locked eyes with Jayla and gave a curt nod before flashing the crooked smile that knocked her world off center.

At the end of class, they headed back into the lodge to warm up. Built of cedar and stone, with a round stone fireplace in the center of the room, the lodge had high ceilings, two full walls of windows, a full bar, and a host of tables in various sizes. It felt cozy despite its large size. Jayla grabbed a table while Rush ordered their food. He came back with two steaming bowls of soup, baguettes, and bottled water.

"Thanks." She pulled off her gloves and set them on the empty chair beside her as Rush took his coat off.

"What'd you think of the classes?" He took off his hat, and his short hair tousled into a sexy state of bedhead.

Jayla reached across the table and patted his hair into submission.

"That bad, huh?"

"Someone has to make you presentable or those MILFs won't be after you anymore." She ate her soup, trying to ignore the nagging twinge of jealousy.

"You know I have no interest." He leaned back and stretched his arms over his head.

Jayla couldn't help but notice how his biceps strained the sleeves of his shirt. Unfortunately, neither could about ten other women in the restaurant.

"Until after next week," she challenged.

"I don't think so." He held her gaze.

His response caught her off guard. What was this new restraint all about?

"All of a sudden you're picky about your conquests?" She looked around at a woman who was still staring at Rush and sighed.

"Maybe I'm done seeking conquests."

Right. And maybe I'm not holding on to my career by a very thin thread.

"You up to the trail that wraps around the mountain?" Rush ate his soup with his eyes trained on her, even with the other woman practically salivating over him at the next table.

This focus on her was new, and it made her a little nervous. "I think I'll wait for our team practice." She dropped her eyes to escape his narrowing gaze. "Thanks for coming over last night."

He nodded. "It was fun. Besides, I love to listen to you snore. Wanna hit the gym?"

"I don't snore. You already went to the gym this morning. I saw you when you went back to your cabin."

"You snore like a chain saw, but it's kinda cute." He crossed his arms, and his eyes shifted to her shoulder.

She dropped her spoon into her soup with a *clank!* "What?"

Rush shrugged. "No skiing? No gym? You tell me." He picked up his empty bowl and walked it over to the trash.

Apparently, you already know.

"I'm going to head out to the slopes."

"Rush." *Why do you always make me face everything?* "Sit."

He did, right beside her.

"It's not what you think." *It's worse.*

"Tell me what I think, Jayla, because I can only think of one reason you'd ever keep a secret from me." He crossed his arms and pinned her to her seat with a dark stare.

"Oh, please. I have lots of secrets." *One. One secret. My injury. Does that count? And my crazy crush on you. Okay, two secrets. That's considered lots in my book.*

His crooked smile nearly slayed her right there in the lodge. She imagined herself sliding bonelessly from her seat to the floor and the EMTs hovering above her. *It's that damn crooked smile. It does it every time.*

"Okay, maybe I don't, but damn it, don't assume

you know everything about me, because you don't."

"Maybe you're right. But I do know that my friend Jayla, the one I know hates when guys call her Jay-Jay and who loves flannel sleeping pants more than lingerie, wouldn't keep something as big, or as little, as an injury from me. So either the therapy band I saw was a precaution, or you're an imposter."

"*Pfft.*" She tossed her napkin on the table. "It's nothing."

"Is that your opinion or the doc's?"

She rolled her eyes and looked away.

Rush moved closer to her, and she turned the other way. Other than her crush—which she could only hope she'd been successful at hiding from him— she'd never been very good at keeping secrets from him, and right then, she hated him for it. A bolt of worry seared through her. *What if he's known how I feel about him all along and he's just pretended not to notice? Oh God. Please just kill me now.* She fought against the thought. No way could he have ignored that and still remained as close to her as he had.

"Even when you look away, I see you worrying," he said quietly.

"I'm not worrying. I'm annoyed that you're pushing me so hard over nothing." *I can handle this.*

"Well, can I judge nothing for myself?" He ran his hand through his hair. "Did you tell Marcus what this *nothing* is?"

She thought she heard a hint of jealousy. "Why would you even ask that? Do you think I'd tell Marcus anything I didn't tell you?"

"I've never shared your bed."

That doesn't mean I never wanted you to. "Is that jealousy I hear?"

He lowered his voice. "Is that evasion I hear?"

She was breathing so hard she couldn't concentrate.

He draped his arm over the back of her chair, and she closed her eyes for a second, wanting to lean in to him and tell him everything, but that would mean admitting it to herself, and she was sure there was a chance that the docs were wrong. Maybe another shoulder injury really wouldn't mean the end of her career. That's the hope she was hanging on to as if her life depended on it.

"What's going on, Jayla?"

"Nothing. I'm just doing exercises to keep my shoulders strong." She kept her eyes trained on the table.

Rush cupped her cheek and drew her eyes to his. "Promise?"

No. How could she look into his trusting eyes and lie? He was the one person who had always been there for her and put her needs above even his own. And why the hell was her heart beating so damn fast? *Think "friend," think "friend." What is happening to me that I can't get a grip on myself?* She took a deep breath and tried to calm her racing heart, hoping he didn't notice.

He leaned forward and whispered, "I know about you and your battery-operated friend. I think I can handle the truth about an injury."

Her entire body shuddered. "Keep..." *Oh my God, why does that turn me on?* "Keep my...*friend*...out of your mind. I don't bring up your secret pleasure."

Rush sat back and cocked his head. "My secret pleasure? Nothing about my pleasures are secret. I tell you everything."

She whispered, "Oh, so other women have walked in and found you beating off to pictures of Victoria's Secret models?"

"Jesus." He looked around, assumedly to see if anyone heard her. "I was nineteen years old."

She shrugged. The distraction worked like a charm.

"Besides, I seem to remember that it didn't send you running from the room."

"I...it..." *Shit.* He was right. In the space of a second she'd realized what he was doing, and in the next second she'd been intrigued. It wasn't until the third second hit that she realized she'd been standing there two seconds too long and had left his room.

He flashed a mischievous crooked smile, obviously pleased with himself.

"I gotta go back to my cabin and take care of a few things." She pushed to her feet.

"I bet you do."

Chapter Eight

JAYLA STOOD BEFORE the mirror and stepped on one end of the Thera-Band and held the other end in her right hand. She raised her arm slowly, gritting her teeth against the pain.

"*Never shared my bed*. Of course you didn't share my bed," she said to her reflection in the mirror.

She lowered her arm and repeated the motion again.

"You never wanted to share my bed."

She wrinkled her brow. "Did you?"

"Oh my God. Could I have missed that?"

She dropped the band and took a step closer to the mirror.

"Are you that stupid?" She sighed. "No. You're not that stupid, and he's a big player. No. No. No way."

She sat on the floor with her legs out straight and wrapped the band around the balls of her feet, then drew the ends toward her with her elbows parallel to the floor, thinking about Rush's biceps. *Stop it*. She winced through her reps and thought about what he'd said about her *battery-operated friend*, which sent a little thrill through her. She should have lied about *that* two years ago when they were punchy after staying up until four in the morning and played a silly game of Truth or Dare. How many times had she used the damn thing while thinking about Rush? A tingle of arousal had her releasing the band.

She'd used it too many times to count after thinking of nothing *but* nineteen-year-old Rush, lying on his bed, his muscular body still wet from a shower, his big hand wrapped around his even bigger erection, and a magazine open with half-naked Victoria's Secret models on display. She hadn't thought twice about walking into his room without knocking, and once she'd seen him in such a compromising position, forcing herself to knock in the future took a concerted effort.

She sank into a warm bath, imagining what might have happened if she hadn't left his room that night. She'd replayed the scene a million times since that day so long ago, and her fantasies always ended the same way. Now she closed her eyes and slid her hand down her hip and between her legs, remembering how he looked back then, when she'd walked in on him. She could retrieve the memory so easily, see him so clearly—his thick thighs, tense hills of perfectly sculpted muscles, and his rippled abs expanding upward to his broad chest and shoulders, droplets of water from his shower still clinging to his skin. Before he'd caught sight of her, his head had been bowed, his eyes slits of desire beneath the fringe of his hair, his jaw clenched. His arm moved swiftly, expertly. The muscles in his biceps and forearm jumped with his efforts, and his formidable erection primed, craving release. A sigh escaped her lips as she sank a little deeper into the water, her fingers slick and warm inside her as she brought herself to the edge, struggling to hold herself on the verge of release, until she could no longer take the tingling in her limbs, the tightening of her inner muscles, and the longing for the man she'd never have. With one final tease, she came apart. Rush's name slipped from her lips, and an ache for him squeezed her heart.

She was drying off when her phone vibrated with a text from Kia. *We're going into town to a place called Fingers. Wanna go?*

Fingers? Heat flushed her cheeks. She texted back. *Bar? Restaurant? When?*

Still warm from her thoughts of Rush, she pulled on a pair of skinny jeans and a sheer camisole, then dried her hair. Kia's response came through a few minutes later. *Both, with dancing. In twenty mins. Come with?*

It sure as hell sounded better than sitting around in her cabin trying not to think about Rush. *Oh crap. Rush.* She texted back. *Who's going?*

A minute later she had her answer. *Me, Teri, and Patrick. The other losers are going to a bonfire the resort is having.*

The resort was having a bonfire? Now she was faced with a real dilemma. There wasn't much Jayla enjoyed more than dancing or a bonfire. How could she possibly choose?

She went to the kitchen and reviewed the resort

events flyer that had been on the counter when she'd first arrived. She'd been so wrapped up with Marcus and her injury that she hadn't had a chance to look it over yet. Two nights of bonfires. Perfect, she could go tomorrow night. She texted Kia back. *Sure. How are we getting there?*

Kia texted back. *We'll come get you. Rented SUV.*

There was a knock at her door five minutes later. She pulled it open with a laugh. "That was fas—"

Rush stood before her wearing a charcoal-gray cable-knit sweater and a pair of faded jeans. He wore a baseball cap, and as he adjusted it, his aftershave wafted toward her in the night breeze and she drank it in.

"Hey."

"H-hey."

His eyes dropped and lingered below her neck. He nodded at her chest with that sexy crooked grin of his and slid his eyes away. "Um..."

She looked down, having completely forgotten that she hadn't finished dressing and had on a sheer camisole and no bra—and very aroused nipples.

"Oh God." She crossed her arms over her chest and spun around, searching for a shirt. In the kitchen or living room. *Great.* She grabbed her parka. "Sorry." She turned back to him, zipped up to her chin.

The right side of his lips lifted, and a little laugh escaped. "Hey, I'm not complaining." He drew his brows together at her ensemble.

She looked down at her parka and felt herself blush again.

"I'm going to head over to the bonfire in a little

while. I was just wondering if you wanted to go."

Yes. Definitely. It took her a minute to remember she'd not only sworn off men, but she'd just had a great orgasm thinking of this particular hunky man. *Very bad idea.* "I...um. I just told Kia I'd go into town with them. Do you want to go?" The words left her lips before she had time to consider them.

"They asked me earlier, too. Actually, I think I'll hang out here for a while. Have fun, though." He descended the stairs, then turned back. "You might want to actually wear a shirt."

She closed the door and leaned against it, breathing like she'd just run up a flight of stairs and wishing she could run back outside and go with him to the bonfire. Something between them had definitely shifted. She reminded herself that the warm, friendly Rush whom she trusted with her secrets was also a womanizer—and because of that, he was not boyfriend material. *No. No, no, no.*

THERE MUST HAVE been fifty people at the bonfire. Families with small children roasted marshmallows, groups of teenagers huddled together—like Rush and Jayla used to at ski camp—and couples snuggled on nearby benches. The threat of snow had passed with only an hour of flurries, leaving a light gray sky and the crisp smell of winter. The pine trees were dusted with snow and decorated with colorful lights, giving the evening a magical feel.

Rush tugged his baseball cap down low. A poor excuse for a disguise, but hey, it had worked so far. He gave a wide berth to the others. After being blown off by Jayla, he just wanted an evening to wallow in his messed-up thoughts. He had always felt most comfortable on the slopes. There was no replacement for the combination of speed and icy air against his face, or the adrenaline rush that came with it. As a boy, the slopes provided an escape from his four-star-general father's scrutiny and the stress of school. For a few blessed minutes, there was only him and the mountain. And over the years, that comfort included having Jayla by his side. Now, as he walked around the bonfire, he longed for her company.

A young couple strolled by hand in hand and paused to kiss a few feet away. His mind moved to Jayla. Her comment about his conquests nagged at him—and pissed him off. He needed to tell her how he'd changed, and damn it, he needed to tell her why he'd changed. Rush remembered with pinpoint accuracy the moment the painful truth had come from his eldest brother Jack's mouth. It was shortly after Jack's wife, Linda, had died in a car accident. Their whole family had been devastated, but of course for Jack, who'd lost his best friend, lover, and wife, it was crippling. Neither Rush nor Jack knew how to handle the overwhelming grief, and one night they'd gotten lost in that grief and they'd said horrible things to each other. Jack's vehemence had seared itself into Rush's head. *You're a spoiled womanizer who wouldn't know how it felt to love if it kicked you in the ass, let alone how it feels to lose the one you love.* Rush had spent two solid years rebelling against the truth of Jack's words, going from one woman's bed to the next as if he were on an endless cycle. Everything changed about a year ago, when he'd woken up next to a woman and had no recollection of her name. For some reason, his mind had traveled straight to Jayla. He'd taken a good, long look in the mirror, and he hadn't liked what he'd seen. Moreover, once he stopped sleeping around, he realized why he'd been doing it. Sure, he liked sex, but he'd been on a hunt, trying to fill the emptiness inside of him that he hadn't realized existed. An emptiness that no amount of sex could ever fill. And over the last year he also realized that the dark hole he'd been trying to fill didn't exist when he was with Jayla.

But Jayla was off-limits, and on some level, he'd always known that. He was certain that knowing he could never be with Jayla was the reason he had been desperately jumping from bed to bed. He was seeking a replacement. Only he could never replace the woman who he now realized owned his heart.

That was the morning he vowed to leave the rebellious, lost child behind and find his grown-up self. He'd made a plan to tell Jayla how he felt, even at the risk of losing their friendship, because Jack had been right. Rush hadn't had any notion of what love was. Rush hadn't known that love could not only embrace a person, but consume him. Once he opened himself up to it and realized his true feelings for Jayla, he understood exactly what his brother meant because that love for her seeped into his every thought.

Rush confided in Jayla about most things in his life, but he'd never told her what Jack had said, or that he had been trying to change. Once he accepted the truth of his behavior and really saw it for what it was—which wasn't a joke, or harmless, or even acceptable—he'd been too ashamed of who he was. For the first time in forever, he'd been touched by fear, and that drove him to keep his efforts toward self-improvement to himself. What if he'd told Jayla he was trying to change, and he couldn't? Then not only would he have still been the person he was ashamed of being, but he'd have also been a failure. No way would he have wanted to see that disappointment in her eyes. He'd even let his family believe he was the same player he'd always been, and since he feigned the part so well during Skype calls or when they met for dinners, they'd never questioned it.

Jayla knew all about Rush's philandering ways, and she accepted him, faults and all. They'd joked about it for years, but she'd never called him on it the way Jack had. In fact, now that he thought about it, she'd never made him feel bad about anything he did. But then again, that's who Jayla was. She'd always stood by him. Now it was his turn to help her through whatever she wasn't telling him.

He crouched by the fire to warm his hands.

"Hey there, handsome."

Rush turned toward Danica's voice. "What are you guys doing here?"

"We come to the bonfires a lot," Danica explained. "My sister's kids love them." Rush had met Kaylie and her family once when he went skiing with Blake. He turned to look for them.

"Oh, they're not here tonight. She's singing in town this week," Blake said. "Tonight's all about romance." He nuzzled against Danica's neck.

Romance. That's what this week was supposed to be about for me, too. Rush rubbed the back of his neck, trying to push away thoughts of Jayla.

Blake and Danica making out wasn't helping any.

"So, everything good with the baby?" He hoped changing the subject might get his mind off of Jayla.

Danica pulled free from Blake's grasp. "Yeah." She settled her hand on her lower abdomen. "It was exciting to hear the baby's heartbeat, which doesn't sound like a heartbeat at all, but more like a swishing sound."

"I still can't believe we're going to have a baby. But I guess it's time, before I get old and gray." Blake ran his hand through his shock of black hair. "You here alone?"

Rush nodded. "Yup. Some of my teammates were supposed to be here, but I guess they turned in early, and the others went into town. Fingers, I think."

Blake and Danica exchanged a look.

"What?" He hoped Jayla hadn't gone someplace dangerous.

"Nothing. It's a bit of a meat market," Blake answered.

A meat market. Great. And Jayla was there with that sexy camisole, tight jeans, and probably those fuck-me leather boots she had in the closet.

"There must be a dozen beautiful women here." Blake nodded toward a group of young women. "Why are you alone?"

"Maybe he wants to be alone." Danica leaned against him.

"It is by choice," Rush said, even though it was the

farthest thing from the truth. If he had his way, Jayla would be in his arms right now. "I need to focus for the competition."

"But you're teaching, not competing." Danica pulled her coat tighter around her.

He shrugged. "I have one last race, the NFC this weekend. So…"

Blake had told Rush all about his premarried, player lifestyle and how meeting Danica had filled every empty spot he had and all the ones he'd never known existed. Rush hadn't been so different from Blake, and seeing Blake with Danica gave him hope that not only could the changes he'd made be permanent, but that a woman could overlook a man's checkered past. *Jayla.* That Jayla could overlook his past.

"Well, you can certainly wait a week." Blake winked.

Rush wasn't so sure he could wait another day, much less a week. His head was spinning. Jayla awakened a sea of emotions within him—and since he was getting hard just thinking about her in that see-through camisole—apparently she affected his body, too.

Chapter Nine

"COME ON!" KIA dragged Jayla and Teri back out on the dance floor for the fifth time in the last hour. Patrick had hooked up with a woman thirty minutes after they'd arrived and said he'd catch his own ride back to the resort, leaving Jayla alone with Kia and Teri, who were obviously on the hunt for men. They used the Olympic ski team card with men the way social wannabes name-dropped, whereas Jayla preferred to keep her identity as far under wraps as she was able, which wasn't very easy in a ski town like Allure. It seemed like everyone knew who they were. On the cramped dance floor, a tall twenty-something guy who reeked of money and testosterone was breathing down her back. She moved over a few inches and he moved with her.

Kia raised her brows and mouthed, *He's hot.* The forest-green minidress she wore set off her flames of red hair as she bobbed her head from side to side while she danced.

Jayla mouthed, *You dance with him.* Dancing kept

her mind off of Rush, but every guy who approached her sent her mind racing back to him.

Kia was all too happy to move in between them, giving Jayla a clear path back to the table. Teri waved from the edge of the dance floor, where she was dirty dancing with a tall, blond guy who was staring at her boobs, and as Jayla turned to wave, someone knocked into her right side, jarring her shoulder. She scrambled back to the table, wishing she'd taken stronger pain meds and wishing she'd stayed home. She needed a plan for her stupid shoulder, and she knew that her original plan to secretly rehab her shoulder was a long shot at best.

At eleven thirty they finally piled into the SUV and headed back to the resort.

"That was so much fun. Maybe we should do it again tomorrow night," Kia suggested as she parked in front of the resort.

"I think I'm gonna go to the bonfire tomorrow." Jayla watched them exchange an eye roll.

Kia climbed from the SUV. "Now that we don't have to drive, wanna grab a few drinks with us at the bar?"

"No, thanks. I think I'm going to turn in." Jayla inhaled the scent of burning wood drifting up from the bonfire pit and thought of Rush.

"I was hoping to get you really smashed so you'd give up your place in the downhill and let me take it." Kia smiled and twirled a fiery curl around her finger as if she were joking, but Jayla knew that Kia, like any competitive athlete, was only half kidding. While Kia and Teri hadn't won Olympic medals, they were strong competitors and both had also gained popularity among their fans, not just through skiing, but also from their clothing sponsorships. They weren't as well known as Jayla or Rush, but they were quickly gaining recognition.

"Yeah, right. If I can endure Marcus, I can ignore peer pressure. Thanks again. I had a great time." Jayla followed the stone path down the hill and around a cluster of pine trees toward the bonfire. A residual of low flames split the darkness. She scanned the handful of people around the fire, hoping she might see Rush. When she didn't see him, she sighed, disappointed and relieved at once. She warmed her hands by the dying fire and looked up at the sky, wishing she had a bag of marshmallows. Maybe she could eat her troubles away.

She wished on the first star she saw. *Star light, star bright, first star I see tonight. I wish I may, I wish I might, have this wish I wish tonight.*

She felt his hands on her waist and smelled his Tommy Hilfiger cologne before she felt the scratch of his whiskers on her cheeks.

"Star light, star bright..."

She opened her eyes. *I asked for a sign about what to do with my injury and you bring me Rush? Boy, did I have the wrong star. Or else...you know my wishes better than I do.*

Rush moved beside her. "I thought you were out painting the night fantastic."

"I was. We did." *I'm so glad you're here.*

"Good. I know you love to dance."

"Maybe a little." *I love that you are thoughtful*

83

enough to think about what I love.

"I saved something for you in case you wanted to come to the bonfire tomorrow." He pulled a plastic bag of marshmallows from his pocket.

She snagged the bag and drew in a breath. She felt guilty for not telling him about her shoulder and maybe a little for fantasizing about him. He was so good to her. She had no business thinking of him like that. *Do I?* She set the bag in his palm.

Suddenly, the things that had always felt natural felt like she was taking advantage of him. The guys she dated didn't think of her in the intimate—though clearly not sexual—way that Rush did. He acknowledged her love of dancing and he brought her marshmallows? Her favorite movies? Her most hated movie? *No wonder I love you so much.* And there was keeping her shoulder injury a secret and crushing on him in a way she had no business doing. Guilt propelled her hand, and the marshmallows, toward him.

"Here."

He wrinkled his forehead. "They're for you."

"I know, but..."

He shoved the bag in his pocket and she saw the muscles in his jaw jump.

"Marcus must have really messed with your head."

Or you are. "Marcus was nothing more than a mistake." She fiddled with the edge of her coat sleeve.

"Then what gives? Did I do something?" He drew his brows together.

I can't help it. You make me hot all over. She looked into his eyes and wanted to crawl into his arms again.

She'd have done exactly that if she didn't think she'd then try to scale him to his peak. *Oh God. No peaks. Not with you.* She looked away. "It's not you, and I'm good. Really."

"You've said that a lot lately. You're *good*. And you know what, Jayla?" He took a step closer.

She couldn't breathe.

He lowered his face to hers. "I'm not buying it."

He stood back up to his full height, and without thinking, she touched his stomach, a nervous habit that she'd done a zillion times before. A playful touch that usually translated to, *Get out of my space.* Only this time it sent a shock of lust right through her. *Oh God. Oh God. Oh God.* She took a step back and let her hand fall away.

"I'm really good, Rush. I'm...I'm fine." *Why is my damn voice shaking?* "Besides, it was my own fault I stayed with Marcus so long, not yours."

He closed the gap between them and reached for her hand again. She was going to screw up everything. Their friendship, her career. Maybe Marcus had done more than put a kink in her armor. *Maybe he saw what I've been hiding.* She wanted Rush, and she wanted him bad. She needed to pull away. She tried to get her hand away from his, but he held tight as he led her over by the trees.

She stumbled along beside him. "Rush?"

He placed his hands gently on her arms, and it sent another thrill through her. It took her a second to realize that he was only skimming her right arm, barely touching it at all. When he lowered his face to hers, she thought he was coming in for a kiss, and she braced herself for what she'd been waiting for since she was a teenager. Damn her for not being strong enough to turn away, but it was Rush, and he smelled so good, and...He pressed his cheek to hers and pulled her close, holding her there as he spoke.

"What was that?" he whispered.

"Wh-what?"

"When you touched my stomach. You felt it. I know you did. And I sure as hell did. What's going on with us, Jay?"

Her body went numb, but her mind had a hundred answers, which all translated to the same answer—*You're finally waking up after all these years.* She opened her mouth to answer, and he brushed hair from her cheek, distracting her before she could get any words out.

"I want to kiss you," he whispered.

Kiss me? She couldn't believe her ears. Jayla tried to pull back so she could see his eyes, check if he was teasing, but he kept her close, and she had no choice but to feel his hot breath on her neck and listen to every word.

"There's something I want to tell you."

He let go of her, but she was rooted to the ground by his admission, by his touch, by the feel of his body against hers.

"Before I tell you, is this messed up? Wait, before you answer..." His eyes were full of sincerity, dark, focused on her. "Jayla, I don't even know how to tell you this, so I'm just going to say it." He brought her hand to his lips and pressed a kiss to it.

Jayla held her breath.

"I've changed, Jayla. I've changed, and so have my feelings for you."

"What? But..." She shook her head, breathing hard, elated, confused—and a little angry. How could he put them in this position? At least she was smart enough to ignore her feelings. "What do you mean you've changed?"

"Jayla." He reached for her again.

She backed away from him. Marcus's words vibrated through her. *It was Rush you were after, not me.* Was that why she'd accepted the date? To make him jealous? Would that make her a woman who sought out men who hurt her? No. She was anything but that. Her other boyfriends had been good to her. She'd made a mistake with Marcus, but she wasn't going back down that road, not even for Rush.

"No." Her lower lip trembled. "What are you even doing? Are you crazy?" Now her limbs were trembling, too. "It's me, Rush. I know you." She laughed then, a nervous, tear-provoking laugh. "I know you all too well. You'll only break my heart. I can take a lot, but not that. Not with you."

"But I've—"

"No."

He moved toward her, and she stepped out of reach. He was saying the things she'd always hoped he would, and she was too scared to think straight—or to hear more.

"Jayla, you're the person whose friendship I value the most. This, whatever it is, scares the shit out of me, too." He paced, then turned back to her. "So you don't feel it? Nothing?"

Of course I do! She crossed her arms over her chest, took a step back, and shook her head.

He eyed her curiously. "I'm not going to force myself on you."

"I...I know."

"I've spent this last year changing, Jay. I'm not the guy who sleeps around anymore. I hate that I ever was. The last thing I expected was to find out that I had feelings like *this* for you. I tried to push them away and forget them, but there's no forgetting you, Jay." The left side of his mouth twitched. "And to be honest, I don't ever want to." He turned away from her and tugged his hat down low.

"I don't know what you want me to say. I can't even believe you're saying this to me. How can I believe you?" She took a few hitched, deep breaths. "Do you really think I want to be one of the women you sleep with and then throw away?" She crossed her arms in an effort to remain erect.

He stared at her for a beat longer, and she almost softened to the sincerity in his eyes. Then he closed the distance between them again.

"No. I don't want you to be one of them either. I'm not like that anymore."

She rolled her eyes.

"You know what? This whole thing is messed up and I know that. You're my best friend, and I have no business thinking of you in any other way, but I do. I am." His voice rose, but it wasn't an angry escalation. She saw his frustration in the way he leaned in close with his muscles tense, as if he were fighting against himself not to come even closer. "And you know what else?" he asked. "It's messed up that you're keeping secrets from me. With the exception of that stuff with Marcus, I've always been there for you. How can you shut me out like that?"

"You *were* there for me when Marcus and I broke up."

"I shouldn't have let you date him in the first place." He stood back again, with his legs planted firmly in the snow and a serious look in his eyes that pierced her heart.

"Let me? You're my friend, not my dating adviser."

"I know that. But I should have been watching out for you. I messed up."

"I'm not your responsibility, and I'm not shutting you out." *Too much.*

He took off his hat and ran his hand down his face, then slid the hat back on. "Let me show you who I am now, so you can see for yourself that I've changed. Jesus, Jayla, the thought of looking at any woman other than you makes me sick. It's you I want."

She could barely find her voice, but self-preservation nudged desire over just enough for it to peek through. "So you're going to, what? Pretend to be something you're not to lure me into your bed, then go your own way after next week and pretend it never happened?" Tears welled in her eyes. "It'll ruin our friendship." He was saying all the things she wished he'd said years ago, and as much as she wanted to wrap her arms around his neck, press her lips to his, and hold on for dear life, she wasn't sure if she believed him. Could he change that much? Was it worth risking their friendship to find out? It was all too much. She had no idea how her jelly legs were holding her up.

"No." It was nearly a whisper. "I'm going to be me. And hopefully you'll see that I've changed and that I'm a better man for it. Because of you. For you." He touched her cheek with his warm, rough palm.

Pull away. Just back up. She couldn't.

His jaw clenched, and his eyes darkened. "I can't help it, Jayla. I still want to kiss you."

Despite the fierce warnings that had been going off in her head, his voice, the love in his eyes, and the way he moved slowly and carefully toward her, pulled the trust she had in him from her heart and that trust wrapped around her like an embrace. All the fear that had been welling inside her slid away. "You want—"

"To kiss you. But I won't if you don't feel the same. I just..." He paused and furrowed his brow. "I...Do you think you're scared, or do you really not feel anything more for me?" His voice was barely a whisper. "You tell me, Jay. What do you want?"

She opened her mouth, but no words came out. She'd fought against her feelings for too long. She wanted him, she trusted him, and she was so goddamn sick of stifling the love that had swelled within her for too many years to count. She nodded, or at least she thought she did. She couldn't think beyond the rush of blood in her ears, the slamming of her heart against her chest. Oh God, how she hoped she nodded.

He was still searching her eyes.

"Kiss...Kiss me. Kiss me, Rush," she whispered.

He lowered his lips to hers and Jayla closed her eyes, feeling as if her body were floating away as she melted against him. His lips were soft and warm, full, delicious, just as she'd dreamed they would be. *I should stop this.* Apparently, the connections between her brain and every other part of her body had shorted out, because her lips parted and her hips rocked into his, and damn did he feel good. *Hard.* He felt good and hard, which made her whole body hot. He dragged his tongue across her lower lip to the corner of her mouth, then along the swell of her upper lip, until she was practically panting for more. Finally, his lips met hers again in a deep, sensuous kiss. One strong hand slid to her lower back; the other found its way beneath her hair, and she realized he wasn't just kissing her. He was searing the feel of his kiss—and his body—into her brain. And he was oh so good at it. Not only would she never forget the toe-curling, mind-numbing feel of the kiss, but she memorized the feel of his chest pressed against hers and the urgency of their tongues as they tasted each other, pulling moans of need from their lungs and catching them in their mouths. She'd been thinking, hoping, fantasizing about this—about him—for so long. Oh no. She would never forget the feel of his hair as she ran her fingers over his ears and touched the back of his head, drawing him closer and hoping to extend their kiss. Or the way his whiskers scraped against her cheeks. And as they drew apart for the desperate need for oxygen, the pain of knowing just how much practice he'd had perfecting that kiss had almost—*almost*—faded away.

"Holy Christ." He was breathing hard. "I think I've wondered what it would be like to kiss you forever."

She could barely think past wanting to kiss him

again, and she couldn't have spoken if her life depended on it.

When he asked, "Can I walk you back to your cabin?" she still couldn't find her voice. She simply followed him.

THE DIN OF the few people still mingling around the bonfire faded behind them as they followed the path back to the cabins. Rush could not ignore the hum of electricity between them. Kissing Jayla was like no kiss he'd ever experienced before. He knew exactly why it felt so different, so magnified. *So perfect.* He'd never felt anything for those other women. Months of introspection had opened doors to his emotions, and behind every one was Jayla. It had always been Jayla.

As they neared her cabin, his heart sank at the idea of leaving her for the night, and he realized that she hadn't been just his best friend for all those years. She'd been the strong girl he admired and the most trustworthy person he'd ever known. She'd known about the pressure from his father, how much he missed his older brother when he was away at school. Hell, she'd known about the first girl he'd slept with. Now he wished that girl had been her. She knew the man he'd been and it had never changed how she treated him. Rush realized that was also the one thing that might keep Jayla from allowing herself to take a chance on taking their friendship to a different level. The thought was like a punch to his gut. She was the one person outside of his family whom he respected and loved—*I do love you*—and he knew he'd do everything he could to prove that he was worthy of her love.

Jayla's porch was dark. Her hands shook as she unlocked the door and pushed it open. He fought the urge to swoop her off her feet, carry her to the bedroom, and love her until they could no longer move. She looked up at him with her lips parted, eyes full of want, need, and...*worry*.

He ran his finger down her cheek, desperately wanting to waylay her concerns and knowing that only time would prove to her who he had become.

"I don't think kissing you was a mistake, Jay, if that's what you're thinking. I really have changed."

"I liked who you were."

Her voice was just above a whisper, and he saw the truth of her words in her eyes. "You liked who I was when I was with you, but we both know that wasn't who I was all the time."

She dropped her eyes, and he lifted her chin, drawing them back to his.

"I like who you are when we're together." She hooked her finger in the pocket of his jeans. "I know that other side of you exists. You've told me all about your...escapades, and each one pinched my heart a little more than the last. But...I've always liked you."

"You've...*liked* me? In that way?"

"Maybe."

"Jayla." He set a serious stare on her.

She looked away.

Holy hell. I should have told her a year ago, when I first realized how much I love her. "Why didn't you say something?"

"Because. What good would it have done?" She

turned in to him and buried her face in his chest. "I love our friendship. I would rather be your best friend and the girl you were honest with than the girl you make love to and then forget."

"Jay." He folded her in his arms. "Give me the chance to show you who I've become. I could never forget you."

She dropped her eyes again and touched his stomach as she had by the trees. Her fingertips grazed the muscles just above his waist, quickening his pulse and making him hard again. She pressed her hips to his, giving him a clear—and conflicting—message. He had no business taking her in his arms and kissing her again, but he couldn't pry himself away. When he felt her leg inch up along the outside of his, his hand found her ass—her glorious, perfect ass. He knew he had to stop. He had no business rubbing the backs of her thighs like he owned them, but Christ did she feel good. When she made a sexy, feminine, whimpering sound of need, he backed her up against the cabin wall and deepened the kiss. Her cold hands slid beneath his sweater, and a shock of desire stole his breath. He pulled back from the kiss with a gasp for air.

"Jayla." He searched her eyes, and through the want, through the *love-me* look in them, a shadow of doubt remained, and he regretfully pulled back. Prying her hands from his body was the most difficult thing he'd ever done. He let out a long, low breath as they slid from his skin.

She looked up at him and smiled. "You always could see right through me. And with me, you're always a gentleman."

A nod was all he could manage.

"Good night, Rush." She turned and went inside, closing the door behind her.

Rush stared at the cabin door like it was the enemy, but he knew better. As he walked away from Jayla's cabin with a hard-on like no other, everything became clear. There was no enemy. There was only the truth of who he'd been, who he'd become, and the bridge of proof that he was going to try his damnedest to construct.

Chapter Ten

JAYLA HAD FALLEN down the rabbit hole with Rush and seriously doubted she'd ever want to climb back out—and it felt so good that she had no idea if it was smart or not. She lay in bed thinking of him and that insatiable kiss until the sun peeked in through the curtains, and then she finally dragged herself from bed. She pulled on sweatpants and argued with herself in the mirror again while she worked through her shoulder exercises. It was a losing battle. She couldn't look at herself for two minutes without feeling guilty for hiding her injury from Rush.

She'd always trusted her own judgment. From knowing that competitive skiing was right for her to choosing friends and the few lovers she'd had. Okay, three lovers wasn't a huge track record, but they were *her* choices. Luckily, she'd realized quickly that dating Marcus had been a horribly bad decision, and though they'd spent a lot of time together, she hadn't yet slept with him. She assumed that was why he forced his way onto this trip, to finally claim that piece of her and win the *gold* that Rush hadn't yet taken. She was beginning to doubt her ability to judge men at all. Jayla didn't often reach out for advice, but when she did, her sisters were only a phone call away. If only one of her sisters were there now. She could always count on Mia, her eldest sister, to give her sound advice. Then again, she could count on Jennifer to be brutally honest. Jennifer wasn't afraid to talk about the more intimate aspects of relationships that Mia avoided at all costs. She leaned against the dresser looking at their picture, debating which sister she'd burden with her love life. She opted for a good dose of honesty. Jennifer answered on the second ring.

"How's my hotshot, supercute baby sister?" Jennifer was only seventeen months older than Jayla, but she never failed to rub it in.

"Baby? Wouldn't that be Jared?" Their parents had a freaky thing about names. She and her siblings all had names that began with the letter *J*, only her older sister Jocelyn went by her middle name, Mia. Apparently, in sixth grade Mia decided that their parents' naming theme was stupid, and she'd been Mia ever since. Her brother Jace was the oldest at thirty-six, then came Mia, Jennifer, Jayla, and her youngest brother, Jared.

"No, he'd be my cute baby brother."

Jayla heard papers shuffling in the background. Jennifer was a high school principal, and she seemed to always have a million things going on.

"You at school?"

"Yeah, rockin' it like a rock star, too."

Jayla pictured her in her pencil skirt and fitted

blouse, her long dark hair pinned up and secured with a pencil or something equally schoolmarmish and equally out of place on her sexy sister.

"What's up with you? How's the asshole? You dump him yet?"

Jayla sighed. The time she spent with Marcus seemed a world away, like a bad dream. "Yeah, finally. You know, as my older sister, you probably should have kicked my ass into submission and made me dump him earlier."

"Do you not remember a certain awesome sister talking to you until three in the morning on more than one occasion and telling you to do just that?" Before Jayla could answer, Jennifer added, "I think your response was, *Nothing is more important than the competition. I can deal with this for another...whatever. Day, week. Ugh.* You made me so angry."

"Yeah, well, at that point I had three competitions I was facing. Next time threaten me or something. Anyway, I need your advice."

"Are you going to listen this time?"

She heard the sarcasm in Jennifer's voice and pictured her perfectly manicured brows lifting above her hazel eyes. "Yes. Maybe."

Jennifer sighed again. "Okay, I'll do my best. But hurry, because I've got a new teacher interview in about six minutes."

"You know Rush..." She winced, expecting a litany of rants. Her family knew all about Rush's history with women. The whole world probably knew. For months after he won the Olympic gold two years ago, he'd been shadowed by the media everywhere he went—

and appeared in gossip magazines with a different woman on his arm in nearly every shot.

"He's only been your best friend forever, and if I might add, one hot playboy." More papers shuffled in the background.

Jayla heard her tapping away on her keyboard and knew Jennifer was losing interest in the conversation. She was great for advice, but she had the attention span of a squirrel.

"The one and only. Well, we're teaching together and—"

"And everything's changed. He's a changed man. You're a changed woman, and you can't help yourself from banging him, right?"

"Jennifer."

"What? We both know how long you've wanted him. Besides, I hear it in your voice. You want my blessing, or do you want me to tell you to be careful?"

"I don't fricking know what I want, which is why I called you." Jayla went to the living room window and looked out over the snowcapped mountains. The sun beamed down between breaks in the clouds, giving the already majestic mountains an even more impressive feel. There was something about the immensity of them that calmed her—and reminded her of Rush.

"Well, here's the thing. Can people change? Sure. Absolutely. The hard part is knowing if the change is permanent or temporary. And I can't answer that because I'm not there and I can't look in his eyes." The keyboard sound stopped. "What does your gut say?"

"That *my* feelings for him have never changed."

"Well, I'm not even sure that's a good thing. You've

always known about his propensity for women—
many, many, women—and you still adored the man.
What does that tell us?"

"That I'm an idiot?"

"Hey, don't be so harsh on my baby sis. Maybe it
tells us that you really do love him? I'm not exactly the
queen of relationships, but I think the real issue is that
if you decide to be with him, really *with* him, then he
can't be doing all that romping around."

"Of course." She leaned against the windowsill and
twisted the end of her hair, debating if she should tell
Jennifer about her shoulder. Her family didn't
understand the mind-set of a competitive athlete, or
Jayla's determination and passion for skiing. Rush
understood both. "Rush has never been a liar or a
cheat. He wasn't in a committed relationship with any
of those women that I knew of. In fact, I can't
remember him ever being in one."

"Hello? Red flag much?"

Jayla sighed. Nope. She'd keep the injury to
herself. No need to overdose on her sister's honesty.
"Maybe. Or maybe honesty all the way? He's never lied
to me about any of it. Not the number of women he'd
been with, or his lack of emotion for them,
or...anything."

"Look, I gotta run, but here's my advice." Jennifer
paused so long that Jayla wondered if she'd gotten lost
in her paperwork. "I have none. For the first time in
our lives, I'm afraid to give you advice. I mean, what if
he's the right guy? But what if he's a bastard?"

"Really, Jen? That's what you're leaving me with?
That's almost worse than if I hadn't called you."

"I know. I kinda suck on this one. Okay, here it is."
She sighed loudly. "Sleep with him, see if you're
compatible and then decide."

Jayla rolled her eyes. "That's horrible advice. I
know sex with Rush will be good. Amazing. Earth-
shattering."

"You'd be surprised. It's the ones who are all hot
and sexy that suck in bed." Jennifer had never hidden
her penchant for sexual experimentation. She'd been a
promiscuous teenager and driven their father batty,
and as she matured, she'd turned that promiscuity
into almost an art form, always searching for someone
to stroke some invisible itch. Jayla wasn't sure Jennifer
even knew what she wanted, and the few times she'd
asked her why she slept with so many men, Jennifer
claimed to enjoy the feel of being in a man's arms and
that she got bored easily.

Now wasn't the time for Jayla to try to figure out
her sister. She couldn't even figure out herself.

"You would know, I guess. But what if it ruins our
friendship? That's more important to me than sex
could ever be."

"Hmm...Okay, so if you don't want to do the dirty
with him, little Miss Purity, then follow your fluffy
little heart. I do know one thing for sure. It's always
been Rush."

"What does that mean?"

"You figure it out. I'm late, sis. Love you tons. Let
me know what you decide. My vote is on dirty, hot,
animalistic sex with no commitment until you see that
he's everything you want in every way."

"My sister the freak. Love you, too." Jayla ended

the call and went to answer a knock at her door. Nerves stifled her smile at the sight of Rush filling her doorframe. *Dirty, hot, animalistic sex.* Heat flushed her cheeks, and she focused on the steaming cups in his hand to keep him from reading the desire in her eyes.

"Hey." Rush handed her one of them. "Hazelnut."

She took the coffee. "Thanks." She fidgeted with the lid of the to-go cup. "You didn't have to do this."

He reached one arm above him and stretched against the doorframe, causing his shirt to lift above his waist and flash a sexy path of skin. "I know. Listen, I was thinking."

"I thought I smelled smoke."

He smiled, making it very hard for her to separate the friend from the man who was vying for her attention—and winning.

"You've seen the friend side of me, and you've seen the asshole side of me, but you've never seen the boyfriend side of me."

She narrowed her eyes. She had always been direct with Rush, and as far as she knew, he'd never lied to her in return. She reached for the doorknob to keep from faltering.

"Has anyone?"

He leaned a little closer to her. "I've never been boyfriend material. I thought that you of all people knew that."

"I guess I always did, but you're thirty-two, and that's a whole lotta years without a real girlfriend."

"It's a damn long time." He leaned his shoulder against the doorframe, bringing him closer to her. He ran his hand through his hair and looked away. When he drew his eyes back to her, his mouth was twitching again.

Instant nervous detector.

If only there was a bullshit detector that she could rely on just as accurately.

His voice grew serious again. "I've been trying to think of all the reasons for you not to give us a shot. And I can come up with a million excuses not to, but I'm not sure they're reasons." He paused and shoved his free hand in his pocket. "I know you think our friendship is a reason, but I see it as a foundation for so much more. There is one thing I want to tell you, and it's presumptive, so don't hate me for saying it."

"Please don't tell me you're one of those guys that are into kinky things, because that might kill any chance you have." She arched a brow.

"Really? Gosh, I thought for sure you'd be into that sort of thing, with your little buzz-buzz friend and all." He sighed. "Guess I'll have to rethink this."

The sensuality in his voice sent a quiver through her.

"Okay, here goes. I can't believe I'm telling you this, but I'm sure part of your brain is tossing it around a million different ways." He trained his eyes on hers again. "I've never had unprotected sex, and I've never had a disease. Not that I expect you to fall into bed with me. I just wanted you to know that on that front, I'm clean."

And there it was. Rush held her gaze without a shadow of guilt or doubt. The look of a steady, honest man. It had been right before her eyes this whole time. *The bullshit detector.* Who knew it was built right into his eyes? Jayla realized that she had always known it was there, which is why she trusted every word he'd ever said. How was she supposed to respond?

She bit her lower lip. "Um. Okay."

"I know it's a weird thing to say, but, Jayla, it's us." He shrugged, as if that explained everything.

It kinda did.

It's us. They trusted each other. Their friendship deserved honesty, and Rush was clearly acknowledging that she deserved the same. *It's us.* There's nothing he wouldn't tell her, even if it felt weird.

The guilt she'd been ignoring since they'd shared the heart-stopping kiss made her throat thicken. With everything on the line, and honesty written all over his face, she couldn't hide from it any longer.

"I didn't tell you the truth about my shoulder."

"I know." He touched her hand. "I figured you'd tell me when you were ready."

"I'm not ready now, either."

He shrugged. "You will be. Eventually. Just tell me this. Should you stop practicing?"

"No." The word came so fast she practically spit it at him.

"You're sure?"

"Yes. I have to practice." That part was true, and not just for now. She was always in training for the next Olympics; they all were. Whether it was two years or two weeks away made no difference. A competitive athlete was always in training for the next big event. "God, Rush. You're turning my whole life upside down. Do you know how long I've hoped that you'd see me as more than a friend?" Before he could answer, she added, "What about your *no relationships during this competition season* thing?"

"It's no secret that I'm all about focus, and women mess with my focus."

"I'm a woman, and focus is precisely the reason I didn't break up with Marcus sooner. It would have been too distracting to deal with a breakup while competing."

Rush pushed off of the doorframe and rubbed the back of his neck. She'd struck a nerve.

"Jayla, I haven't been with any women this season because I only want to be with you. It's that simple. Yes, I'm about focus, and I don't know how our relationship will interfere with my focus because I've never cared enough about a woman before to test it. I've never had a real relationship; you know that. But don't kid yourself. You were distracted just by dating Marcus."

She chose to ignore that particular truth. "And I have other stuff to deal with. Big stuff."

"Let me help you." He took a step toward her, and she stepped back.

"There are some things I need to figure out on my own. But, Rush, the more important issue is focusing and dating. You'll lose focus and you'll resent me for it. If not now, then if we stay together, next season. What happens after the summer, when we go back into full-blown training?" *We?* The way her shoulder was aching, she had serious doubts that she'd be training with the team next year. She pushed the thought away before it could take hold and distract her from their discussion. "You think I want to be responsible for messing up your focus? Or worse? You'll realize it won't work and you'll dump me? Then I've lost my best friend and boyfriend." She crossed her arms like a shield against the truth.

"We've always trained together."

"No. We've always been together as *friends* when we train. Not a couple. There's a big difference." She could hardly believe she was talking Rush *out* of wanting to be with her. She had no idea what they'd find with her shoulder, and if the doctors were right and she ended up unable to compete, would he still look at her the same way? Until she figured out her own life, how could she drag him into it?

Rush stepped inside the cabin and closed the door behind him. "Jayla, we're both competitors. We both know what it takes. If any two people can make a relationship work while competing, we can."

"So you'd chance losing your focus that easily?" *Why am I shaking?*

His eyes were sincere. "For you? Yes."

She was breathing so hard that her words tumbled fast from her lips. "You say all the right things, but you forget. I know who you really are. You said yourself that you've never had a real girlfriend. Why do you think we'll be any different?" She sank down on the couch and pulled her legs up beneath her.

Rush sat beside her. "Because we *are* different. We've not only been friends for fifteen years, but we've been best friends. We've shared the good and the awful. We've cried about losing races that we had no business crying over. We celebrated wins by making snow angels." He cocked one side of his mouth up. "Do you really think I'd do that with anyone else? Come on. We both know about hard work, hours of practice, and determination. We won't hold each other back or whine about not getting enough attention."

Jayla shook her head, trying to ignore the lump in her throat.

"You're not a quitter, which can mean only that I must have totally misread you. That you didn't feel what I did when we kissed."

When she didn't answer, his eyes glazed over, and she swore she saw the hope in them float away with his next breath. It nearly broke her. Between her shoulder and Marcus, she'd lost time and focus. She had to prove to herself, and to the coach, that she could still compete. And when she added that to Rush's need for tunnel vision when he trained, it weighed her down like a lead coat.

Rush pushed to his feet. "I didn't realize."

She grabbed his hand and jumped to her feet so fast she nearly knocked him over. "It's not that, Rush." She felt him pull away and tightened her grip. "Kissing you was better than winning the Olympics."

Tension rolled off him in waves. "But?"

She wrapped her fingers around the waist of his jeans. "But we both know this can't go very far. There's a reason you're so focused when you train, and there's a reason the coach is giving me the stink eye."

And I have to find out if I'm going to be a competitive skier next year or a nobody, which just might change the way you think about me.

Chapter Eleven

AS EXPECTED, THE second day of teaching was more trying than the first, not only because several of the kids had more confidence than skills, which meant Rush and Jayla had to be hypervigilant about their safety, but also because Rush could barely think past his conversation with Jayla. She had exposed the elephant in the room—real relationships and competition didn't mix—and the wind had once again changed, cooling the heat between them. Now Rush stood at the top of the bunny hill with Suzie Baker, thinking about Jayla.

"I really don't think I can do this."

Suzie's voice pulled him back to the more immediate issue, getting her down the hill safely. He tucked away his worry and brought Suzie into focus. Her blond hair stuck out beneath a pink knit cap, which matched her new pink and black parka and her black snow pants. Her mother had bought her all the right clothes. Too bad she hadn't put as much effort into building her confidence outside of her reliance on gaining the attention of men.

"Suzie, tell me something you feel like you are really good at."

She wrinkled her nose. "I guess dating doesn't count?"

Jesus. He knew Jayla should have taken her up, but Jayla had her hands full with a few of the other kids. "A sport, Suzie. Dating's not a sport." There was a time he'd have disagreed with that statement. He felt proud knowing he'd changed and knew that only Jayla could have had that sort of impact on him.

She sighed and rolled her eyes. "Swimming."

"Swimming. Cool sport. That takes strength, confidence, and agility. Okay, and what makes you good at it?"

"I'm fast." She pushed her hat farther up on her forehead.

He ignored the incessant blinking of her heavily mascaraed lashes.

"Okay, you're a strong swimmer. Tell me what scares you about this hill." Rush watched her look down the slope. The color drained from her face, and if she didn't lose that fear, she'd never make it down on her feet.

"Falling."

"What happens if you fall?"

She shrugged. "I could break a leg."

"True. You could, but I highly doubt you will. Look at me a minute."

She looked at him and smiled.

He waited for her smile to falter, so he knew she was doing more than just trying to get his attention. "I bet you don't remember what it was like to learn to swim, do you?"

"No, but my mom said I pitched a fit because I thought I'd drown."

"And did you? Drown, I mean?"

She laughed. "No."

"This is the same thing. In here"—he pointed to his head—"you think you're going to fall. But also in here"—he pointed to his head again—"your brain sends messages to your body about what to do to keep from falling. You fell twice, right?"

She nodded.

"Once while learning the wedge and once while walking up the hill sideways, when you lost your balance."

She nodded again. "But then I did the sideways thing fine the next time."

"Exactly. When you look down that hill, I want you to remember that when you swim, you don't drown, and if you feel yourself falling—"

"Center my balance." She grinned and her eyes widened.

Rush smiled. "That's exactly right. I knew you were a good listener. When you're on the slope, I want you to stop thinking about boys, and clothes, and school, and anything else that steals your focus."

She nodded and drew her brows together.

Rush knew that the instant he saw the confidence in Suzie's eyes, he had to act on it. Otherwise, she'd have time to talk herself right back into her worries. "Do you remember how I showed you to ski in an S rather than straight down the hill?"

She nodded. "To control my speed."

"Good, then you're all set. Remember, faster is not always better." He pointed to his head. "You control everything, and just like swimming, you're strong, you're confident, and I have faith in your skills."

He skied close by her and was impressed at how she kept her body centered, her arms tucked in, and her chin level, just as she'd been taught.

When she reached the bottom and had to catch herself with one of her poles to keep from toppling over, she faced Rush with wide smile. "Can I go again?"

"You know what you just proved?"

"That maybe I can ski after all?" Suzie looked back up at the bunny hill.

He felt the stare of Suzie's mother like a laser beam. He'd made an effort not to make eye contact with her after the way she'd leered at him yesterday.

"Can I talk with you a minute?" Suzie's mother called to him.

Shit. He held up a finger and answered Suzie. "Yes, that you can ski and that the power of positive thinking can pull you through even the things that you're most afraid of. All that peripheral stuff slows you down. Focus, Suzie. You can absolutely do it again. I'm proud of you. Join Jayla and the others and I'll be right there." He wondered if the power of positive thinking could bring Jayla into his arms—or get rid of Suzie's mother.

Team practice started in less than an hour, and he had hoped to catch up with Jayla and clear the air beforehand. They both needed clear heads for practice. Dealing with a mother with hunger in her eyes was the last thing he needed. He knew exactly what Ms. Baker was after in her knee-high black boots and tailored coat—instead of the bulky parka she'd worn the day before—and if he wasn't mistaken, much more makeup than she'd had on yesterday. He cast a quick glance at Jayla, her face free of makeup, a thick hat pulled down low over her ears, and ten times more beautiful than Ms. Baker or any other woman could ever hope to be, because Jayla had a warm heart and good intentions. When she looked up and met his gaze, she smiled—until her eyes shifted to Suzie's mother, and she quickly turned away.

He could almost hear her thoughts—*See? You haven't changed*—as if he were up to his old tricks.

Only he had changed.

Chapter Twelve

JAYLA WAS READING a text from Jen—*Any decision yet about RR?*—when Rush joined her after their last workshop was over. She texted back, *Thinking.*

Rush pulled off his hat and ran his hand through his hair. "Did you see Suzie?" His cheeks were pink from the cold, and his eyes shone with pride for Suzie's success.

"Mm-hm."

He bristled at her cold response, and it sent a wave of guilt through her. She'd been stewing over their conversation all day, trying to dissect it, to make the truth of how relationships and competing didn't mix come apart. As if that wasn't enough to make her belly twist and her nerves burn, to then have to watch Suzie's mother flirting with Rush? She'd watched women flirting with him for years, and she'd never been clutched by jealousy the way she was today. *Our kiss changed everything.* Not to mention the dull ache that decided to set up camp in her shoulder. She had no idea how she'd focus at practice.

Rush took her hand in his. "We have twenty minutes before practice. Let's go someplace and talk."

Talking leads to kissing, and kissing got my head scrambled in the first place. He led her into the lodge. Rush pulled out a chair for her by a small corner table that overlooked the slopes.

"Want me to get you something warm to drink?"

It struck her how considerate Rush was of her. Always.

"Sure."

"Hot chocolate with mini marshmallows or hazelnut java?"

She smiled up at him. "You choose." As she watched him walk away, she noticed several other women also watching him. Rush had always been *Rush* to her. He was above all else her confidant and friend, but he was also handsome, funny, kind, and now she could add a *damn good kisser* to that list. But if she pushed away all that she knew of him and saw what the other women did, she wondered what she'd find.

Jayla closed her eyes for a second, then opened them and pretended that she didn't know that his father was controlling or that his mother evened that out with her soft nature. She tried to forget the tattoos on his upper back and his arm and the scar he'd gotten during camp one summer that ran along the index finger on his right hand. She pushed away the sound of his young voice as he'd whispered urgently to hide so the counselors didn't catch them out after curfew and the way his heated breath had made her entire body shudder last night. And as he came toward her with two steaming mugs in his hand, she saw a man who

116

looked at her like she was the only woman in the room. He had a kind, handsome face, which, if she were really a stranger, would seem open and welcoming. She dragged her eyes down his body, and a shiver ran through her as she remembered the feel of him against her. Oh yeah, she knew just what the other women were seeing. He was not only damn hot, but as warm and inviting as a summer's breeze.

Rush set the mug of hot chocolate in front of her and sat down. "I gotta admit, I felt a little like I was being checked out just then."

She felt her face flush and covered her eyes with her hand. "I just wanted to see what all the other women saw."

"And?"

She glanced up at the amused look on his face. "And now I'm completely mortified that you caught me doing it."

"Why? I check you out all the time." His smile reached his eyes, and when he lifted his mug and took a sip, his smiling eyes were still locked on her.

"You do?"

"Hell yes. I'd be crazy not to. But to be honest, I used to check you out from a different perspective. You know, to make sure you didn't have spinach between your teeth or anything." He laughed under his breath.

She was still stuck on *Hell yes.*

"I've only been checking you out like *that* for the past, oh, I don't know, year or so. But now..."

"Year?" *Year!* "Now?" *Stop, stop, stop.*

He leaned across the table and motioned her

117

closer. "Since we kissed," he whispered, then sat back with a satisfied look in his eyes.

She tugged at the end of her hair. "You're just trying to rattle me." She took a drink to buy herself time to learn how to breathe again. "Brat."

"Okay, so we should talk about this." He ran a hand between the two of them. "Us."

Why does jumping across the table to kiss you suddenly seem like an option? Not only was that a crazy-ass idea that went against everything she was trying to accomplish, but it would not go over well with clunky ski boots weighing her down.

"Us? I don't remember committing to an *us*."

"No. You sure didn't, which, I might add, is not great for my tender ego." He set his mug down. "But don't you think we should at least talk about it?"

"I can't even think about all this. I'm still reeling from..." She noticed Patrick and Cliff sitting at another table and she lowered her voice. "You know."

He laughed. "You can't even say it? The kiss?" He leaned in close again. "The hot, sexy, passionate kiss that left me practically unable to walk?"

"You're doing it again, saying things just to get to me." Her eyes darted to the other tables.

"Get to you?" He cocked his head.

"Make me uncomfortable. You *know* I'm private about that stuff."

"I probably know about at least ninety percent of the men you've kissed." He furrowed his brow. "How can you say you're private about it?"

"Well, private between us. You're my closest friend, but I don't like other people to know those things."

"I'm sorry." He lowered his voice. "I wasn't doing it to get to you in that way. But I *was* doing it to bring it back to your mind so that it would be tougher for you to put me back in the friend zone."

Coach Cunningham walked by their table, square chin held high, broad shoulders squared. He paused, shifting his serious eyes between the two of them. "Ten minutes."

"Yes, sir. We'll be there." Rush nodded and watched him walk away.

"Rush, maybe we should table even talking about it until after the competition this weekend. Then we'll have a few weeks to decide if it's worth it." Her stomach sank thinking about all of it—her shoulder, the competition, delaying what she really wanted...being with Rush—but she was already on thin ice with the coach. The women's coach had spoken to her about her loss of focus before they came to Colorado, and she was sure that was why Coach Cunningham had zeroed in on her during the meeting. What she wasn't sure of was whether her coach had attributed her lack of focus to her shoulder injury or to her relationship with Marcus—or both.

His jaw twitched. He pressed his lips together, then scrubbed his face with his hand and nodded. "If it's worth it?" His eyes filled with pain. "Is that what you *want* to do?"

"I..." *No.* She was staring at the man she'd loved forever, and she couldn't form a single sentence to save her life.

He gripped the edge of the table. "I'm gonna make

this really easy for you. The competition is only a couple days away, and by the look in your eyes, you're more than a little conflicted about the two of us."

He rose to his feet, and her heart nearly stopped.

"Friends. Until you decide what you want."

He was being considerate, and still his words pierced her heart. She knew all it would take was for her to stand up and tell him that wasn't what she wanted at all, but she caught sight of Coach Cunningham and a different worry gripped her. She had to get back on track.

"Is that what *you* want?" she finally managed.

"I think you already know the answer to that." He picked up his mug and looked toward the door. "Ready to hit practice?" He asked the question without an ounce of resentment, and it stole the air from her lungs.

No. I'm not sure my legs will work any better than my mouth.

RUSH SQUINTED BENEATH his goggles against the frigid air pelting his face as he raced down the slope. Coach Cunningham's words rang in his ears. *If you can feel your face, you aren't going fast enough.* The coach was a hard-ass, which made him the perfect mentor for Rush, who had grown up under the strict tutelage of his father. *Do your best. Be better than every other person in everything you do.* He leaned into the curve with his heart slamming against his ribs, and his mind drifted to Jayla. He fought to pull it back to the slopes, knowing damn well that any distraction would cost him time. He hunkered down lower and leaned forward, eking out a little more speed. Racing at speeds upward of fifty miles per hour meant that the smallest mistake could cost him his career in injuries—or his life.

The lights of the lodge came into view, and he pushed himself harder, drew forth more speed as he hit the last leg of the run, and finally plowed to a stop at the bottom, spraying snow in his wake.

Coach Cunningham looked at his stopwatch and shook his head.

Shit. "How bad is it?" He skied over to the coach. His lungs burned from the cold air—a good burn.

The other team members came in after him, and the coach and his assistant, Chad, clicked off their times.

Rush knew better than to hound the coach. He'd tell Rush when he was damn good and ready and not a second before. He skied over to Jayla as she took off her goggles, which left marks just below her eyes. She was breathing hard, and she wasn't smiling.

"How'd it feel?"

"Not as good as it should have." She turned to look at the coach, and Rush didn't miss the way the coach narrowed his eyes. She shifted her poles to her left hand.

He had the urge to take her in his arms and tell her everything would be okay. It wasn't okay, and he of all people knew that.

"Well, then, we did the right thing. You need to train harder and focus more. The last thing you need is me messing with your sexy little brain. Big brain. Shit. Never mind."

121

Another week and the competition season is officially over. One week. That's all it is.

Only it wasn't. Even when they weren't in training or actively in competition, they lived and breathed for the day they would be. The sadness in Jayla's eyes told him that she knew it as well as he did.

"You'll fix this, Jayla. I know you. You're just distracted. First there was Marcus; then I came roaring in with feelings you didn't know were there. And damn it, I knew better." He shook his head, feeling guilty as hell.

"Rush."

The way she said his name was a halfhearted effort at best, and he didn't blame her one bit.

"Jayla, look at me."

She lifted her eyes, her lips slightly parted.

He focused on her eyes, because focusing on her lips would bring his directly to them. He leaned in close. "You sure your shoulder is okay?"

She rolled her arms backward, as if proving to him it was. Her eyes turned to liquid steel. She wasn't about to show any sign of weakness. Not even to him. The Jayla he knew had returned, and she'd booted vulnerability to the curb.

Unfortunately, she might have booted him right along with it.

Friends. Despite the fissure he felt in his heart, he had to be supportive of her. He wanted to, even if he was hurting. "You've worked your whole life to get here."

He saw determination in her eyes and in the lift of her chin. When he touched her left shoulder, he felt her gathering strength through the slight pull of her muscles as she drew her shoulders back.

"All that matters right now is that you fix this," he said. "Concentrate. Practice until that run feels like fucking heaven. You got it?" His eyes drifted to her shoulder, and he wished like hell he knew what was really going on.

She nodded.

"Remington." Coach Cunningham's arms were crossed; his face was set in a stern grimace.

He skied over to the coach.

"Follow me," Coach Cunningham said gruffly as he led the way toward a grouping of trees, then glanced back at Jayla before setting his sights on Rush. "You're not a dumb kid, Rush. You know damn well why I put you with Jayla for the workshops."

"Because of Marcus, I assumed. He's out of the picture. She ended things with him."

"Yes, because of Marcus. He messed with her head, which messed with her times, which you know is everything." He ran his hand across his jaw and blew out a breath. "Rush, I won't tell you what to do with your personal life, but Jayla's a strong competitor, and she needs to pull it together. She can't do that with you looking at her like she's one of your fan girls."

Fan girl? More like the love of my life. "Coach, you're the one who put me with her."

"Because I've seen the way you are with her. You're protective, even when you say nothing at all. One look from you stifles the riffraff. Except it had the opposite effect on Marcus because of that asinine competition between you two. He only went after her

123

to get your goat."

"No offense, Coach, but I don't think Marcus's dating her had anything to do with me."

He smirked and shook his head. "Then you're blind as a bat."

No way.

"Now, I respect the hell out of you as a competitor, Rush. And I expect you to respect her, given your long friendship. At least enough to give her a fighting chance to get back on her feet. You guys have the whole summer to figure out what to do with those looks you're giving her, but she needs to get back on track or she'll lose her edge, and I'm seeing her going easy on her right arm, which worries me."

"Got it, Coach."

If he had any doubts before, the coach just sealed their fate. Rush wanted no part of hindering Jayla's career.

Chapter Thirteen

JAYLA STARTLED AWAKE at four thirty the next morning. She sat up in bed, trying to figure out what had woken her. Someone knocked at the cabin door, and she picked up her cell phone and clutched it to her chest. Marcus? Panic ran through her. She pulled on a T-shirt and sweatshirt with her flannel pants. As three more hard knocks rang out, she texted Rush. *Someone's banging on my door. Marcus?* She stood frozen in the bedroom, hoping Rush was awake. Her phone vibrated a few seconds later. *Morning, sunshine. Open the door.*

She pulled the door open and Rush stepped in.

"Let's go." He ran his eyes down her body. "Boots. Now."

"Now?" She shoved her foot into her boot as she rubbed her eyes. "What the hell is wrong with you? Do you even know what time it is?"

"I do. Take something for your shoulder and hurry up. The coach is worried."

She sighed loudly as she stomped into the

bedroom, took Motrin and Tylenol, then joined him in the living room.

"Rush, if you think this is the way to a girl's heart, you've got your head on backward."

He grinned. "Want to put on real pants instead of pajamas?"

"That depends. Where are we going?"

"To whip your ass into shape. Shit. I almost forgot. Stretch."

"What?"

"Do your stretches. Here. Now."

"I'm not even awake yet."

Rush frowned at her. "Come on, whiner. I'll do them with you."

They sat on the floor and stretched their legs, then progressed up through their muscles. When they reached their arms, she felt him scrutinizing her movements, and she fought to keep from revealing the pain in her shoulder.

"Look at Sleeping Beauty doing her thing." He pointed to the bedroom. "Why don't you change out of your sexy pj's and then we'll go."

She went into the bedroom, mumbling under her breath. *Sexy pj's. It's four thirty in the morning.*

Jayla yawned as they headed up to the equipment room in the dark. To their right, the slopes snaked up the mountains like fingers reaching for the clouds. The resort stood tall and imposing at the crest of the hill. White lights lined the peaks and valleys of the roof, like hundreds of stars shining down on them. The top layer of snow had frozen overnight and crunched beneath her boots.

"Why are you even up?" She curled her shoulders against the cold air, her hands buried deep inside her coat pockets.

"Because you and I both need to shave some time off of our speed, and God knows you're not going to get your butt out of bed early without a friend to give you a little push."

A friend. How many times had he pushed her to practice for extra hours at camp when she complained about someone beating her time? "How are we going to get up the slope? The lifts don't open this early."

They went into the equipment room, which was eerily silent, and collected their skis and poles.

"Don't underestimate the power of Rush Remington." He winked as they made their way to the ski lift.

"I've missed you these last few weeks, you know. Even the way you push me further than I might push myself."

"Don't kid yourself. You'd push yourself as hard as you needed to by this afternoon if I hadn't shown up."

He was right. It didn't matter how much she liked him, or that for the first time in forever she felt whole despite her injury. She'd already decided that she'd come too far to let her focus falter for anyone. Including Rush.

"Then why did you wake me?" They climbed onto the chairlift and settled in as it rumbled to life.

"Because I've missed you, too, and it was a great excuse to watch the sunrise with my best friend." He nodded at the sliver of pink bordering the crest of the mountain.

"That's beautiful."

"By the time we reach the top, it'll be up a little higher. That's worth getting up early for, don't you think?"

Resting her head on his shoulder came naturally, and when his arm slipped around her, she soaked in the comfort of him. "I think it's definitely worth getting up early for."

He took out his phone and clicked a picture of the two of them, then turned the phone around and took a shot of the mountains before tucking it back into his pocket. He kissed the top of her head. "Hey, Jay?"

She heard the strain in his voice and readied herself for what she knew was coming. "Don't say it, okay?"

He didn't respond.

"I know *we* can't happen, Rush. Just let me watch the sunrise with my friend without worrying about it." She wondered if he heard the pitch of her voice change with the fib.

Two hours later, they were making their way over to the lodge for coffee and Jayla was trying to ignore the burn in her shoulder. "That was fun." She inhaled deeply.

"You shaved three seconds off of yesterday's time. Keep this up and you're gonna nail the competition."

"I appreciate you dragging me out, Rush." She smiled at him, but it was wasted. His eyes had been trained on the lodge since they'd started walking back.

Rush stopped before they reached the lodge. "You know what? Go ahead in. I just remembered something that I need to take care of. I'll see you at eight for the class, okay?"

She watched him walking back toward the cabins, and somewhere deep in her belly, she knew he was purposely putting distance between them. How could she blame him? It was what she said she wanted, even if it hurt like hell.

Three seconds. Focus on the gains.

Maybe I made a mistake.

RUSH CURSED UNDER his breath as he unlocked the door to the cabin and threw it open. He tossed the keys on the counter and stared at the empty room. He had no idea what he was doing, or how to read Jayla's conflicting messages. He thought he could handle practicing together without being distracted by thoughts of how he wanted to be doing so much more, but as they walked toward the lodge, he'd been one second from draping his arm over her shoulder. That would have been normal, easy, except that when he'd done that on the chairlift, it had brought his mind right back to their kiss. The truth was, he didn't know how to be just friends with Jayla now that he'd opened his heart to her.

He paced the cabin floor. She'd been upset with him for risking their friendship, and maybe she was right. He ran his hand through his hair and stared out the window, trying to push away anger brewing in his gut. Anger at putting them in this position in the first place. Anger at her for not reciprocating—even though he knew that wasn't fair at all. Hell, he was goddamn angry at the world, and he needed to get it out before it screwed up their friendship and this weekend's race.

He picked up his cell phone and called his brother Jack. Someone had to pay for this shit, and it all started with him.

"Hey, little brother," Jack said all too happily for Rush's mood.

He hated to crush Jack's spirit, but he was unable to stop the shit storm of emotions from spewing forth. "You fucked me up, man, and I'm pissed."

"Whoa, bro. I haven't even seen you in weeks. What's going on?"

Rush paced again. His mind told him to calm down, but he was unable to quiet the rage. "You told me I was a womanizer. You made me open my goddamn eyes when I was perfectly happy with them closed, and now...Now..."

"Now you've fallen for some chick and you're pissed at me for whatever reason, right? Well, guess what? We both said shit we probably shouldn't have, and I'm sorry, but I wasn't exactly in my right mind when I lost Linda. Remember that, little brother? So before you rip me a new asshole, think. I had just lost my wife."

Jack was a model of controlled anger, speaking in a serious, authoritative tone. A tone Rush had heard a million times when he was growing up and Jack had made it his business to set him straight. Even during the years when Jack was away at college, if he'd heard that Rush had done anything remotely out of line, he'd call him up and speak in that same tone, and it made Rush swallow his words and think. It still had the same effect.

He sank to the couch, elbows on his knees.

"Goddamn it."

Jack didn't say a word. He was good at waiting out Rush's internal battles.

Rush pushed to his feet again. "Damn it, Jack. I changed my whole life because...of what you said." *And because of Jayla.* "And now I wish I hadn't."

"What the hell are you talking about?"

"Feeling shit for a woman sucks."

"Now you're just talking crazy. Are you drunk?"

"No. I'm not drunk, you ass." He needed air. He flung open the front door and stood on the front porch. He caught sight of Kia and Teri walking out of Kia's cabin, and he went back inside and closed the door.

"You want to tell me what this is really about, or do you just want to vent? I'm cool with either. I just need to know if I should brew another pot of coffee."

"Goddamn it, Jack."

"You said that already."

He flopped on the couch again. "Right." He pressed his palm to the tightening muscles in his chest. "Jesus, Jack."

"Some people call me Jesus, but you can just call me Jack."

Rush laughed despite his anger. "Okay, here's your chance to use your big brother skills and talk me off the ledge."

"Where are you?"

"Colorado. Teaching a ski workshop for Danica Carter's company."

"Now I get it. I thought your season was over."

"One last competition. Now you *get* what?"

"This isn't about some random woman, is it?"

"No. It's about Jayla. Jack, listen. I fought what you said I was for a long time, and then one day I woke up next to this woman and couldn't even remember her name. And I might be thickheaded, but it finally set in. I realized you were totally right, and then...I realized all those women were space fillers. It was Jayla I wanted all that time." His gut twisted, and before Jack could say anything, he continued. "Anyway, I've spent months cleaning up my act. Christ, the thought of all that time I spent sleeping around makes me sick."

"And Jayla?"

He blew out a loud breath. "She's everything. I think I love her. I do love her."

"You're just realizing this after fifteen years? No wonder you're messed up." Jack laughed. "Hey, remember when Mom made me have a talk with you about respecting women?"

"Mom? I remember the snore of a talk, but she put you up to that?"

"Yeah. She called me at some point, worried about how often you and Jayla talked. You were getting ready to go to camp. She thought you and Jayla were headed for the bedroom. It was way past the point of you needing to hear it, but she said Dad wasn't the right person to do it."

Rush laughed. "Well, she was right about Dad but not Jayla. We were never like that. We've always just been friends. You know, as we got older, I was hooking up with every woman under the sun, and she was in the friend zone."

"And now?"

Rush rolled his shoulders, stretching out his muscles. "Right now...Now I can't look at her without wanting more."

"Okay, so? What's the issue? Why are you so pissed at me?"

"Maybe if you'd never said that shit to me in the first place, I wouldn't have changed, and then I wouldn't feel all these crazy emotions every time I see her. It's like I just want to protect her, and touch her, and—"

"Whoa, okay. You could have led with that and saved us an assload of time."

"No, I couldn't have, because you needed to know that I'm not the dick you think I am." Rush let out a breath.

"Man, I have no idea how your mind works. Look, none of us judge you by what you do with women. But let's cut to the chase."

Rush sighed. "I finally realized what she means to me, and she's worried that being together will screw with our focus. She might be right. I don't know that I can be in a real relationship and compete. It might screw with my mind and I can't chance that. She can't chance that."

"Then you need to fix that. Does she think you're still screwing every woman in your path?"

"No, I don't think so, but...I think she's still trying to see it with her own eyes. She's about the only one who can see right through me."

"Then what's the issue? Can't you compartmentalize? Put away thoughts of her while you compete, or train, or whatever. Tons of athletes have relationships."

"I don't know. What if I can't? What if she can't?"

"Can't? You wiped that word from your vocabulary years ago, Rush."

Jack had him there. "I'm not sure we can ever go back to just being friends. I think about her day and night. I want to be with her every second. Jack, I can't lose Jayla altogether."

"Then fix it. There's nothing you can't do, Rush. You're one of the most focused people I know. She's probably scared, and you sound scared, too."

"Of losing her, maybe."

"Makes sense," Jack said. "If you need to separate your relationship from your training, then do it. Look, you're the king of concentrating on what matters. This is no different from training. When you train, you push the rest of the world away. Just make sure that if you decide to really have a relationship with Jayla, you put her away with the rest of the world when you train. It might take some getting used to, but you can do it. There's nothing you *can't* do." Before Rush could respond, Jack continued. "Talk to her, Rush. Ask her what she needs and what she really wants. I'd imagine she's just as scared as you, but if she doesn't want this, then you can't force it."

"I never would."

"I always thought she liked you. Look, this is simple even if it feels like the hardest thing you've ever done. And I'm sure it does, because when I fell in love with Savannah, I had all sorts of scary shit going on in my head. You know how to overcome obstacles. Face it head-on like you do everything else in life. And all that bullshit about not being able to focus? I got news for you. That's all smoke and mirrors, buddy. You've built a wall around yourself for whatever reason, and it's made of bullshit excuses. Tear it down."

"Just what I needed, a therapy session. I could have gone to Danica for that."

"Hey, you called me."

Rush glanced at the clock. "Oh shit. I'm late. I gotta run. Sorry to dump on you like this." Rush headed out the door and jogged up the hill while he spoke to Jack.

"That's what family's for. Call and bitch me out anytime."

"Thanks, bro. Love you." He raced up the hill to join the workshop, which was already in progress, and as Jayla came into view, he knew Jack was right.

Head-on was the only way.

Chapter Fourteen

"JAYLA, CAN WE just go up already?" Taylor Harper was fifteen. He wore no hat, a black hoodie beneath a ski vest, and a pair of stonewashed jeans. He was the focus of every teenage girl within viewing distance, and despite the heated gazes cast upon him, he'd be damn cold when he got to the top of the mountain. But Jayla's job was to help him learn to ski, not parent him.

Jayla glanced at Jeffrey in his nondescript black parka, standing beside two of the other teenage students, Chris and Meg. Jeffrey fidgeted with his gloves, his eyes bouncing between Meg, a cute, dark-haired girl, and Taylor. Meg's eyes were locked on Taylor, and Taylor beamed at Jeffrey with in-your-face pride. *Ugh!* Teenage love triangles weren't fun when Jayla was a teenager. She wasn't looking forward to dealing with them on the slopes.

She caught sight of Rush heading toward them and stifled the urge to give him hell for leaving her hanging. He'd given her such conflicting signals all morning, and she couldn't decide if she was to blame for them. Was he just respecting what she'd asked for, or was it something more? He acted like her best friend, but he looked at her with eyes that said so much more. Maybe she *was* losing her mind.

Focus on the class.

"Sure. Taylor, you and Chris take the lift up together. Jeffrey and Billy. Suzie, you're with Meg. Remember, no messing around on the chairlift." She stepped into line behind the kids and watched Rush put on his skis. A pretty woman about Jayla's age got in line behind her, and when Rush joined them, he was paired with the woman for the ride up the mountain.

He leaned closer to Jayla. "Sorry I'm late. Got stuck on the phone and forgot about the time."

She wondered who he was so lost in a conversation with. *It's none of my business. I'm the one who said I didn't want more right now.*

"It's fine." Jayla settled onto the lift and tried not to think about Rush and the pretty woman behind her. Rush was right; she needed to remain focused.

At the top of the mountain, she counted heads and gathered the kids in a group as Rush skied off the lift. He reached out to steady the pretty woman he'd ridden with. The woman flipped her long dark hair over her shoulder and fluttered her lashes. Jealousy prickled Jayla's nerves again.

She had to distract herself before she literally turned green with envy. "Does anyone have any questions before we start?"

Meg had her eyes locked on Taylor, and Taylor was soaking up the attention, playing the disinterested attitudinal teen, checking out the woman who was still talking to Rush. The others were perched at the edge of the slope and ready to ski. Jeffrey stood off to the side, and Suzie was busy eyeing Rush. Jayla remembered what it was like to look at Rush that way at that very same age. *I still do it.* She only wished that Suzie was more focused on skiing, or even boys her own age. She wondered if her mother's infatuation with Rush had anything to do with Suzie's obsession with him.

It's none of my business.

She went over to try to distract Suzie. "You're going to do great. You know that, right?"

"I know. I'm a little nervous." She lifted her blue eyes to Jayla and brushed her hair from her face.

"I am, too. I'm always nervous when I'm up here." She looked over the beautiful sea of white below and sighed. "But once I'm on the slope, it all comes together, like my legs weren't made for walking at all, and I should have been born with skis for feet."

Suzie laughed and stole another glance at Rush.

Jayla wanted to tell her that she was pretty and strong and didn't need to put herself out there in inappropriate ways, but that wasn't her place any more than it was her place to tell Taylor that he didn't need to be a show-off.

"Come on. Let's show everyone just how good of a skier you are. I'll go down with you." She cast a glance over her shoulder at Rush. "You guys ready?"

"Always," Rush answered.

In her mind she heard a sexual innuendo in his tone. Unfortunately, she knew it was in her mind because he hadn't even looked over when he'd said it.

Taylor descended the slope fast and confidently as the others tried to keep up. Meg tumbled over a small bump in the snow. Rush helped her up, then followed her down the slope.

Jeffrey was the last to join them at the bottom.

"About time," Taylor said with an eye roll.

Jeffrey looked away.

Stand up for yourself. She knew better than to come to Jeffrey's defense. It would only make him look weaker to the others. Rush slid Taylor a dark stare and Taylor turned away. Problem solved, for now.

"Hey, Rush!" The dark-haired woman who had ridden up the slope with him waved as she skied over to the lift. "I did what you said and it worked perfectly. Thanks."

She smiled, and even Jayla couldn't look away from her glistening white teeth and flawless olive skin. She could have been the face of Dove. Jayla didn't even have the right to feel the jealousy that gripped her—she'd turned Rush away.

"Glad to hear it." Rush cocked his crooked grin.

"Ride up with you?" the woman asked.

Rush glanced at the kids, then at Jayla.

She shifted her eyes away.

"Can't, sorry," Rush said to the woman. "I gotta stick with the class."

The corners of the woman's mouth turned down.

Can't? This was new. It gave Jayla pause.

"Grab a drink later?" she asked.

Wow, you're persistent. Jayla settled into the chairlift and turned away from them. It was hard enough listening to her flirt with Rush. She didn't need to watch them, too. And if Rush was the guy he'd always been, then she already knew what he'd do. He'd meet her for a drink, get his ego—and particular body parts—stroked, and forget her name by the next morning.

"Sorry. We have practice, but thanks anyway," Rush said as he settled into the chairlift beside Jayla.

She whipped her head around. *You turned her down? You turned her down! Oh wait...we're still officially in competition season.*

But you kissed me and we're still in season.

JAYLA SAT RIGIDLY beside Rush, her eyes narrowed and maybe a little angry. She was still so goddamn beautiful it made Rush ache. After a minute of uncomfortable silence, he said, "I'm really sorry I was late."

"We were fine, but I can't take them down the mountain alone, so..."

"Today was a fluke. I was talking to Jack."

She turned toward him, and his whole body went hot.

"How is Jack?"

Although Rush had never shared what Jack had said to him, he had shared with Jayla how Jack had basically escaped to the Colorado Mountains for two years after Linda's death, maintaining connections as a survival training guide and bush pilot and not much else. That is where he met his now-fiancée, Savannah Braden, when she'd taken one of his survival courses, and the connection finally helped Jack heal.

"Good. He and Savannah set a wedding date." He

felt a fissure between them and wondered if it was due to his being late that morning, or the feelings they were trying to ignore.

They joined the group. Meg was talking with Taylor, and Taylor was staring at Jeffrey with a challenging look in his eyes. Jeffrey was bent over, tightening his boot dejectedly, and Suzie stood with the other kids. At least Suzie was starting to blend in with kids her own age.

"Can I go?" Taylor asked Rush.

"In a minute." Rush skied over to Jayla. "Want me to take the moody teens or the others?"

"I'll take the attitudes. They suit me today."

He watched her ski away and was beginning to think that he had made a huge mistake by telling her how he felt. He'd managed to screw their friendship up even more by practicing together and then leaving her high and dry. He should have left well enough alone.

By the end of class, Taylor and Meg were a unit. Where one went, the other followed—and Jeffrey's sad puppy eyes trailed behind them. If Rush had one week with Jeffrey, he knew he could bolster his confidence, and he'd never have to look that way again. Then again, his own love life was messed up beyond control. He had no business trying to help anyone else.

After class, Rush watched Meg fidgeting with her gloves as she and Taylor stood inches apart, and it made him think of kissing Jayla at the bonfire. Rush had the whole womanizing thing down pat. That didn't take emotions. It wasn't complicated. Find a hot woman, gauge her interest, and the rest was a given. He'd known Jayla forever. He loved her. Kissing her should have been anything but nerve-racking. Instead, it had made him feel like a kid going in for his first lip-lock.

"Hey there."

Suzie's mother, Kelly, smiled up at him with an I'm-yours-for-the-taking look in her eyes. She licked her lips and flipped her blond hair over one shoulder. *That's where Suzie learned it.* It was a look that Kelly had probably practiced in the mirror a thousand times, and it was spot-on hot.

"Hi." Rush looked around for Jayla. *Where are you?*

"So, I was thinking..." Kelly glanced at Suzie, standing a few feet away and talking with Chris. "Suzie's dad has her this weekend. I know it's sort of forward of me, but I figured, what the hell. Any chance you'd like to have a drink Friday night?"

"Mom, are we going?" Suzie called over.

Rush wondered if he was wearing a sign around his neck that read, *Test me. See if I've really changed.* "Thanks, but I'm in training. I really can't. Sorry."

"Mom!"

Kelly sighed without answering Suzie. She furrowed her brow. "Well, if you change your mind..." She shoved a piece of paper in his hand and turned away. She glanced over her shoulder at Rush and smiled.

Not a chance in hell. He crumpled the paper in his fist and stuffed it into his pocket as he spotted Jayla walking away.

Chapter Fifteen

JAYLA CLOCKED IN at two seconds faster than she had the evening before, and when Coach Cunningham patted her on the back and smiled, it was all the encouragement she needed to know she was doing the right thing with Rush. She'd watched him with Kelly Baker after class, and she'd been surprised to see his eyes darting around instead of giving Kelly his swoon-worthy stare. She'd gone back to her cabin to take medicine for her shoulder, which ached like a bad tooth, and when he didn't text or stop by, she panicked a little. Rush had to go and open his mouth and say all the things she felt. She didn't like the awkwardness between them, and she never would have believed that anything could rock their friendship.

This is so stupid. We need to talk. Clear the air. I just need to get through the competition, then go to the doctor to see if I can compete next year or not. Then we can figure out if there's an "us" to think about.

She rode the lift up with Kia and focused on the next run down the mountain. Focusing on training kept her mind off of Rush, which drove away the thoughts of whether she could trust him or not. That wasn't the most important thing at that moment. Neither was the hot pain spearing her shoulder. All that mattered was bettering her time and winning the competition. If she could make herself believe that, the rest of the week would be livable.

"You were out early this morning. I heard you leave at, like, five." Kia's cheeks were bright pink, and she had mischief in her eyes. "How'd you get them to turn on the lift? Teri said she saw it running."

It was Rush. Isn't it always? Jayla wasn't about to say that he had arranged it. Kia gushed over him, and just about every other guy around, and she'd seen enough women swooning over Rush today. She shrugged.

"Are you going tomorrow? Can I come with you? I'd love to hit the slopes for some extra practice."

"I'm not sure if I'm going tomorrow or not, but if I do, I'll let you know." She definitely wanted to hit the slopes in the morning, but she had to find out from Rush who ran the lift, and she'd been doing all she could to avoid him.

After practice, Rush caught up with her on the way to the cabins. "Hey, good job out there."

"Thanks."

He whipped off his hat and shoved it in his pocket. "Everyone's getting together for dinner. Wanna go?"

Go, like together, together?

He must have read her mind, because he followed that up with, "Don't worry. Not a date. Just friends. All of us."

"You're not meeting Suzie's mom?"

He glared at her.

"Sorry. I couldn't help it. Sure, I guess I'll go, if you're sure you won't mind."

"Why would I mind? Friends, right?"

Then why is your jaw twitching? "Right, yeah," she practically whispered. "Hey, who can I talk to about running the lift tomorrow morning?" The cabins came into view, and she fought the urge to slow her pace just to spend a few more minutes alone with him. Maybe they could just be friends, even after those mind-blowing kisses. She snuck a glance at his profile, and butterflies fluttered in her belly. *Nope. Friends won't work anymore.*

"They're set for the next few days. They'll have them running by five each morning."

"Really? Thanks. That's great."

When they reached her cabin, Rush slowed but didn't stop to say goodbye. "I'll see you at dinner." He turned and jogged up to his cabin, and she longed to relive the moments of intimacy they'd shared that went beyond friendship. She wanted to relive all of them—the looks, the kisses, the feel of his hands on her waist, his whiskers against her skin, the taste of him...

JAYLA SHOWERED AND changed three times, finally deciding on a see-through sweater with the lacy cami that had drawn Rush's attention the other night. With that, she wore a short black skirt and knee-high black boots. Maybe she'd garner a few glances and give Rush a dose of jealousy so she wasn't the only one sweating over wanting what she couldn't have.

Her phone vibrated with a text from her sister. Every time Jennifer texted about Rush, it was a reminder of what she was trying so hard to push away, and it made her nerves pinch.

So???

She texted a message she hoped would stop her sister's constant inquiries.

Decided not to pursue it.

Her phone vibrated a minute later with a text from Kia. *Ready?*

She had assumed that Rush was coming to get her, but now she realized how stupid that was. He'd asked her to go as part of the group. Why would he stop by to get her? *Because he always has.*

She texted Kia. *Yup. Where should I meet you?*

Jennifer's text came in next. *Chickenshit.*

She texted back an emoticon of a person sticking out their tongue, then read the text from Kia. *Parking lot. Now if you're ready.*

She grabbed her coat and purse and headed out the door.

Chapter Sixteen

LAYERS OF DEEP blues and pinks danced above the mountains as the sun descended behind their snowy peaks. The cold air stung Jayla's legs as she headed for the parking lot. She contemplated going back to the cabin and throwing on a pair of jeans, but when the others came into focus, she didn't want to hold them up. Her eyes fell on Rush, leaning against the hood of the black SUV, his muscular legs crossed at the ankles, his face partially hidden by a baseball cap, and his attention completely captured by Teri and Kia, who stood in front of him wearing ungodly short skirts.

Glad I didn't go for my jeans.

"Oh good. You're here," Kia said to her as she clicked the key fob and unlocked the doors to the SUV. "I almost forgot to tell you. I heard Marcus already moved on to some other chick. He's such a dick." Kia rolled her eyes.

Thank God. "You won't get an argument on that from me."

Rush's eyes landed on Jayla's boots and ran slowly

up her legs, lingering at her skirt, then roved north, finally landing on her face. He narrowed his eyes and pressed his lips together. She took his dark stare as a compliment, and when he climbed into the passenger seat without saying a word, she knew she'd chosen the right outfit.

While she was busy watching Rush climb into the passenger seat, Patrick, Cliff, and Teri claimed the three rear seats.

"Looks like you're on Patrick's lap," Kia called to Jayla.

Rush whipped his head around and shot her a narrow-eyed dark stare. His jaw clenched, lips pressed tightly together. She knew he wouldn't offer for her to sit up front with him when they were trying to remain just friends. She'd felt the effect she had on his body when they'd kissed, and given his reaction, she was pretty sure the short skirt had an even stronger effect. The thought sent a thrill vibrating through her.

"Oh yeah, climb in, baby." Patrick patted his thighs.

Patrick was known for having roaming hands. She was just about to offer to squeeze between Cliff and Teri when she had another idea. Why not torture Rush a little? She climbed onto Cliff's lap.

"Okay, ready." She could feel Rush's eyes on her, and at the same time, she realized she had the same effect on Cliff as she had on Rush. *Ugh.*

They drove into the next town over, Allure, and parked at Bar None. Rush sidled up to her as they walked across the parking lot. "What the hell was that?"

"What?" *Oh, this is fun.*

"You could have sat on my lap." He latched on to her arm and slowed her pace.

"I didn't hear you offer." *Jealousy isn't fun, is it?*

"I didn't hear Cliff offer, either."

Good point. "Trust me, he didn't seem to mind. Besides, I'm not trying to walk a fine line with my feelings for Cliff."

Patrick held the door open, and she broke free from Rush and followed the others to a table. Cliff settled in beside her. Patrick and Teri claimed the chairs at the ends of the table, and Rush sat across from Jayla, with Kia—of course—sitting beside him.

Jayla had no idea how to do whatever it was she and Rush were doing, but by the way the muscles in his jaw were jumping, she'd clearly struck a nerve. She drew her eyes away, thinking about their predicament. Was she being stubborn and stupid? She loved him. Oh, how she loved him. What if they didn't work as a couple? She couldn't stand losing their friendship—but look how awkward things were now. Wouldn't it be ten times worse if they dated and then Rush realized he couldn't date and still focus? All that left them with was remaining friends. *Forever.* And that made her ache all over.

Her phone vibrated. She pulled it out to read a text and was surprised to see Rush's name on the screen. She lifted her eyes and saw him staring down at his lap. She couldn't help but smile as she read the text.

Cliff?

She texted back. *It's not like we're dating. No*

dating during competition remember?

Her phone vibrated a few seconds later. *That's my rule not urs.*

She tried not to enjoy his jealousy, but it was damn hard. *Oh. Right. But we said we wouldn't date each other bc of distractions. So...it's kind of the same thing.*

He texted back right away. *Good.*

She needed a drink, or twelve, to weed through this friendship of theirs. And she could only have one. Any more than that and she'd never get up at four thirty to practice.

AFTER DINNER THEY moved to a table in the dimly lit bar, where a band was playing. Teri and Patrick headed for the dance floor. Rush pulled out a chair for Jayla, but before he could claim the seat beside her, he felt a tap on his shoulder. He turned and found Rex Braden smiling down at him, a leather Stetson set high on his head. Rex was one of Savannah Braden's brothers. All the Braden men were tall and well built, and Rex was no exception. At six four with thick black hair and a body built from years of hard work on their family ranch, Rex had a formidable presence.

Rush opened his arms and embraced him. "Rex. What are you doing here?"

Rex nodded at the woman singing with the band. "That's Danica's sister, Kaylie."

Rush squinted at the pretty blonde. "I didn't recognize her."

"I came out with my buddy Cal Hayden." Rex stepped to the side, and another man of equal stature and immense breadth came into view. His hair was as blond as Rex's was black, and he also donned a leather hat and boots.

Rush held out his hand. "Rush Remington."

Cal flashed a friendly smile. "Howdy. I hear y'all are on the Olympic ski team. That right?" His eyes dropped to the others, lingering on Jayla.

Jayla smiled up at him, and Rush felt the muscles in his neck tighten.

"Yeah. We're here to teach a few ski workshops. We'll be gone before you know it." *So take your eyes off of Jayla.*

"We were just about ready to leave," Rex explained. "Then I saw you and thought I'd say hello." Kaylie began singing a slow song. "Mind if we join you? I want to hear this last song before heading home."

Yes. "Of course not. Pull up a chair."

Cal sat beside Jayla, and Rex grabbed two chairs from a nearby table and handed one to Rush.

"Hi. I'm Cal." Cal tipped his hat at Jayla.

"Jayla." She leaned closer to him as she introduced Kia.

"I knew Colorado was full of cowboys, but seeing two big, strong cowboys donning Stetsons at once?" Kia fanned her face.

Jayla laughed.

Great. "This cowboy is spoken for." Rush pointed a thumb at Rex, hoping Cal would say he was, too.

"Very," Rex confirmed.

No such luck. "How about you, Cal?" Rush hoped for confirmation.

"Nope. Single as the day is long." He tipped his hat

at Jayla.

I'll tip your hat. Every muscle in his body corded tight. His hands fisted below the table.

"Has Treat come by the resort?" Rex asked.

"Not yet." Rush caught movement in his peripheral vision and watched as Jayla and Cal joined Teri and Patrick on the dance floor. She looked damn hot in that sexy little skirt. He couldn't help but wonder what she had on underneath it. In the next breath he wondered if Cal was thinking the same thing. He gritted his teeth against the thought and tried to concentrate on what Rex was saying, but he was having trouble keeping his eyes off of Cal's hand, which was sinking dangerously close to Jayla's ass.

"Then you may not see him," Rex said. "He and Max headed out to Nassau today for a last trip before the baby's born."

Rush had forgotten that Max was also pregnant. "Good for them," he finally managed.

"Hey, Rex, wanna dance?" Kia asked.

"Thank you, but my dance card is reserved for my girlfriend, Jade."

"Aww." Kia pouted. "Rush?" She came around the table in her sexy little dress and pulled him by the hand. "Come on. Dance with me."

Rex motioned *up* with his hand.

Rush reluctantly rose to his feet. "I'm no dancer."

"It's a slow dance. If you can ski, you can slow dance." Kia dragged him to the dance floor and wrapped her arms around his neck.

Rush tried not to stare at the contented smile on Jayla's luscious lips, or to read too much into the look in Cal's eyes. He tried not to think about how good Jayla had felt against him when he held her, or how he'd do anything to be dancing with her rather than Kia, but it was flipping impossible. So he did the only thing he could. He wrapped his arms around Kia's waist and danced, gritted teeth and all.

When the song ended, Cal kept his hand possessively on Jayla's waist as they walked back to the table, and Rush fought the urge to...He didn't know what. He felt like a caged beast, and he had a feeling fists would be involved.

Rex rose as they joined him at the table. "I have to get home, but I'm glad I got to see you." He glanced at Cal. "Looks like he might want to stay a while. Do you mind?"

Rush downed his beer. "Absolutely not. Any friend of yours..." *Is apparently a friend of Jayla's, too.* "Good to see you, Rex. Tell your family I said hello."

"Will do, and we'll see you at Savannah and Jack's wedding."

"Right. Definitely." After Rex left, Rush flagged down the waitress and ordered another round of drinks.

"None for me. I'm driving," Kia said with a wave of her hand. "Jayla, are you training in the morning?"

Jayla leaned forward, listening to something Cal was saying much too closely for Rush's comfort.

"Jayla?" Kia called her again.

"Sorry, what?"

"Are you training in the morning?" Kia asked.

She shrugged. "I'm not sure, but the lift will be open at five, so you can definitely go."

"You're not sure if you're training in the morning?" Rush pinned a glare at her. The whole reason for them to nix seeing each other was so that they could focus on training. What the hell was she up to? "Jayla?"

She lifted her eyes to Rush. "Yeah? Sorry. It's hard to hear in here."

"Dance with me?" Damn if it didn't come out as a command rather than a question.

"Um, I'm kind of in the middle of a conversation." She slid her eyes to Cal and smiled at him.

"Darlin', you go right ahead and dance with your friend. I'll be here waiting for you when you return." He stood when Jayla did and tipped his hat again.

Goddamn gentleman cowboy.

It was all Rush could do not to drag her to the dance floor. It felt so good to have his arms around her again, to feel her body against his. He kept his mouth tightly closed to keep from sounding like a jealous ass.

"Thanks for dancing with me." Jayla looked up at him with her trusting eyes, and he felt like a heel.

"I have to admit, I asked you to dance because I was jealous."

She grinned. "Really? Why? You've seen me with guys before."

"Not *after* kissing you," he reminded her.

She pressed her hand to his chest and he covered it with his own.

"Is this as painful for you as it is for me?" He had to know, even if the answer was no.

"Oh, I don't know. It's not too painful talking to a handsome horse trainer who has a sexy accent and sultry eyes. Not to mention the way he pays attention to every word I say."

Every muscle in his body flexed. "Now who's the brat?" Rush turned them so Jayla's back was to Cal.

"Nice move." She narrowed her eyes and spoke in a hushed whisper. "Before we kissed, you didn't care who I danced with."

He was too busy telling himself not to lower his mouth to hers to respond.

"Before we kissed..." She licked her lips. "You'd never even looked at me like you do now. Well, maybe you did, but not before we got to Colorado." She stroked his cheek, and it sent heat straight to his groin. "Before we kissed, you never messed with my concentration." She ran her finger down his jaw to his neck and he felt himself breathing harder. "Before we kissed, you were just a fantasy that I knew would never come true."

"A fantasy." *Christ Almighty.* Rush conjured up images of Jayla lying in bed thinking of him, touching herself where he'd like to be buried deep.

She rose up on her toes and whispered, "Before we kissed, you never got hard when I was close to you."

The hell with this. He took her hand and dragged her across the crowded dance floor, past the tables, and down the hall leading to the bathrooms. He pressed his body to hers and backed her against the wall, his hands on her rib cage, both of them breathing hard.

"Don't move."

He opened the men's room door and came out a

second later, grabbed her hand, and pulled her inside the restroom. He backed her up against the door and, so thick with need he was barely able to see straight, he took her in a deep, hard kiss. They stood there chest to chest, hip to hip. He buried his hands in her hair, and she opened her mouth wider for him, making him ache for her even more. This. This was everything. She was everything. Kissing Jayla sent his world spinning. He couldn't help but drop his hands to her breasts, and rub his thumbs over her hard nipples.

"Rush."

Hearing his name come from her lips filled with want, need, desire. It spurred him on. He covered her mouth with his again and ran his hand down her hip, over her thigh, to the silky, damp material between her legs. Heat radiated from her as her hands found his ass and she rocked her hips in to him.

"Holy Christ, Jayla," he said, before lowering his lips to her neck and sucking until he drew an erotic moan from her lungs. The scent of her perfume heightened his arousal, and he pulled back and searched her eyes, gauging her desire.

She gripped the back of his neck and pulled him into another kiss. Holy hell, he loved her. He ached to touch her. To taste her. To claim her. He opened his eyes. He couldn't make love to her in a men's room. He had no car.

"Goddamn it." He kissed her again.

She rocked against him again and reached for his ass again. He gripped her wrist. If they went on too much longer, he'd take her right there.

"I need to make love to you." He had to say it.

There was no holding back what he felt, what he needed, and it wasn't just sex. He craved a deeper connection with her. He wanted to be hers as much as he wanted her to be his.

She looked down at his hand on her wrist and arched a brow.

"Not here," he said.

She drew her brows together.

"Not like this. Not with you." He pulled away and took off his hat, cursing under his breath. He ran his hand through his hair, then looked down at his hard-on, trapped beneath his zipper. He felt like he would come apart if he didn't get inside her soon. He closed the distance between them again and kissed her. "I need to feel you close to me."

"Yes," she said in one long breath.

"We gotta get outta here."

"Now," Jayla said in a harsh whisper.

Her hair fell forward, covering half of her face. She looked so damn sexy he could barely stand it. They were both breathing hard.

"Jayla, there's no turning back. If we do this, you know there isn't a chance in hell we're gonna walk away from each other."

"I know." She wrapped her fingers around the waist of his jeans and held on tight, holding his body against her.

"We both may lose focus." *No more hiding.*

Jayla held his stare. "I don't care."

He wrapped her in his arms and kissed her again. "I'm sorry about the men's room."

"Shut up and kiss me," she said in a throaty voice

that made him shudder.

The door pushed opened and sent them both flying backward. They stumbled against the wall. He caught her with one arm and glared at the blond man who looked from them to the door and back again.

"Sorry, dude," the guy said.

He was too focused on Jayla to respond. "Your shoulder?"

"Fine." She stifled a laugh, looking too damn cute not to kiss again, which he did the second they were out of the bathroom and clear of the door.

He smoothed her hair and straightened her sweater. "You have that just-been-fucked look, and we never even had the pleasure."

"You have that cock-blocked look." She went up on her tiptoes and pressed a kiss to his lips.

"We can't go back to the table like this. Or at least, I can't." He looked down at his pants and arched a brow. "You go. I'll be there in a minute."

She leaned in close. "You may be hard, but you left me wet." She pressed her cheek to his and whispered, "I think I have to take off my panties."

Jayla disappeared into the ladies' room. There wasn't a chance in hell Rush would lose his erection with that image in his mind.

JAYLA BURIED HER panties in the trash, then leaned against the bathroom wall and tried to catch her breath. Her heart was racing, but that didn't compare to the aroused hum that vibrated through her entire body. She pressed her hand over her heart and closed her eyes, breathing deeply, trying to calm her racing heart.

"There you are." Kia came through the bathroom door and went directly to the mirror to check her hair and makeup. "One minute you were dancing, and the next, you and Rush were gone."

Oh shit.

"I saw Rush out in the hall. He said you weren't feeling very well." She lifted her eyes to Jayla in the mirror. "Are you okay? Do you need some Midol or something?"

I need some Rush Remington. "No, thanks. I think it was just the heat from dancing. Is Rush still out there?"

Kia shrugged and applied a fresh coat of lipstick. "But that singer came over and stole that hunky cowboy of yours away from the table."

"Oh my God. Have I been gone that long?" She washed her hands in cold water and patted her face with a wet paper towel.

"Fifteen minutes, maybe. You okay? Should we leave?"

Yes! Yes! Yes! "Actually, yeah, I think we should." It was all she could do not to run out of the bathroom and to the parking lot.

Chapter Seventeen

JAYLA RODE HOME sitting on Rush's lap in the passenger seat of the SUV. Within seconds of getting on the road, Rush slid his hand beneath her jacket, and in turn, beneath her clothes to her bare skin. The car was dark and the others were busy talking about the evening, which was a good thing, because Jayla could barely breathe, much less think as his thumb grazed the underside of her breast. By the time Kia pulled into the parking lot, he was rock hard, and she was damp again. She stepped from the SUV and Rush drew her against him in a blatantly possessive embrace.

And she loved it.

"I'm going to take Jayla home." His voice was gruff, commanding.

"Feel better, Jay," Kia called.

She'd almost forgotten that she'd feigned feeling sick. They walked quickly down the stone path toward the cabins, and as soon as they were out of eyeshot of the others, Rush pulled her behind a grouping of pine trees and took her in a kiss so deep and sensuous, her body went warm despite the cold night breeze. His hand slid down her hip, and her knees weakened.

"I'm sorry. You're probably cold," he said between heavy breaths.

She shook her head. "Hot."

His eyes widened, then narrowed before he lowered his lips to hers again. He felt so good, so right. She wondered how she could have ever thought that competing was more important than him. Than this. Than them. She could feel his love in his strong and careful embrace. When they finally drew apart, his gaze was soft, assessing, and she loved that about him. He was always considerate of her.

"My place?"

She nodded, knowing her voice would never work.

Rush moved behind her as he unlocked the door, forming a protective shield from the wind as it whipped around the side of the cabin. He pushed the door open, pressing his hips into her from behind. She leaned her head back against his chest, loving and relishing in the electricity that hadn't replaced, but added to, the quiet comfort of their friendship. He reached an arm around her waist from behind, then lowered his mouth to her neck as he guided her inside and kicked the door shut behind them. Jayla's body was on fire. His stubble grated against her neck, and he ran his tongue along the tender scratches before gently turning her to face him and gazing lovingly into her eyes. He brushed her hair from her shoulder and held her cheeks between his large palms.

"Jayla." His voice was thick with desire. "You're sure?"

She nodded again. His glorious, masculine scent was everywhere, in the air, on his skin, in her lungs.

He lowered his hands to her hips. "One hundred percent? Because I can't make love to you and then go back to just being friends. Hell, I'm not sure I can go back to just being friends now anyway. I damn near wanted to kill that cowboy for putting his hands on you."

"Yes. One hundred percent. Yes." *I have no idea what I was thinking before. You're all I've ever wanted, and even if I lose focus, I want you. All of you.* "I love that you care enough to ask," she managed.

"I care too damn much. Way too damn much."

His lips were an inch from hers. One little movement and they'd meet again, but guilt stabbed at her and her shoulder ached. She couldn't cross this line with Rush without being perfectly honest with him.

She swallowed past the urge to remain silent and kiss him and forced herself to speak. "I...I have to tell you something."

He leaned his forehead on hers, his chest rising and falling with each heated breath.

"Okay, but if you're going to tell me that you just want to be friends, shoot me instead."

"No. I want this. I want us. I just need you to know something before we do this." She grabbed hold of his coat collar and held on tight.

"Afraid I'll run away?"

"No," she whispered. "I'm afraid I will."

"Oh, babe. Really?" He took her in his arms and held her close. "Is it that bad?"

"My injury might be," she said against his shoulder.

He drew back and searched her eyes. She saw him measuring the truth of her words.

He narrowed his gaze. "You're serious. Oh, Jayla. I'm so sorry." His eyes danced over her shoulder.

She shrugged.

"No, this isn't a shrug. Did I hurt you when I touched you? Kissed you? Oh God, when you were against the wall?"

"No, no."

"Have you talked to all the team docs?"

She shook her head.

"Specialists?"

She shook her head again. "Remember when I tore the lining of my shoulder socket? This feels worse, and they told me last time that another tear would probably stop me from competing."

Rush tossed his baseball hat on the floor and ran his hand through his hair. He gently rubbed her shoulder. "How much pain are you in?"

She swallowed hard.

He shook his head. "Jayla, why didn't you tell me?"

"Because I thought I could build up the muscles and still compete. Some people can. I read about it online, and it depends on the tear—where it is, the size, circumstances."

"Jayla, that's what these docs do for a living. They can figure all that out."

She hooked her finger into the waist of his jeans. "Can we talk about it tomorrow? Right now I've got advertising contracts and sponsors, and...I've got you.

Tonight. Now. I just want to enjoy it, because if I have this surgery, that all may go away, and that's too much for me to think about right now."

He kissed her forehead. "You know I'm not going anywhere, right? Whether you're a competitive skier or not makes no difference. I love you for you, Jayla. Whatever needs to be done for your shoulder, or anything else, we'll get through it together." He lowered his lips to hers, and relief swept through her.

Her breath caught in her throat. "L-love?"

He gazed into her eyes. "Yes. Love. Without an ounce of doubt, Jayla, I love you."

"Rush, I..." *Don't cry. Don't cry.* She'd held the words in for so many years that she had trouble setting them free. "I...Oh God, Rush. I love you, too."

"Even with my past? You aren't going to regret those words tomorrow?"

She shook her head. "I haven't regretted saying them in my head forever, so I can't imagine ever regretting saying them aloud to you."

He kissed her softly "Why did you decide to tell me about your shoulder now?"

"So that if you wanted to change your mind, you could do it before I knew what it was like to be close to you. To be loved by you."

"You can't get rid of me that easily." Rush helped her off with her coat before removing his own and tossing them both on a chair.

Jayla glanced nervously around his dark, tidy cabin. Canisters of protein powder sat atop the kitchen counter along with a crumpled paper, a handful of change, and a few skiing magazines. She eyed the open bedroom door and her pulse kicked up a notch. Butterflies swarmed in her stomach. She closed her eyes at the feel of Rush's hands on her bare legs as he slowly unzipped her boots. When he slid the warm leather from her legs, it was the most erotic thing she'd ever felt. His hands traveled up her legs, hesitating at the edge of her skirt. When he touched the bare skin of her hips, Jayla sucked in a breath and opened her eyes.

His eyes went dark. "You weren't lying about your panties."

She bit her lower lip and he smiled, then pressed soft kisses along her chin, pulling a sigh of pleasure from her. He kissed her softly as his hands found her waist; then he deepened the kiss. Every stroke of his tongue stole a little more of her breath. He rocked into her, and she clutched at his chest, feeling his muscles jump beneath her fingertips. Lord, did he feel good. When he slid his lips to her neck again, she shivered and snuck her hands beneath his shirt, grasping handfuls of muscle and skin on his strong back, grabbing for any piece of him she could hold on to. His hands roved over her breasts, bringing every nerve to the surface, heightening every sensation.

Her knees weakened, and she couldn't hold back her desire. "Rush," she whispered.

She held her breath as he gently removed her sweater without lifting her sore shoulder too high. He tossed it onto the counter and stepped closer. His breath became hers, and the heat of his body enveloped her.

"I dreamed about you in this sexy little camisole,"

he whispered against her neck.

She shuddered. "And?"

"And I might not have been sleeping." He drew her camisole over her head, exposing her bare breasts. "Good Christ, you're beautiful."

He lowered his mouth to her breast, hungrily devouring every inch of skin and driving her out of her ever-loving mind. He moved his attention to the other breast, pulling a gasp from her lips. She clawed at his back, craving skin-to-skin contact and spurring him on to lavish her nipple with slow strokes of his hot tongue.

She tugged at his shirt. "Off," she managed.

He pulled his shirt over his head and tossed it away, then took her in another kiss, pinning her against the door. His hard length pressed against her, pulling a moan of need from her lungs. She lifted her knee along his outer leg, and he gripped it with his hand and held on tight, grinding against her.

"Rush," she said against his lips.

His hand found her center with a moan of his own. He captured her mouth in his again, and his fingers teased her until her body felt ridden with pins and needles. She reached for the button on his jeans and he shook his head.

"Not yet."

She whimpered a plea, and he slid his fingers inside of her. She sucked in another breath. His thumb moved expertly, caressing the sensitive nub that drove her hands to clutch the waist of his pants as he kissed her harder, thrusting his tongue in rhythm to his fingers. Her thighs tensed, and she gasped for air as he brought her up to the edge and held her there. She could feel the pull of an orgasm, taunting her, driving her up on her toes, pulling whimpers from her mouth to his, until she thought she might go crazy, and finally, he softened the kiss and quickened his tease, sending her over the edge. She drew back from the kiss with the need to breathe, crying out against the explosion of sensations that coursed through her. She felt her muscles pulsating around his fingers. His tongue on her neck, his teeth grazed her skin as she came down from the peak. And he took her in another hard kiss, still holding her leg by his hip, teasing and taunting her again until she was right back at the precipice of another orgasm, begging, pleading for more. He took her over the edge again, and she threw her head back and clawed at his skin.

"Oh God. Oh God."

Her legs trembled as he lifted her into his arms and carried her into the bedroom. She slid down his body until her feet hit the floor. She clung to him, unsure whether her legs still worked. He must have sensed her unsteadiness, because he held her against him with one arm and used the other to unbutton his jeans and step from them. She couldn't shimmy out of her skirt fast enough. She'd seen Rush in his boxer briefs a million times, but she never could have imagined how his lean, hard frame could arouse her as he stood naked before her. She tried to look away but was held captive by the look of love in his eyes.

He reached for her hand, then for his wallet.

She grabbed his wrist and shook her head. "I'm on the pill."

He hesitated, and she knew what he was thinking. He'd told her straight up about his past, but he'd never asked about hers.

"Three men, and never without a condom." She saw the question in the narrowing of his eyes, the parting of his lips.

"Because it's you, Rush. I want all of you. I've always wanted all of you."

He kissed her then, and they came down on the bed together, his strong body perched above her, the tip of his arousal against her center, and his eyes—those sensuous blue eyes—reached right inside her and touched her soul.

"I love you, Jayla. I think I always have."

As he slid inside her, she closed her eyes. She'd dreamed of this moment forever, and she never wanted to forget the feel of his chest against hers, the scratch of his stubble as he kissed her, his hard length buried deep and moving inside her like she was all he ever wanted, too.

Chapter Eighteen

RUSH LAY ON his back beside Jayla with one arm arced over his head, his other hand interlaced with hers, and his heart beating faster than during a downhill race. Their naked bodies touched from shoulder to ankle, and he felt full. Satiated. Happy. He never realized that sex could make him feel so fulfilled. Then again, he knew that this wasn't just sex.

He pushed up on one elbow, and Jayla shifted her eyes away from him. He assumed she was embarrassed and pulled the sheet from the bottom of the bed up and covered her.

"Better?"

She closed her eyes, and Rush sank back down to the mattress with a sigh.

"That's not the reaction I was expecting, but..."

She smiled, opened one eye, then closed it again.

"Not doing much for the old ego here, babe." Rush had more experience fleeing beds than he did remaining in them, but strangely, the need to flee was coming from her side of the bed. He didn't quite know how to handle that.

"I'm trying to figure out if I should lie here and fall asleep, get up and eat gummy bears, take a shower, or go to my cabin." Jayla opened her eyes and finally met his gaze.

"All those things are going through your mind right now? Hm. And my mind is just...blown. I can barely think past, *Wow, that was amazing.*" He came back up on his elbow and kissed her lips.

"Who knew my alpha badass was such a chick?"

She bit her lower lip and it made him want to climb right back on top of her.

"Like I said, you're not exactly great for my ego."

She laughed. "I'm teasing. I'm trying to decide if you want me to go to my cabin or not. Don't forget, I know you. You've already had me in your bed longer than you're comfortable with."

It killed him that she'd even think that way, but if she'd been anyone else, she'd have been right. "Yeah, you do know me, but as we've already determined, I don't think either of us knows what to expect from the new and improved boyfriend-worthy man I've become."

She pushed up on her elbow. The room was dark, with just a hint of moonlight peeking in between the curtains. Her hair tumbled over her breasts, and she had that freshly loved look of sleepy contentment in her eyes. His heart squeezed a little.

"So? Go or stay?" she asked.

"Stay. Definitely stay."

"You do realize that if I come out of your cabin in the same clothes I was wearing last night, people are going to talk."

"You know they won't, but if you're worried, let's get cleaned up and go to your cabin. They're used to seeing me come out of your room at all hours of the night." Rush wondered if she was just nervous, and if she was, he'd do whatever it took to calm her. He ran his hand through his hair and sighed. "It's weird, isn't it? No one has ever questioned us about that, and if it had been anyone else, they would have."

"We are so thickly seeded in the friend zone that they probably don't even think that way."

"Were. We were thickly seeded in the friend zone." *The others might not, but the coach thinks of us in that way.*

Jayla wrapped the sheet around herself and walked to the bathroom.

"I've seen you naked, you know."

She glanced over her shoulder with a shy smile and flushed cheeks and pushed the bathroom door partially shut behind her. Rush heard the shower turn on and debated joining her.

He lay back down. He didn't want to smother her on their first night together.

"You coming or what?" Jayla called from the bathroom.

Oh hell, yes.

Seeing her in his shower, water running over the planes of her lean body, got him hot and bothered again.

She ran her eyes down his body as he stepped in beside her. "If you're careful with my shoulder, I just might let you show me how great shower sex can be."

He backed her up against the wet tiles.

"Jayla Stone, I'm gonna love you until you can't even think about a shower without blushing."

THIRTY MINUTES LATER, Rush helped Jayla into one of his long-sleeved shirts, which hung to the middle of her thighs. She had no panties from the night before and only a skirt, so she threw on a pair of his sweatpants instead, which hung several inches past her feet and looked like they'd swallowed her.

Rush had the urge to take a picture and Instagram it with the caption, *Eat your heart out, America. She's my sweetheart now.* Seeing Jayla in his clothes should have sent his mind right back into the friend zone. Instead, his pulse ratcheted up and heat pulsed through him. He took her in his arms and nuzzled against her neck.

"I want to take you right back to bed." He pressed his hips against her so she could feel what she was doing to him. He felt her fingers tighten around his waist.

"Then do it," she said in a breathy whisper.

Chapter Nineteen

SOMETIME DURING THE night, Rush had gone to Jayla's cabin to retrieve her clothes for the morning, and now, with the sun streaming through the windows, having worked painfully through her shoulder exercises, showered, and dressed, Jayla listened to the sounds of Rush in the other room. His footsteps crossed the bedroom floor. She heard the shifting of skin against denim, the sound of the zipper of his jeans. They were familiar sounds, and yet they were completely new and exciting. She'd known that coming together with Rush would be earth-shattering, but what she hadn't expected was how quickly her mind would flip from being his friend to being his girlfriend. It not only happened quickly, but easily, as if all her stubbornness and worry had been for naught.

He'd loved and lingered over every inch of her. She felt her cheeks flush, thinking of all the naughty things they'd done as they discovered each other's pleasures for the first time.

She stood in the kitchen, her heart full of him and

a throbbing pain in her shoulder. *Totally worth it.* She wondered how they'd handle their relationship with their teammates and coach, and the pain in her shoulder made her wonder if they'd even have to worry about it next year. She refused to think about that.

Jayla carried a cup of coffee into the bedroom for Rush.

"Thanks, beautiful." He kissed her cheek.

Beautiful. Not *Jay. Beautiful.* She loved that.

"I grabbed a premade protein shake from the convenience store at the resort after the gym so I wouldn't wake you with the blender. Sorry I kept you up so late, but that's what you get for being so damn cute."

"Maybe I'll borrow your clothes more often. How was the gym? Did you have any energy to work out?"

"You mean while you snored away? I was tired after two hours of sleep, but no biggie."

She'd slept in instead of going to either the slopes or the gym, and at first she'd felt guilty, but between clinging to Rush last night, teaching during the day, and evening practices, the dull ache in her shoulder had worsened. She'd opted for rest, light shoulder exercises, and recuperation.

He pulled her close and she winced.

He narrowed his eyes. "Where are your pain meds?"

"I'm taking Motrin and Tylenol."

"That's insane. You must be in tremendous pain."

She walked into the living room and sank into the couch. "Oh, please. It's not anything I can't deal with."

She would give her eyeteeth to take stronger pain meds, but she knew they would slow her down.

Rush sat on the coffee table across from her and set his coffee cup beside him. He rested his hands on her knees and gave her the serious look she knew so well. The *you know I'm right* look.

"So, let's talk about this. No more avoiding it. No more hiding the truth."

She dropped her eyes. "Truth? My shoulder is going to end my career." She fought against the tears that came too easily.

He reached for her. "Come here."

"No." She pulled away. He searched her eyes and she shifted them away.

"You're shutting me out of this? Talk to me, Jayla. What's your plan?"

"I don't really have one. I want to keep trying to build strength, and after this weekend's competition, I'll see the doctor. If it's definitely a tear, maybe I'll have the surgery, but I don't even know if that's the right thing to do. What if it can heal on its own and surgery just messes it up more?" She pushed to her feet so he wouldn't see the tears in her eyes.

"Jayla." His voice was laden with concern. "You know the chances of the doctors being that far off."

She turned with anger in her chest and worry in her belly—and goddamn tears in her eyes. In the next breath, he was on his feet and she was wrapped safely in his arms.

"What if they're right? They told me last time that another shoulder injury would probably end my career. What if I really can't compete again?" Her tears soaked into his soft T-shirt. She clutched his chest, and she was sure she'd taken purchase of his chest hair, which had to hurt, but he didn't shift away. He held her tighter.

"Then you won't compete."

Four simple words that cut her to the core. She clenched her eyes shut against the pain of them. It was Rush who pulled her from her hiding place against his chest. She reached for him, and he placed his hands firmly on the sides of her head and made her look up at him, tears and all.

"You are not just a competitive skier. I know you, Jayla. You're just like me. You're thinking that your life is over if you can't compete. And it's not."

"You know that's...not true," she said through the stupid tears that made her feel weak. "Our whole lives we've been scared of this, Rush." She pushed away from him as her voice escalated. "Remember? Shoot us. That's what we said we wanted to happen if we couldn't compete. Because what's left?"

"What's left? You. Me. Us. And even if you can't compete, you'll probably still be able to ski."

"You don't know that. What if they screw up my shoulder so badly that I can't?"

"What if you damage it so badly that they can't repair it?"

The challenge in his eyes pissed her off. She turned and walked away.

He was half a step behind her. "You can't pretend this isn't happening, and I won't let you hurt yourself so badly that it can never be fixed."

She spun around. "You know what? I get to make

that decision. Not you. Not the coaches." She pointed at her chest. "Me, Rush. It's my body, my decision."

He ran his hand through his hair, and she saw his biceps flex and his hands curl into fists. Determination gave way to frustration, and he paced, breathing fast and hard.

"Damn it, Jayla. Fine. Okay, fine. You're right. You're an athlete, and a damn good one. You get to make that call. I was out of line." He ran his hand over his face.

She went to him, feeling guilty for being so full of herself when he was only trying to help.

"No, you were in line with your worry, but it's my decision." Her entire body trembled, but she managed to speak calmly. She reached for the counter and leaned against it, trying to clear her thoughts. "I'm sorry I'm such a wimp, and I'm sorry I'm so angry, but…"

He reached for her again, and this time she didn't pull away.

"Wimp? An army of women could never be as strong as you. It's okay to be angry, but don't confuse what you're angry at. I get it, and I'm a patient guy, but I'm not the enemy."

"I know you're not."

"Okay. Good. I want to go with you to the doc. I want to hear what they say. I want to see the scans. Whatever it is, Jayla, we can get through it together."

She held his gaze. "Okay, but I'm competing this weekend."

"Fine."

She let out a breath. "Really?"

"Your body, your decision. Besides, it's what I would want if I were you, so even though as your boyfriend I can't stand to think about you in pain, as your teammate, I'd expect nothing less from you."

"Oh, thank God." She fell into his arms and held on tight. "Thank you." His body was tense, and she didn't blame him. She knew he hated not being able to fix this for her, but she wasn't going to back down. She already felt better having shared the truth with the one person she knew would understand.

"Don't thank me. You know damn well that you could end up with a worse injury from practicing, much less competing. And if that happens, I'll have to live with the guilt of not forcing you to stop."

"You can't force me."

He looked down at her with a crooked grin. "I've got a foot and about a hundred-plus pounds on you, and it pisses me off to know that you're goddamn right. Can we at least talk about options in case you can't compete in the future?"

"Only if you want my fangs to come out."

He didn't ask again.

Rush made egg-white omelets and toast, and after they ate breakfast, Jayla washed the dishes as Rush dried them.

"We need some rules," Rush said.

"Oh God, please tell me you haven't been hiding some freaky side of yourself all these years, because without skiing and without my best friend, I might lose my mind."

"No freaky sides. Unless you want there to be." He arched a brow.

She rolled her eyes.

"I just mean that I think there are a few things we should talk about. I do have some rights as a boyfriend."

She touched his stomach. "I like that, you know. *Boyfriend.*"

"Probably not as much as I like knowing that I get to claim you as my girlfriend." He set down the plate he was drying and leaned against the counter with a sigh. "Before we get to boyfriend rules, what about Coach C and the team? How do you want to handle them? And before you answer, you need to know that Coach asked me not to get involved with you."

"No, he did not." *What the hell?*

Rush nodded. "Yup. He said you needed to focus and I'd screw that up for you. He's right, you know. We'll probably both lose focus."

"No, we won't, because until after the competition, we're keeping our relationship just between us. I don't need Coach on my back, and you don't need him on yours, either."

"I'm not sure I can promise that."

"Sure you can."

He leaned close to her. "When I see you, I want to touch you." He kissed her. "Like that."

"Mm. Oh, wait, I'm not supposed to enjoy that." She sighed. "You'll have to think of it as a competition, then. We both will. Which one of us can hide our affection in public the longest?" She smiled, and he shook his head.

"I'm defeated the minute we walk out this door."

She laughed. "You can do this. If I can go without

pain meds, you can go without kisses. Besides, you've always held my hand and put your arm around me. As long as you aren't looking at me like"—she looked into his eyes and nearly melted at the desire she saw there—"*that*, we'll be okay."

"Like what?"

"Maybe you won't be okay." She lifted his shirt and pressed a kiss to his belly.

"Christ Almighty. There's no way in hell we'll fool anyone."

She lifted up on her toes, and he took her in a deep, delicious kiss. She came away dizzy.

"There can't be any of...that," she whispered.

"You're trying to kill me. Now I get it." He pulled her into another kiss; then he took her hand and placed it on his bulging, hard zipper. "Just one more reason there can be none of that in public. That's girlfriend rule number one."

She glanced at the clock, calculated in time for a quickie before the workshop, then groaned when she realized they'd never make it.

"Now that we have that torturous stuff out in the open, my turn. Boyfriend rules. If your shoulder shows any signs of getting worse, you tell me. Right away."

"Okay."

"I mean it, Jayla." His voice filled with seriousness, and he held her gaze. "We have to trust each other on every level."

"Fine, then I need to be able to trust that you're not going to take any women's numbers anymore." She watched his brows pull together.

"I haven't done that in ages. You heard me tell that

woman on the slopes that I wouldn't meet her."

"Yeah, I did." She turned back to the sink. "But I also saw Kelly Baker's phone number on your counter."

"What are you talking about?"

She closed her eyes. "No way, Rush. There's not a chance in hell I'll play games with any man. Especially you."

He touched her arm, and when she turned and looked at him, she read honest confusion in his eyes.

"Jay, I'd never expect you to. What number?"

"There was a crumpled paper on your counter and I...got curious."

He looked at the paper on the counter. "Shit. You're absolutely right. She shoved that in my hand after class and I never looked at it. I crushed it in my fist and shoved it in my pocket."

She searched his eyes again. "I believe you, but..."

"But what? Anything you want. Just tell me."

"I want to know that next time you won't take it. That I won't have to worry about finding a number on the counter or in your pocket. Mostly, though, I want to know that you're sure you don't want to accept any more numbers, because if you ever hurt me like that, it would be more than I could take."

His lips spread into a smile.

"Stop looking at me like that. I'm serious. You have no idea how it feels to watch women lust after you."

He pulled her close and looked into her eyes. "Oh, I don't?"

"No, and you know I'm right."

"How about the handsome cowboy with the sexy

accent?"

Gulp.

"I believe that's what sent us onto the dance floor and into the men's room," he reminded her.

"I didn't take his phone number." *Touché!*

"No, you didn't. You just hung on his every word and looked at him like you should have been looking at me."

He had her there.

"So, let's make sure we're both clear." His serious tone returned. "I know that you are the only woman I will ever want. No phone numbers and no more flirting." He held her against him.

"Careful. I'm not sure you know how not to flirt, Rush."

"I do, too."

"I know you don't, which is why I didn't ask you to promise not to. That's something that can only change if *you* want it to."

He stepped back. "Well, I don't want you flirting with other men."

"I won't."

"How can you say that and not ask the same of me?"

"Because I don't need to. I trust that you'll figure that part out on your own."

Chapter Twenty

FLURRIES FELL THROUGHOUT the morning and turned to steady snowfall by midafternoon, causing the students to be too excited to focus. Rush couldn't wait for the classes to be over so he could hit the real slopes. The need nagged like a relentless itch, and his thoughts drifted to Jayla. He'd been watching her closely, and he had no idea how he could have missed the way she cringed when she gripped her pole too tightly or leaned too heavily on her right side. He had to remind himself that she wasn't just a woman with a hurt shoulder. She was *Jayla Stone*, Olympic medalist. Athlete. She knew her limits, and he knew she'd push them. Even though it went against every protective bone in his body, he knew he had to accept that.

The students were perched and ready to ski down the intermediate slope. Suzie flipped her hair and threw Taylor a flirtatious smile. Rush was relieved that she'd at least set her sights on someone her own age, even if Meg was giving her the stink eye. He skied next to Jeffrey.

"How's it going?"

"All right." He fidgeted with his poles.

"Nervous about going down?" Jeffrey had already proven to be one of the strongest skiers in the class, but as Rush knew, skill didn't preclude nerves.

"Not really." He shot a look at Taylor.

Rush eyed Taylor, who was talking behind his hand to Suzie. Suzie looked at Jeffrey and giggled.

"Ignore them, Jeffrey. Focus on your run down this mountain." He shot Taylor a hot stare, and Taylor looked away.

Jeffrey nodded and, satisfied that he could hold his own for a few minutes, Rush made his way over to Jayla.

"Hi." Jayla's cheeks flushed. "You're looking at me like you're not supposed to."

"I'm...Really?"

She nodded.

"Then we have a problem." He leaned in close and lowered his voice. "Because this is what it looks like to fight the urge to kiss you." He knew from the way she bit her lower lip that she was fighting the same urge. "How's your shoulder?"

"Rule number two. No asking about it. The more I think about it, the more it hurts."

"Okay. Fair enough. Just remember your promise." He pulled down his goggles. "See you at the bottom." He addressed the kids. "All right. You know the rules. Give each other plenty of space, and take it easy. Safety first."

Rush watched them launch down the hill. Taylor led, followed by Suzie, Meg, and Chris. Jeffrey wisely gave Taylor a wide berth before taking his turn. Rush bided his time, waiting for Jayla to go down ahead of him so he could gauge how much she was favoring her right side.

At the bottom of the slope, Rush heard Jeffrey's father's voice above the din of the skiers.

"Good job, Jeffrey," Mr. Dager said with pride.

Jeffrey waved to his father as Rush called the kids over to conclude the class.

"You were all over that slope, daddy's boy," Taylor said as he skied past Jeffrey.

Jeffrey looked away.

Rush was about a breath away from grabbing Taylor by his collar and knocking his head into tomorrow. He didn't want to step in and embarrass Jeffrey, but he wasn't above a little visual intimidation.

Rush locked his eyes on Taylor. "You all did a great job today. Let's review rules of safety before you leave. Taylor, three rules of safety. Go." He took pleasure in the way Taylor fidgeted against his stare.

"Yield to others, observe signs." Taylor sighed.

"And?" Rush pushed.

Taylor shrugged.

"These are the most important things you need to know before stepping onto the slopes. Anyone else?" Every other student raised their hand. Rush looked at Taylor and raised his brows with a smirk. *Little smart-ass.* "Jeffrey, three rules. Go."

Jeffrey kept his eyes trained on his skis. "Um, skiers ahead of you have the right of way. Safety on the slopes is everyone's responsibility, and keep off of closed trails and slopes."

"Excellent. Suzie, help him out."

"Don't stop on trails and obstruct others. Don't ride any lift you don't know how to get onto and off of safely, and use cords and whatever other devices you have to keep your equipment from running away. Wait…" She scrunched her nose. "To prevent runaway equipment. Yeah, that's it."

"That's right. Taylor, I suggest you learn those before tomorrow. We gave your parents a handout the first day of class and that information was in it. Who studied it?"

Everyone raised their hand except Taylor.

"Way to go, guys. I'm proud of you. We'll see you tomorrow." Rush put his hand on Taylor's shoulder and held him back from leaving. "I want to talk to you."

"What?" Taylor lifted his chin, as if challenging Rush.

Rush looked down at the ornery teen's defiant gaze. "I heard what you said to Jeffrey."

"So?" Taylor shrugged.

"So if I hear you pulling that with him again I'll have a talk with your parents."

"Whatever." Taylor shrugged again.

Taylor's father waved Taylor over, and Rush touched his shoulder again. "I mean it. It stops here and now."

Jayla joined him, and as they removed their skis, she said, "What was that about?"

"The kid's a jerk."

"Yeah, but that usually comes from the parents, so you can't really fault him for it."

"Rush?"

Kelly Baker. Goddamn it.

Jayla took a step away, and Rush grabbed the sleeve of her coat. "Please stay."

She blinked up at him and said quietly, "I don't need to watch."

"Well, I agreed to girlfriend rules. I want you to see that I'm sticking with them." He walked over to Kelly.

"Hi. Suzie's doing great. She's become much more confident over the last two classes."

"Yeah?" She ran her hand down her hip and flipped her hair over her shoulder. "That's good, I guess."

You guess?

She took out her cell phone and held it up to Rush. "I was surprised that I didn't hear from you."

"Surprised?" A year ago he'd have jumped on the chance to be with an easy, pretty woman like her. That felt like a lifetime ago, and he had no desire to go back.

"I gave you my number. Remember?" She smiled and tilted her head in that overtly practiced fashion again.

"Kelly, I'm sorry if you thought I wanted your number, but I have a girlfriend." He took off his hat and shoved it in his pocket.

She took a step closer and lowered her voice. "Well, that doesn't have to stop us from seeing each other. I'm all about discretion."

Rush glanced over Kelly's shoulder at her daughter. Suzie rolled her eyes and looked away. A sick feeling washed through him. "I wouldn't dream of hurting my girlfriend that way." He walked back to

Jayla, slung his arm over her shoulder, and they headed toward the lodge.

"See? Easy." Rush kissed her temple.

"Why do I feel guilty?" She rested her head on his shoulder.

"Because you're not used to asking me for anything, and in your beautiful mind, you think that you're asking me to change who I am. But I already have changed, and I have no intention of going back. I just feel bad for Suzie. Can you imagine having a mom like that? To be honest, it kinda kills me knowing that I used to be the kind of guy who would have added to all that mess."

AS THEY NEARED the cabins, Jayla's stomach was doing flips. *Do we go to my cabin? His? Do we have time to rip off our clothes and make up for all the years we missed?* She glanced at Rush, who was probably calculating how much time it would take him to prepare his protein shake, get a few push-ups and sit-ups in, and...*And what?* Was he thinking the same thing she was?

She pulled out her keys. "I guess I'll see you at practice?"

"I'll...Do you want me to stop over so we can go together?"

She heard it in his voice, an awkwardness that had never been there before, and she hated it.

"Sure, okay."

He leaned down to kiss her.

"Hey, guys!" Kia hollered from the path.

Rush pulled back fast. "Hey."

"Jayla, missed you this morning. It was a perfect practice, too. I'm heading over early to the meeting. Wanna go with?" Kia ran her eyes between them. "Did I interrupt a BFF thing?"

"Um, no. I'm just heading inside." Jayla hurried up the stairs and unlocked her door.

Rush drew his keys from his pocket. "We've got some stuff to do, but we'll meet you there, Kia."

"Cool. Okay."

Jayla went inside and leaned her back against the door. Why was she such a mess? *Who cares if Kia knows about us?* It took her a minute to realize that then the coach would find out, and Rush had already been warned away, which pissed her off even more. She stomped to the kitchen and took Tylenol and Motrin, then headed into the bedroom to do her shoulder exercises.

Her phone vibrated on the floor beside her. She glanced at the screen. *Rush.*

She read the text. *Was that weird, or was it just me?*

She breathed a sigh of relief. At least she wasn't losing her mind. She texted back. *Def weird. But it shouldn't have been. Are we making a mistake?*

When he didn't return her text right away, she worried. *Ugh.* She never would have believed that anything could make things awkward between them. *This sucks. Royally sucks.* She finished her exercises and checked her phone for the fourth time. Still no text. Her stomach sank.

There was a banging at the door in the bedroom that led outside to the back of the cabin, and it caused her to jump. She peeked through the curtains and saw Rush looking at her with a serious scowl on his face. Butterflies took flight in her stomach as she opened the door.

Rush pushed past her. "Mistake?"

He closed the distance between them. Then his lips met hers and his tongue swept away all of the uncertainty and awkwardness. Wrapped in his arms, pressed against him, she could barely think. When he drew back from the kiss, a little sound of longing escaped her lips.

His forehead wrinkled and his eyes filled with sadness. "Mistake?" he whispered.

She swallowed hard to remind herself how to breathe again and to try to form a sentence in her desire-laden mind. She shook her head.

"No," she finally managed. "I didn't mean mistake between us. I don't think we're a mistake. I could never think we were a mistake."

He let out a breath. "You're going to give me a heart attack, you know that, right? Please don't say something like that unless you really mean it. I've waited months to finally tell you how much I love you."

"I've waited years," she admitted.

"Oh, babe."

She snuggled in to his chest. "It just seemed awkward."

"It was. It's because we're worried about the coach finding out. I need to talk to him so he doesn't find out by accident."

"It's more than that. I mean, do we go to my cabin?

Yours? Do we act like we always have? Am I supposed to wait for you to say you want to see me, or ask me out? I never thought it would be hard or confusing, but it's kind of complicated."

"It's a little complicated. But what isn't?" He smiled down at her. "We'll figure out all the details that are worrying you. I promise." Rush placed his hands on her arms and she winced. His eyes fell on her shoulder. "You said you'd tell me if your shoulder worsened. I can't even touch your arm? Babe, you're in no shape to practice."

"I'm fine." She shrugged away from him. "And we decided it was my decision, remember?" Her shoulder had been worsening all afternoon, and she knew practice would be a bear. She felt like the whole world was spinning around her, and somewhere among the chaos was Rush—sweet, caring, supportive, loving Rush—and she was stumbling to find her footing and a clear path to him that didn't include injuries or trouble focusing.

"Yes, but, Jayla, this is only one competition. It's not the Olympics, and it's not even a huge competition. You're taking a risk by—"

"Really, Rush? Not a huge competition? You and I both know that the minute I start thinking like that, I'm done." She stared him down and knew that regardless of the words he said, somewhere in his mind, he agreed.

"Before last night I would have been right there telling you to push through the pain. You know I would. That would have been hard, but now?" He narrowed his gaze and nearly stopped her heart.

"There's no more pretending. I can't even fake myself out. I love you, and making love to you revived every emotion I've ever stifled. Now I'm supposed to just stand by and watch my girlfriend take a risk that you know damn well you shouldn't?"

She took a step closer to him and spoke far more calmly than she felt. "I'm an Olympic skier, like you. We compete. We train. We push through our aches and pains."

"And you're also my girlfriend."

"So support me," she pleaded. "Don't ask me to do less than you would if you and I were still just friends." She hooked her finger in the waist of his jeans. "If we hadn't admitted our feelings to each other, or slept together, you'd be pushing me, not mollycoddling me. So act like we never did."

His eyes softened as he lowered himself to the bed. "You thought that was awkward with Kia? What the hell do you think practice will be like?"

If my shoulder is any indication—it'll be two hours of hell.

Chapter Twenty-One

RUSH MADE A point of standing a good distance from Jayla, knowing there wasn't a chance in hell that he'd be able to keep from reaching out and touching her at some point—even with Coach Cunningham's steely stare burning a path between them.

"Today is Thursday. You've got less than two days before the North Face Competition, the last competition of the season. Less than forty-eight hours to shave time and prepare. That means no more late nights. No more partying in Allure or coming in at three in the morning." He locked eyes with Patrick, then paced a path with his heavy boots. "Any injuries, ailments, issues I need to know about?" He slid his gaze to Jayla. "No colds? No aches or pains? Jayla? How's that shoulder?"

"Fine, Coach." She stood with her shoulders back.

Rush watched the coach narrow his eyes as they drifted to her right shoulder and held for a beat.

He nodded. "Good." He addressed the group again, his dark stare rolling over each of them with the fierceness of a rabid dog. "Press will be all over this mountain during the next few days. You need to be on top of your game at all times." He stopped pacing and crossed his arms over his thick chest. "Training. Let's really kick it up out there. If you can feel your face, you're not going fast enough. If your leg muscles aren't rubber when you leave the slope, you haven't trained hard enough. If you don't fall into bed at night barely able to keep your eyes open, you haven't trained hard enough. Get out there and make me proud."

The coach held Jayla back from the group. Rush could tell by his hooded eyes and serious face that he was lecturing her. It took all his willpower to keep moving forward toward the chairlift and to keep from *coddling* Jayla. He wanted to tell her she could do this—and at the same time, tell her she didn't have to.

He caught up to Cliff and Patrick by the lift.

"What're you doing out until three?" Cliff asked Patrick.

"You mean who am I doing?" Patrick winked at Rush. "Let's see…You want a list?"

Cliff shook his head. "Kia was out here at five practicing yesterday and she said you and Jayla were here the day before," he said to Rush. "Patrick and I have been hitting the downhill in the mornings. You wanna come tomorrow?"

"I'm usually at the gym by six thirty. Can we go earlier? Five thirty?" Rush glanced behind them and saw Jayla making her way toward the slopes with her head down.

"Yeah. As long as Patrick can get his ass outta bed." Cliff elbowed Patrick in the ribs.

"Shit, I can skip sleep altogether if I need to. I'll be there. What about Jay?" Patrick asked as they reached the lift.

"I'll ask her." Rush waited for Jayla while Patrick and Cliff took the lift up the mountain. She wasn't giving away anything with her blank stare. "What's up?"

"Nothing."

"Is that how we're playing it?" *Goddamn it.* The boyfriend in him warred with the competitor as they settled onto the lift.

Jayla stared in the direction of the snowcapped mountains as the lift rumbled and swayed beneath them. The clear night sky was picture perfect, and it should have been a romantic ride up the majestic peak, but Rush's stomach and chest tightened.

"Hey, you okay?"

"Yeah." She leaned against him as they neared the top of the mountain.

"If you want to talk, I'm right here."

She finally looked at him, but before he could read her eyes, she lowered her gaze and fiddled with the edge of her ski pole.

"Thanks," she said as the lift slowed at the top of the mountain. "It's nothing, really."

The first two runs down the mountain sucked. Rush was sidetracked by Jayla and dying to know what the hell the coach had said. Jayla was right. If they hadn't slept together, he would have pushed her for information and wouldn't have thought twice about pushing her harder when she refused. Now the dynamic had changed. By the stern look on Coach

Cunningham's face, he assumed that Jayla's times weren't cutting it.

And now the coach was heading his way. *Christ.* Just what he needed.

"You didn't take my advice seriously."

It wasn't a question or a statement. It was an accusation. Rush pushed his goggles up on his forehead. Best to play ignorant.

"Coach?"

Coach's eyes turned to liquid steel. "One of the students' mothers said she had an issue with Jayla's teaching style."

Goddamn Kelly Baker. He clenched his fists.

"Now, I talked to the other parents, and I got a pretty clear picture of what Jayla's teaching style is like, not that I had any concerns, but I have to follow through. She's a damn good teacher, but you know how these things go. It doesn't take a rocket scientist to figure this out, Rush. She couldn't say enough about *you.* Wanna tell me what the hell you're doing? I usually don't hear about your sexual escapades until they hit the gossip magazines, and that's usually after the season's over when you blaze a path through whatever women are in your way."

"It's bullshit, Coach. Kelly Baker has been coming onto me after every class, and I told her I wasn't interested. *That's* what this is about. You know Jayla's an awesome instructor. Shit, she's ten times better than me." He saw Jayla heading back over to the lift. "I assume you've told Jayla?"

Coach Cunningham glanced at Jayla, then back at Rush. "Not yet."

"Then what...?"

The coach raised his eyebrows.

He realized it was none of his damn business in his coach's eyes. "Sorry, Coach. Out of line."

"You've got one more day of that damn workshop. Do whatever you have to, to keep yourself away from that woman, and for shit's sake, Remington, you couldn't have picked a worse time to suddenly start turning away women."

No shit. Rush joined Jayla by the lift, wondering what in the hell she was hiding.

Chapter Twenty-Two

JAYLA KNEW SHE was shutting Rush out, but she couldn't help it. She could barely process her conversation with Coach Cunningham without wanting to either kill somebody or cry, and neither of those were viable options. She hated weakness and she wasn't a killer, so she was left shutting out the world.

Her shoulder burned like a son of a bitch as she tried to take off her skis. She switched to her left hand and finally freed her boots from their tethers. Rush sat beside her and unclipped his skis in a matter of seconds.

"Patrick, Cliff, and I are hitting the slopes at five thirty tomorrow morning. Want to go?" He took off his hat and gloves and stuffed them in his pockets.

She shrugged. "Maybe."

"Great."

He started toward the equipment room, and when she didn't follow, he returned to her side.

"You okay?" His eyes drifted to her shoulder.

She gathered her gear and gritted her teeth against a sharp pain that radiated down her arm.

"Here." Rush took her skis and carried them with his. "Come on."

A command.

You know.

Rush put the equipment away with sharp movement and without looking directly at Jayla. He also didn't say a word about her shoulder. And she hated him as much as she loved him for it. It was really hard to stay silent with him doing all the right things. As they headed out of the building, he lifted his arm to sling it over her shoulder. Then he lowered it back to his side, and her heart squeezed a little again.

"Are you hungry? Want to grab something to eat?"

The tension in his voice eased in a defeated sort of way, and as she looked into his trusting eyes, she knew she didn't want to hide anything from him. She stepped closer and touched his stomach. The right side of his lips lifted into the sexy little grin that made her knees weak.

"Are you hungry?"

He lowered his forehead to hers. "For you."

Okay, so maybe telling him could wait a little longer. She needed the comfort of her best friend turned lover, and as they made their way down the hill toward the cabins, she felt that funny little twinge in her nerves again. Whose cabin should they go to? Would he have to run out at four in the morning to grab her clothes again? Should she bring clothes if he wanted to go to his cabin?

As if he'd read her mind, he asked, "My place or

yours?"

The idea of him running out at four in the morning didn't sound good at all. "Mine?"

"And here I was looking forward to seeing you in my clothes again."

She climbed the porch steps, and he stood behind her as she unlocked the door. He gathered her hair over one shoulder and nibbled on her neck. Her hand froze, and her entire body shuddered.

"Aren't...? Aren't you...?" She closed her eyes.

He settled his mouth over the curve where her neck met her shoulder.

More. Yes. Oh God.

"Worried about...everyone seeing?" she finally managed in one long breath.

He took the keys from her hands. "Only if you don't get inside before I take this further." He unlocked the door and then closed and locked it behind them, tossed the keys on the counter, and kissed Jayla as they kicked off their boots and stumbled by the kitchen, dropping their coats to the floor. On their way into the bedroom, he pulled back from their kiss long enough to pull his shirt over his head, and when he moved to gently do the same for her, she gasped a breath as he lifted her arm. He froze and his eyes went dark.

"I'm fine."

She covered his mouth with hers as he removed her bra and went to work divesting himself of his jeans before helping her do the same. When he lowered his mouth to her breast, her mind went blissfully blank. She buried her hands in his hair and

205

held him against her, urging him to take more of her. He ground his hard length into her, and—*oh God*—she wanted to disappear into him. She brought his mouth back up to hers. He deepened the kiss, taking her right up on her toes as he loved her tongue, her teeth, the roof of her mouth, then brought his mouth to the column of her neck and drove her into a frenzy of need. She ran her hands down his chest, feeling the muscles pulsate beneath her fingertips. She lowered her mouth to his nipple and licked him lightly, drawing the sexiest, hungriest moan from his lungs, which sent her hands roaming and groping his rippled chest and stomach, the muscles along his sides. Breathing hard, kissing, tasting his salty skin, her hands wandered south.

"Jayla." One lust-filled word sent her head lower, kissing the path of his muscles as they led her to his thick, hard length. She took him in her mouth with fervor, sucking, touching, stroking him and taking pleasure in the way he rocked into her. He tasted salty, hot, and oh so good. She felt his hands in her hair, urging her to take him deeper. She grabbed his hips and felt his body shudder as she drew him out slowly, then licked the length of him, lingering on the sensitive, bulbous tip, before taking him back into her mouth and eking out a deep, masculine groan from Rush that made her go weak.

"Christ, you're gonna make me come." Rush's thighs tightened.

A few more deep sucks and she felt him—impossibly—swell a little more. She loved torturing him, owning him in that possessive way. She sank lower and licked his balls as he writhed against her. When she found the courage to meet his gaze again, the heat in them drew her up to his succulent, sweet mouth. He laid her down on the bed and tasted every bit of her flesh. She clutched the sheets as his hands gripped her thighs and spread them apart. And his mouth found her, loved her, teased her, until her body felt like it was wrapped too tight and needed to escape her tingling skin. She clawed at his shoulders. Every stroke of his tongue drew a sound from somewhere deep within her.

"Oh...Ru..." Every word ended with a heavy breath.

He shifted his position and took her inner thigh in his mouth. She sucked in a breath at the new sensations—hot, wet, sharp. He slid a pillow beneath her hips and her legs fell open. His strong hands moved up her thighs in an erotic slide of strength and heat that rattled her insides. He gripped her hips, holding them still as he devoured her once again. She struggled against the force of his hands, needing to arch her hips into him, clenching the sheets so hard her fingernails speared her palms. An orgasm tore through her, and she cried out his name. And then Rush was above her, her scent still on his lips. She opened her eyes, unable to think past her sex-fogged mind. She wrapped her legs around his waist as he pushed into her, deep, sure, and strong, over and over, as she clawed for purchase. His skin, his muscles, and—*Oh shit*—she gasped at the pain in her shoulder and stopped him cold. His eyes met hers, filled with worry.

"I'll stop."

"Don't," she panted.

Her right shoulder throbbed. It was all she could do to let it fall to the mattress, and she saw in his eyes the worry pulling him away. She pulled his mouth to hers again, rocking her hips into him over and over. And in the space of a breath, the pain forgotten, they were back in sync, and he was tasting every speck of her flesh he could reach, while still driving her up, up, up to the edge and holding her there as she gasped and panted for air.

"More."

He shifted his weight and drove in deeper, and they both stilled with the shock of intensity that curled Jayla's toes and tightened her insides around him.

"Oh...God. More."

His hands slid down her ribs, gripping her hard, holding her in place as he moved within her and gazed into her eyes, making her whole body tingle and her insides squeeze tight. In the next breath, his eyes widened and then went dark before slamming shut as his body shuddered against her and he groaned out her name.

MOONLIGHT CUT THROUGH the dark bedroom, illuminating a path across Jayla and Rush's legs on the bed where they lay side by side, breathing heavily.

"Holy Christ, Jayla." Rush reached for her hand and brought it to his lips. "How did we go from talking about dinner to that?"

"I have a better question. Why would we ever leave our bed?"

Our bed. A little thrill ran though him. He rolled onto his side and drank in her silhouette against the darkness.

"You are truly beautiful, Jay." Even in the dark he sensed her modesty and knew she was blushing. He ran his hand along the curve of her stomach and over her lean, muscular hip, then back up her ribs, along the side of her breast, to the arc of her shoulder. His heart ached for the pain in her shoulder and for the accusation of Kelly Baker, which he knew he should tell her about. But tomorrow was their last workshop with her daughter, and after tomorrow, that particular headache would be gone. Besides, with her shoulder and the stress of what it might mean, the last thing Jayla needed was more to worry about. If the coach didn't think it was significant enough to talk to Jayla about, then he could table it, too.

He moved closer and caressed her sore shoulder with his fingertips. Her muscles tensed at his touch.

"Relax. Close your eyes and let your muscles relax."

"Yeah, that's not going to work. You're naked and you're touching me. The two don't really add up to relaxation. In fact, they have quite the opposite effect on me."

"I know it hurt your shoulder when we were..."

"A little."

He moved in close and gazed into her eyes. The pain she was hiding, and the fear that lay beneath, tore at his heart.

"Can I get you some pain medication? Anything?" He pressed a kiss to her lips.

She shook her head. "I'm good."

"I know. You're good. You're strong. You can take anything." He fell back on the pillow with a sigh. "Would it be so bad to really let me in? It's not like I'm going to run to the coach and tell him that you're in pain. I told you I'd support your decision to compete before you see a doctor, and I will."

"I know you will."

"Then what's the issue?" He leaned over her again and ran his finger down her cheek. "I know how strong you are, babe. I respect you for your strength, but I also love you, and you can let your guard down when we're together."

Jayla blinked several times. She reached for his hand and laced her fingers between his. "Coach asked about my shoulder. He said he noticed that I was favoring it." Her forehead wrinkled and her eyes dampened.

"It's okay," he whispered.

"He said..." She swallowed hard. "He..."

A tear slid down her cheek, and Rush brushed it away. He pressed his cheek to hers and held her. "It's okay, babe."

Tears slid between their cheeks like secrets. Her body rocked with sadness. It killed him that he couldn't fix this for her, and he knew the last thing she wanted was for him to *try* to fix it. They lay together for several minutes, until her breathing calmed and her tears dried. Then Rush held her until he felt the tension in her body ease as she sank into him. And then he held her a little longer. He wanted to protect her from all of it—the accusations, the pain, the sadness, and the fear they conjured. He wanted to be the person who brought a smile to her beautiful face and who made her lose her mind when they were close. When the emotions became too much to hold in, he let them free.

"You're everything to me, Jayla. You don't have to say anything. I know this is all overwhelming." Her fingers pressed into his skin. "Why don't I draw you a warm bath? It'll help you relax."

He pulled the sheet over her to keep her warm and went into the bathroom, which was tiled in earth tones with white ceramic floors. The mirror was framed in dark wood to match the antique-style double sink and the brushed bronze faucet. The oversized Jacuzzi tub was big enough for the two of them, but he didn't want Jayla to feel like he was smothering her. He took a shower while the bathtub filled. When he returned to the bedroom with a towel wrapped around his waist and Tylenol and Motrin in his hand, Jayla was sitting on the edge of the bed with the sheet tucked under her arms.

"I need to bring you one of my T-shirts so you don't have to cover yourself with a sheet."

She blushed.

"Let me remind you again. I have seen you naked."

"I know. It's weird, isn't it? I mean, I always knew what you looked like, but now I really know what all of you looks like." Her cheeks flushed.

He lifted her chin until their eyes met. "And we know exactly how the other tastes, too." She dropped her eyes again, and he had to kiss her again. "You're too damn cute for your own good. If I wasn't worried about your shoulder, I'd lay you down and enjoy dessert."

She pushed him playfully away. "Rush."

"What? Just being honest." He handed her the Tylenol and Motrin and went to the kitchen to get a glass of water. "Are you sure you don't want something stronger?"

"No. I'm good."

He picked up his briefs from the floor and handed her the glass of water before dropping his towel and stepping into them. Jayla's eyes shifted to his naked body, and the edges of her lips curled up.

"You better be careful, eyeing me like that."

"Come here." She swallowed the pills, took a drink of water, and set the glass on the nightstand.

Rush crouched before her so they were eye to eye, and for a minute Jayla just looked at him. She tilted her head to one side, then the other. She ran her fingers along the tattoo on his left arm and knitted her brows together. Finally, she sighed and touched his cheek.

"Coach said I need to think about the team, and if I can't win, then I need to let someone else take my spot."

"That's bullshit. How can he say that? If you're ready, you'll compete." The *man* in Rush reacted viscerally before the athlete or the boyfriend in him had a chance to weigh in. Rush didn't like to be told what he could or couldn't do.

"And if he's right?" Her voice was a thin thread.

Rush weighed his answer, and in the silence, the sound of the tub caught his attention. "Hold up a sec." He turned off the tub and then brought Jayla a towel.

"Here you go, Little Miss Modest. Why don't you get in the tub and relax, and we'll figure this out."

She tucked the sheet under one arm and slid the towel beneath, exposing her naked body for only seconds when the sheet dropped to the bed and she stood, before wrapping the towel fully around her.

"So how does this work? After we have sex, I shouldn't see you naked? Because if that's your plan, I'm kinda hating it already."

She laughed as she passed him on the way into the bathroom, looking adorable in the thick white towel that barely covered her ass. The bathroom was warm with steam, and when she set the towel on the sink and stepped into the tub, Rush realized he was staring and turned away.

"You don't have to turn around."

He faced her again with a wide grin. "Really? So I'm not banned from the naked Jayla show?" One look at her and he got hard again.

She shook her head.

He looked down at his tented briefs. "Maybe banning me isn't such a bad idea." He went to retrieve his jeans, then came back and leaned against the doorframe, putting a little distance between them, and hopefully, allowing himself to concentrate on something other than wanting to touch her again. "Sorry. What do you want to do about the competition?"

"I want to compete more than I want to breathe."

Rush crossed one ankle over the other. "Okay then. That's what we tell the coach."

Jayla leaned her head back, exposing her long,

graceful neck, and heat swept through him again. The way his body reacted to her took him by surprise and confirmed what he'd already known. He'd been burying his feelings for her for a very long time. He just hadn't been anywhere near equipped to recognize or handle them before now.

She turned toward him with a tentative smile.

Rush couldn't maintain the distance. He knelt beside the tub with a washcloth, dunked it in the water, and began gently washing her. He'd never bathed a woman before, and with Jayla, the desire came naturally. She closed her eyes as he washed her arms, chest, and shoulders.

"I'm not sure it's fair to the team," she said.

"You know that as a member of that team, I want to say he's probably right, but as your best friend, I want to stand behind you and tell you to compete if that's what you want to do. But as your boyfriend, I want nothing more than to take you to the doctor and find out what's going on. You're the strongest female competitor I know." He bathed her legs with the cloth. "But you're trying to make a decision without any concrete information. Why don't we see the team doc and get a feel for how bad the injury really is? Then you can at least make an informed decision, knowing if this is a labral tear or something else altogether."

She looked away, and he set the cloth on the side of the tub.

"Baby, level with me. How bad is the pain? One to ten?" He reached under the water and took her hand in his. Every silent second that passed held what-ifs and worst-case scenarios. She wasn't going to budge, and he knew not to push. "This is your decision, and I'll support whatever it is that you want to do."

Her eyes found his again. "I'm not a quitter."

"Everyone knows that."

"I can do it. I want to do it. Even if I don't win first place. I have to try. I haven't come this far to just throw it away because of a little pain."

It killed him to support her decision to compete, but if there was one thing Rush understood, it was a competitor's mind-set. He'd feel the same way if he were the one injured. "Damn right."

She nodded. "Okay."

He had to try one more time. "Okay. Do you want to talk to the doc just to get a clear picture of—"

"No. No way. If he thinks I can't push through the pain, he'll pull me from the competition." She sat up straight and tall. "And I can push through anything."

"I know you can."

She wrinkled her brow. "I think I need pizza."

"And gummy bears."

"Definitely."

"I'm on it."

Chapter Twenty-Three

TWO HOURS LATER, they were cuddled up on the couch in Jayla's cabin watching *Dirty Dancing*. An empty pizza box sat open on the coffee table beside a half-full bag of gummy bears. The remnants of Hawaiian Punch pooled in the bottom of a wineglass on the end table.

"I love Patrick Swayze." Jayla snuggled against Rush, his arm draped over her chest, her legs stretched along the couch. Rush's feet were propped up on the coffee table, and Jayla traced the seam of his jeans. "He's like the total package: hot, badass, and sensitive."

"And what am I? Chopped liver?"

Teasing him as his lover was so much more fun than teasing him as his best friend. "Hm..." Jayla looked at his feet and tapped her chin. "Let's see. Fuzzy slippers, and you're watching *Dirty Dancing*." She sat up a little and turned to him, using her left hand to steady herself as she raked her eyes down his tight T-shirt. "Not bad to look at." She ran her hand along his tattoo. "You do have cool tattoos." She touched his chin. "And stubble is definitely rugged and sexy."

He clenched his jaw, and she touched the jumping muscle.

"And the jealousy is hot. Definitely hot."

He kissed her, deeply and sensuously, sending her world spinning again.

"Definitely hot," she whispered.

"Tease."

Rush's phone rang, and they stared at it like it was a foreign object.

"Who is calling this late?" Rush grabbed his phone from the coffee table. "It's Jack. Hey, man. Is everything okay?"

Jayla mouthed, *Want me to pause it?*

He nodded and she did.

"That would be fantastic. Yeah." He listened. "What are you doing up so late?" He mouthed, *Everything's fine,* to Jayla. "Bummer. No, no problem. I'm just watching a movie with Jayla." He listened again. "Mm-hm. I can't really...Right. Mm-hm. Okay." He pulled the phone away from his mouth and said to Jayla, "Some of my family's coming to watch the competition on Saturday."

"Great." Jayla admired the way Rush's family supported one another, and she was looking forward to seeing them again. As she listened to him wrapping up the call, the nervous flutter returned to her stomach.

"All right. Yup. See you then, bro." Rush ended the call and tossed the phone onto the table. "So, looks like there's going to be a Remington reunion here on Saturday. Apparently, Kurt has a book signing about two hours from here this weekend, and Siena and her boyfriend, Cash, are visiting his brother in Allure. I guess Jack's flying my parents and Savannah in. Dex and Ellie can't come because of some deadline or something, and Sage and Kate are in South Africa with their company, but Jack and the others are excited to see you."

"I'm excited to see them. I love your family, but..."

"But what will they think of us as a couple?"

She reached for the bag of gummy bears, and he pulled her back against his chest.

"My family loves you, and if I'm happy, they're happy." He kissed the back of her head.

She popped a bear into her mouth. "Yeah, but what if this injury sinks me?" It was a little easier to say that time than it had been the first. "You fell in love with an Olympic athlete. What will they think if I can't compete anymore? Oh God, Rush, what will you think? I'll be like one of those has-beens. A hanger-on."

She set the bag of candy on the couch, and he picked it up and took a bear between his finger and thumb; then he put it in his teeth and leaned in close. She laughed at him, loving how he tried to pull her out of her darker thoughts.

"You know you want me," he teased.

She brought her lips to his, and he pushed the gummy bear into her mouth.

"There's more than one way to win you over." He pressed a kiss to her lips as she chewed the sweet, delicious candy.

"I'm pretty sure I fell in love with you way before you won your Olympic gold. And if you think I'm wrong and that I fell in love with you *because* you won it, then why would I have waited until two years after you won to make my move?"

"Because you had no idea you loved me."

"Well, you're right about that. I didn't realize how much I loved you until, I don't know, a year or so ago, but I fell in love with Jayla Stone, and whether you're an Olympic athlete, a ski instructor, or a gummy-bear-eating ski bunny makes no difference to me. I love who you are, not what you do."

"No difference? What if I were a pantyless ski bunny?" She heard his breathing quicken. "Candy might be one way to my heart, but I think I've learned a little something about the way to yours, too."

"Babe, the organ you tweaked when you took your panties off was far lower than my heart."

She slid her hand behind his head, where it fit perfectly against his short hair, and her pinky rested on the soft skin below. She loved this. Him. Being who they'd always been—only more.

She pulled him into another kiss and tried to ignore the worry wrapping its prickly little tentacles around her nerves.

Chapter Twenty-Four

BY FIVE THIRTY the next morning, Rush and Jayla were on the chairlift heading up the mountain with Cliff and Patrick in the chair behind them. The morning was bitter cold and windy. Night clung to the last thread of itself as a graying sky fought to keep the sun from rising.

"You sure you want to do this?" Rush asked.

Jayla exhaled a fluffy white burst of air. "You've asked me this four times already. Do you think I'm going to change my mind?"

He knew damn well she wasn't going to change her mind, but once again the boyfriend side of his brain was having trouble stepping back after watching her cringe and wince while getting dressed that morning and then again when she put on her skis. She was so damned stubborn that he wanted to shake her and was proud of her in equal measure.

"Nope, just giving you the option." He kissed the side of her head.

She turned to face him, looking a little like an

Arctic robber. Her black balaclava covered her entire face, exposing only her beautiful—and at the moment, challenge-filled—eyes.

"Cliff and Patrick are used to seeing us together, but kissing might draw their attention, don't you think?"

He pulled the cloth from in front of her mouth and kissed her again. "I don't care. The coach knows, or at least strongly suspects, and no one else matters."

The corners of her eyes wrinkled, and he knew she was smiling.

He watched her carefully as she skied off the lift. If he hadn't been looking for it, he probably wouldn't have noticed that she was leaning to the left, but he couldn't ignore what was now blatantly obvious, and it made his gut wrench.

Patrick came to a stop beside him. "What was that?"

Rush pulled down his goggles. "What?"

"The lip-lock on the lift."

Rush set his jaw and flashed a serious don't-fuck-with-me stare at him. "Exactly what you think it is."

"What about your no-pussy rule for this competition season?"

Instinct and pent-up frustration over Jayla's decision to compete drove Rush's hand to Patrick's collar. Through gritted teeth, he said, "Don't ever refer to Jayla as that. Got it?"

Patrick's jaw gaped in surprise and annoyance. He pushed away from Rush. "Dude. Whatever. Sorry, man."

Rush released him but held his stare. His heart

thundered against his ribs. He hadn't expected such a visceral reaction to Patrick just being Patrick, but then again, when it came to Jayla, he hadn't expected his emotions to take over like they had.

The morning light crept over the mountain, illuminating the slope and bringing with it a surge of adrenaline that made Rush break out in a sweat. He watched Jayla launch herself from the crest. Her form was immaculate, her speed immediate, and he worried like hell about her. He skied slower, more worried about her than his time. There was no hint of the leaning he'd noticed earlier in her positioning as she flew down the slope at lightning speed. Satisfied that she was okay, he let his body take over and sped past her to make the most of the remaining trail.

He waited for Jayla at the bottom and they rode the lift up together.

"How's your shoulder?"

"Fine. Cliff asked if I was dating you." Jayla scooted closer to him.

"And?"

"I told him that I was just making the rounds to see if our male ski team was as well endowed as the rumors say they are." She leaned her head against his shoulder.

He laughed. "Well, then, I guess I'll win that contest."

"There goes that ego again."

"Someone's gotta stroke it." He thought of the way she looked as she came off the slope and lifted her goggles, flashing the fierce, determined look he'd come to know so well over the years. *God, I love you.* As their legs pressed against each other's, he wished for the millionth time she'd see a doctor, and at the same time, that she didn't have to.

Chapter Twenty-Five

WHILE RUSH WAS at the gym, Jayla checked her cell phone messages. She had one from her sister, Jennifer and one from her brother, Jace. Jace owned a number of motorcycle shops, and he was also, *for fun,* he claimed, a tattoo artist. At six five, Jace was an imposing sight with his scruffy goatee and leather jacket. To Jayla, he was her sometimes annoying, funny, and way-too-smart, eldest brother who had always looked out for her from afar. He wasn't a hovering, in-your-face type of protector, but she knew if she ever needed him, he was there. She had absolutely no idea why he would have texted her at four in the morning.

She scrolled through the texts, and the slight movement of her thumb made her whole arm ache. *Damn it.* She knew she was pushing herself, maybe even past her limits, but if she could just make it through Saturday...She sighed as she read the text from Jennifer first.

Ready to spill yet?

Jayla laughed. She had to hand it to Jen. She had a knack for seeing right through her smoke and mirrors. She texted back. *Rush...Me...Couple. And he's more amazing than I thought. Chew on that. Talk later. Need to get ready for ski class.*

She read the text from Jace, feeling the seconds tick away and wanting to get to her shoulder exercises.

Guess where I am? Typical Jace. His life moved a mile a minute, and his texts were as random as his tattoos. She hadn't heard from him in weeks, and the last time they'd spoken, he was telling her about some motorcycle he was building. Jace had gone on about technical details and comparisons to other motorcycles for so long that she'd zoned out. That was Jace, a strange mix of too many facts and not enough focus.

She texted back.

Sorry so late. Was on the slopes. R u in LA?

She tossed her phone on the bed and began her shoulder exercises. Her shoulder screamed when she tried to lift her arm above midchest level. She tried a few different exercises and experienced the same deep, excruciating pain. Jayla gave up and sat on the edge of the bed and stewed over the way her body was working against her.

Her phone vibrated with a response from Jace. *New Mexico. Opening new shops. Guess where I'll be tomorrow?*

She rolled her eyes and texted, *Where?*

She sucked in a deep breath and pulled her shoulders back. "I can do this," she said to the empty room. "I can goddamn do this." *Then I'll go to the doc.*

Her phone vibrated again with his response. *Colorado. Coming to see ur race.*

She smiled despite the ache in her shoulder, knowing that the one competition he'd see would probably be her worst race of the year. She texted back. *Can't wait to see u. Gotta go teach a ski workshop. Text me when ur here?*

He texted back right away. *Getting in right b4 ur race. Will see you after. Love you. Good luck.*

She thought about mentioning her relationship with Rush to Jace. Jace knew Rush and he liked him as a person, but he also knew Rush's history with women. Would he like him as much as his younger sister's boyfriend? She decided the fewer issues she dealt with at the moment, the better, and texted him back, *Love u too. Can't wait to c u. Xox.*

Without thinking, she pushed off the bed with her right hand. Searing pain radiated down her arm.

I'll see the doctor right after the race.

She went into the bathroom and reached for a washcloth, cringing in pain.

The second my race is over.

BY MIDAFTERNOON JAYLA'S shoulder and arm were throbbing. She downed a few Tylenol and Motrin before her last class. Rush had gone to get something to eat before the class started, and she braced herself as Coach Cunningham approached with an assessing gaze.

"How're you holding up?" He held her gaze.

"Great. Fine." *Other than my arm feeling like I*

should amputate it right this very second.

"Good. You know, backing out of one competition to prepare for the coming season wouldn't be the worst thing you've ever done."

"I'm fine, Coach. I'm going to compete; then I'll do whatever needs to be done."

He narrowed his eyes. "Your choice. Until I see that you cannot compete, or you or a doc tells me you can't, you're in."

The pain was a constant reminder of their denial. "Thank you." She noticed Rush heading their way.

Coach watched him approach. "I guess Rush told you about the Baker situation."

"Baker situation?" Her stomach clenched at the thought of anything having to do with Kelly Baker.

He shifted his feet so he was facing her head-on. "He didn't tell you?"

Her stomach sank. What could Kelly Baker have said that would have an impact on her or Rush? Despite her trust in Rush, her mind went down an old, painful, and familiar path connecting Rush and Kelly. She fought against it.

"Hey." Rush's eyes darted between Jayla and the coach.

"Coach Cunningham was asking me if you told me about the Bakers." She tried not to sound accusatory or annoyed, but when his smile faded, she wasn't sure she succeeded.

His eyes shot to the coach, then back to her. His mouth twitched.

Jayla felt like she was going to be sick.

"Coach?" Rush put a hand on Jayla's lower back

and she took a step forward, causing his hand to slide off. He shot her a confused—and too apologetic—look.

"Can..." She looked at the coach. "What's going on?"

Coach Cunningham glanced at Rush and then shook his head.

"Jayla, remember when I told Kelly that I wasn't interested?"

How could I forget? "Yes." She broke out in a cold sweat.

"She complained." He shot another look at the coach. "She complained about you."

That wasn't at all what she was expecting, and it was a relief—at first. "Me?" she practically yelled. "What? Why?"

"Because she's a nutcase, and I guess she decided that she'd hurt me by hurting you." He ran his hand through his hair with a sigh. "We walked away arm in arm, remember?"

"Wha...Coach?"

Coach Cunningham shook his head. "I know." He narrowed his eyes at Rush again. "You don't have to worry. I know this is about Rush, and not about you."

She stepped away from Rush.

"Jayla, it's not like I did anything wrong."

"No." Coach Cunningham scrubbed his hand down his face. "For once you did the right thing where a woman was concerned. You just picked the wrong woman to scorn." He turned his attention to Jayla with a rare, empathetic look in his eyes. "Listen, all this crap will pass. I didn't say anything to you yesterday because you've got enough to worry about with your shoulder, but just in case she pulls anything else, I thought you should know."

Anger pooled in her gut. "Thank you, Coach. So what do you want me to do? What happens now? And what could she possibly have had to complain about?" She saw the kids getting ready for class and scanned the group of parents standing off to the side for the blond bitch who had it out for her—and Rush.

"Not much. She had concerns about your skills as an instructor, which we all know is nonsense, Jayla. As for what you do from here on out?" He locked eyes with Rush. "I don't want you anywhere near her or her daughter. Got it? God knows if this woman will try to take things to a crazier level, and with the press coming in, we need that like we need a heat wave. Jayla, you just keep doing what you're doing. You guys are doing a great job and a really good thing by working with these kids." He ran his eyes between them. "And if you two have gone from friends to something more, then I want a promise from you both that when you're training, you'll goddamn focus. No fights or drama on the team, got it?"

"Got it," they said in unison.

With a curt nod, he left them alone.

Jayla was sure there was steam coming from her ears as she and Rush put on their equipment.

"I should have told you, but we were so sidetracked last night, and with your shoulder, I figured—"

"Stop, okay. I can't even think about it right now." Jayla struggled getting her equipment on with her left hand. Every muscle in her body was tense, her nerves burned, and her goddamn right side from her shoulder to her ribs felt like she'd skied into a tree.

"Jayla..."

She blew out a frustrated breath. "Look, I know you didn't tell me to protect me from stress overload. I get it, okay? But with your history with women, I don't think there can be any secrets between us. Ever. Not to protect me, not to protect you, and not to protect us as a couple."

"I agree, but—"

Finally having secured her equipment, she pushed to her feet. "No buts. I trust your feelings for me, and I thought you had always been honest with me about everything. Even the things I didn't want to hear—like you having sex in the back of someone's pickup truck while they were driving down the highway."

He ran his hand down his face, his eyes full of sorrow and maybe even shame.

"But stuff like this makes me wonder if I only thought you had been honest with me. Maybe there's more I don't know, and I don't want to think there is."

"Jayla, there's not. There's nothing. You gotta know that."

"Maybe I do, but just stop protecting me. I'm a woman, not a child, and the last thing I need is you treating me like I can't handle something." She skied toward the kids and paused to take a deep breath. She loved that Rush wanted to protect her, and in equal measure, she hated that he felt he had to. Driving that hate into a little bit of crazy overreaction was the pain in her arm that no one—not even Rush—could protect her from. The realization that she'd kept that pain

231

from him, and that in doing so, she was equally as guilty, gave her a twinge of guilt.

RUSH STEWED OVER the trouble Kelly Baker had caused, and it pissed him off even more knowing that his anger was exactly what she'd wanted to achieve. *Fuck with my girlfriend and make me suffer.* Why did chicks do that? He'd never pine over a woman who didn't want him. What a waste of energy. *Move on already.* His gaze moved to Jayla, who was watching a group of students practice standing from a fall. He realized that if Jayla ever *really* pushed him away, he'd not only pine like a lost child, but he'd do his damnedest to get her back. The cold shoulder she was giving him at the moment would eventually blow over, but knowing Kelly had started the trouble because of him made him madder than hell.

He managed to make it through the class without letting the stress get the better of him, and when they took the kids up the lift for a last trip down the mountain, he caught up with Jayla.

"Hey, I'm really sorry. I thought I was doing the right thing."

She held both poles in her left hand and watched the kids lining up along the crest of the hill. "I know you did."

He touched her lower back on the right side and she sucked in a breath. She was definitely leaning to the left. Her jaw was clenched, and her eyes darted away from his.

"Hey," he said too harshly. She didn't want protecting, but he couldn't goddamn help it.

She snapped her head toward him, wincing at the movement.

"One to ten?" When she didn't answer, he asked again. "One to ten?"

"I'm competing." She didn't give him time to respond. She pushed forward and skied over to the group.

Rush spent the rest of the class fighting the urge to convince Jayla she was making a huge mistake. They were nearing the end of class when he noticed a news crew standing nearby. He glanced at Jayla to try to get her attention, but as she'd been doing all afternoon, anytime he looked over, she looked away. Kelly Baker, however, spent the class moving parallel to him. When he took the kids to the lift, she walked along the path at the bottom of the slope. When they gathered for instructions, she walked over to where they were. He kept her in his peripheral vision for the sole purpose of avoiding coming into contact with her, and as Jayla was doing to him, he avoided eye contact like the plague.

Rush waved the students over, noting how much more confident they were on their skis now than they'd been at the beginning of the workshop. It pained him to see Jeffrey keeping distance between himself and the other skiers, but on the upside, Suzie had made friends with the other kids and had stopped vying for his attention. Taylor leaned in close to Meg and said something he couldn't hear, and they both looked back at Jeffrey. Rush was not in the mood for Taylor's antics. He was running on shoestring patience, and Taylor yanked it at every turn.

Jayla took her place beside Rush in front of the group, and he did a quick visual assessment of her. She held both ski poles in her left hand again. Her right arm was bent at the elbow and pressed to her side, and her jaw was clenched tight. She was in pain. Big, honking, unavoidable, competition-threatening pain.

Distracted and feeling like his nerves were on fire, he addressed the kids. "We're really proud of you guys. You were courageous, you listened well, and you all came out on top, with few falls and no injuries. I'd say that's a success and you should be proud of yourselves." Rush glanced at Jayla, offering her a chance to speak.

True to her nature, she pulled her shoulders back—both of them—then looked over at the kids, a forced smile curling the edges of her lips.

"You guys did great. I hope you'll continue to take more lessons and really hone your skills." Her voice was softer than normal, her breathing shallow.

She was obviously still angry and in pain.

And I'm not allowed to help.

Rush returned his attention to the group. "Does anyone have any questions?"

"Who was the best skier?" Taylor slid a nasty look at Jeffrey.

Rush silenced the look with an icy stare. "This wasn't a competition. You're all equal."

"But if you had to choose?" Taylor pushed.

"The best never have to ask," Jeffrey said, as if he'd been asked. "Only the insecure need verbal acknowledgment."

Rush glanced at Jayla, but the look was wasted.

Her eyes were trained on Kelly Baker, standing a few feet away. If emotions could melt snow, there would be a river running between the two women, and he'd be drowning, dead center.

"Who asked you?" Taylor asked.

Jeffrey stood with his back pin straight, his poles securely in his hands. He blinked up at Taylor as if he'd asked a ridiculous question. "Isn't that obvious by my response?"

Rush wanted to high-five Jeffrey, but Taylor's gape-jawed look was celebration enough.

"Competition can be crippling," Jayla said, surprising Rush. "Let's not make this workshop about that kind of foolishness. You guys all did great, and as you progress, remember that the only competition you have is with yourself. Just have fun and ski safely."

Rush smiled. Maybe she was rethinking the competition after all. He hoped so, because the teammate and boyfriend sides of him had merged over the last two hours, and he wanted to take her straight to the hospital to find out what the hell was going on with her shoulder.

The kids thanked them for teaching the workshop and went to the bench at the bottom of the slope to remove their skis. By the time Rush went to find Jayla, she was gone. Thankfully, Kelly Baker was no longer standing nearby. He scanned the area and spotted Kelly standing by the other parents and—*oh shit*— Jayla was heading directly for her.

Chapter Twenty-Six

I DON'T DESERVE this. Jayla left her skis by the bench and stomped through the snow toward Kelly Baker. She'd had enough of Kelly watching Rush, following him like a puppy as they taught the class and giving her nasty looks. *I'll be damned if some blond bimbo is going to spread lies about me.* She hated herself for the next thought that popped into her head, but she was in tremendous pain and was battling her own demons about competing, and goddamn it, the thought was true. *Maybe if Kelly Baker would concentrate on her daughter a little more and on Rush—or men in general—a little less, then Suzie wouldn't be heading down Slut Street with no hopes of being pulled over.*

She slowed her pace when she was about twenty feet from Kelly, who was frustratingly prettier up close, which pissed Jayla off even more. When she got close enough to see the red nail polish on Kelly's fingernails and realize her snake eyes were green, not brown as she'd thought, she thought about her own reputation—*the face of Dove, a role model for young girls*—and stopped cold.

What am I doing?

Kelly's high-pitched voice sent an icy chill down her back. "Yeah, Jayla might be America's sweetheart, but what she has in looks, she lacks in teaching skills."

Jayla breathed harder. Her hands fisted, sending a bolt of pain through her right side. She saw Suzie off to the side, talking with Taylor and Meg and shooting glances at her mother. Jayla took another step toward bold-faced-lie–telling Kelly.

Kelly flipped her hair over her shoulder and locked eyes with Jayla. "But Rush Remington?" She was speaking to another young mother, while narrowing her eyes at Jayla. "Now, that's a man I wouldn't kick out of bed for eating crackers. What he's doing with..." She opened her eyes wide, feigning sudden recognition. "Oh goodness, if it isn't Rush's girlfriend." She dragged her eyes down Jayla with a scowl on her lips, then turned to the other mother and said something Jayla couldn't hear before the other woman walked away. Kelly set her eyes on Jayla, shedding her beauty like a snake sheds skin.

Jayla closed the distance between them. *I probably should have thought this out better.* Her phone vibrated in her pocket, distracting her from her thoughts. She pressed her palm to her pocket, against the offending sound, and focused on handling the situation she'd come to face. She couldn't say what she wanted to. *Look, ho, put your claws away before I rip them out with my teeth.* No, that wouldn't be cool at all. She thought about what Jennifer might say to a student, and in a flash, she knew how to handle Kelly.

"Miss Baker, I understand you have issues with my instructing. I've worked diligently with Suzie, and I'd like to address whatever issues you have."

With a smile on her lips, as if she were telling Jayla how much she loved her outfit, Kelly said, "Careful now, sweetheart. You wouldn't want the press to hear about how America's sweetheart is really a nasty, jealous bitch who said heinous things to an innocent bystander."

"You wouldn't d—"

"Jayla." Rush's hand landed on her shoulder.

She twisted from his grip, sending another shock of pain through her. "I've got this, Rush."

"Jay..."

Her entire body went hot with anger. Her muscles flexed so tight that even turning to face him hurt.

"Please, just go away and let me handle this." That's when she saw the reporter she'd noticed earlier, microphone in hand, heading directly for them with a camera already rolling. *Holy crap.*

"Mom, what are you doing now?" Suzie's voice drew her attention back to Kelly.

Suzie. Oh God, Suzie.

Suzie stood, red faced, with her hands on her hips between Kelly and Jayla. "What are you doing? Why do you always do this?"

Kelly reached for her daughter, who shrugged her off.

"First you sleep with my skating instructor, and now you pull this?" Suzie pointed to Jayla, and Jayla was struck mute and still as a statue. She couldn't have moved if her life depended on it. "They're great ski instructors. They helped me ten times more than you ever could." Suzie stomped off toward the parking lot, leaving Kelly to chase after her and Jayla to feel like a complete ass for letting Kelly get under her skin in the first place. She obviously had bigger issues fueling her inappropriate accusations.

In the next second, the reporter shoved a microphone too close to Jayla's face. She pulled back, trying to feign a smile and knowing she was too confused to pull it off.

"Jayla, are you ready to compete?" the reporter asked.

She was reeling from the altercation, causing the camera to feel too close and the sun too bright, and she couldn't keep her eyes from darting around in search of Rush. Definitely not her best moment.

"Yes. I'm looking forward to it." She focused on the camera and finally managed a smile. "The whole team is ready."

"How do you feel about the season coming to an end?"

"I'm excited to spend time with family and friends and happy for the success we've had."

By the time she turned away, Rush was gone. She'd sent him away and he'd listened. Damn him. Damn her. Damn Kelly. She was messing everything up again.

She felt her heart crumble inside her chest and realized that the injury that had chased away her sanity was nothing compared to the pain of an aching heart.

Chapter Twenty-Seven

WELL, THAT SUCKED. Being a boyfriend was about a million times harder than Rush had ever imagined. If he had walked into the same scene between Jayla and Kelly a month ago, he would have told Jayla she was off her rocker to think he'd let her handle a situation that had arisen only because of him. *Like hell you will.* That's what he would have said instead of allowing Jayla to call the shots when her body was riddled with pain. He'd had to walk away. There was no other option. If he'd stayed, he would have spoken his mind—and Jayla would have leveled him for it.

He walked around for thirty minutes, trying to figure out what to do and how to navigate his new role. When that didn't help, he stopped at the convenience store in the resort and picked up a few things. Now he sat on Jayla's porch, elbows on knees, hands fidgeting for lack of purpose, and he still had no idea what to do. The coach expected them at practice in half an hour. How the hell would Jayla manage that, given the way she was favoring her shoulder? His hands were tied, and he fricking hated it. He lifted his eyes just as Jayla came around the corner of the resort. She was looking off to the right, and there was no hiding the way her right shoulder drooped. He rose to his feet, wanting to carry her back to the cabin and take care of her, but he didn't move.

She lifted her eyes and caught sight of him, slowing nearly to a stop. Her mouth opened, but no words came.

"Hi," he said.

"Hi."

She moved toward him, and he fought the urge to reach for her hand. His pulse kicked up for the awkwardness between them. He searched her eyes for some indication of where they were headed.

"What are you doing here?" she asked.

"I came to…" He couldn't say, *make sure you were okay*. So he told her the other side of the truth. "Because I had to see you." Rush didn't make a conscious decision to move forward, or to take her left hand and bring it to his lips. He wasn't even sure he was capable of thinking. His world was tilting, and all he knew was that if Jayla wasn't on the right side of that tilt, it would kill him.

He followed her up the porch steps and waited as she unlocked the door to her cabin. *Do I follow you in? Do I wait to be invited?* He wondered when he'd traded in his pants for a skirt, shook his head, and followed her inside.

"Want a drink?" Jayla asked without looking at him.

"No. I'm good, but let me get it." He moved around

her and she glared at him. He held his palms up. "Sorry. Forgot you didn't need help."

She used her left hand to open the refrigerator door and pull out the two-liter Hawaiian Punch bottle. She wasn't using her right arm at all. Rush shoved his hands in his pockets to keep from helping her as she struggled with the cap, and when she tried to lift the bottle with one hand to pour, he couldn't take it anymore. Rush moved behind her. His arms encircled her body as he poured her a drink. He kissed the top of her head and remained there, close, feeling her against him.

"I can only watch for so long before the man in me takes over." He helped her off with her jacket, and as she drank the punch, he went down on one knee and removed her boots, then set them by the door. Jayla leaned her back against the counter, silently watching him. That's what worried him the most. He had no idea how to read her silence.

She looked at the clock. "Practice starts in fifteen minutes."

He lifted her chin and pressed a soft kiss to her lips. "What are we doing? You just went through hell out there and you're worried about practice? How about if we deal with all this stuff first?"

"I'm fine."

"Yeah?" He searched her eyes and she looked away. "Well, I'm not. I respect your need to take care of things on your own, and maybe I was out of line. I don't know." He ran his hand through his hair to give himself a second to get his emotions in check. "Hell, I don't even know what the hell went on out there."

"I was mad."

That was simple enough. Maybe it should have cleared it all up for some other guy, but not for Rush. "Mad. Mad? Okay. Fine, you were mad. But what the hell, Jayla? Aren't couples supposed to show a united front and all that? I don't know what you think I'm like, but after all these years, I was sure you knew me. I mean, really knew who I was."

She moved toward the living room and leaned her back against the wall.

He moved in front of her and softened his tone. "Did you think I'd be able to watch my girlfriend go up against a manipulator like *her* and not say something?"

"I don't know what I thought. I was too mad to think."

She ran her fingers over his stomach, and he looked down at them, completely thrown off by her conflicting signals.

"Okay, I've been there. I get it."

She moved her fingertips along his abs as she spoke. "Do you know what it was like watching her stalk you like prey, knowing that she'd made up that stuff about me after I tried to help her daughter? And that she was doing it all to hurt you?"

"I do know, because I hated it, too." He had a hard time thinking past her fingertips walking across his stomach. While she'd always had a nervous habit of touching his stomach like she was calculating an equation and it held all the answers, and gummy bears and movies were her go-to emotional revival tools, he also knew that holding her close and loving her, mind, body, and soul, would help her even more. He wasn't

244

thinking of sex, but of coming together as a couple. She needed to understand that he wasn't minimizing her strength and abilities; he was complementing them with his own. He wanted to fill the tub again and settle in behind her this time, then hold her until her frustration dissipated and comfort and security filled those empty spots.

She leaned in to him with a grimace. His eyes traveled to her shoulder, and he lowered his cheek to the top of her head.

"Please take something stronger for your shoulder," he pleaded.

"Practice."

He rose to his full height again. "Please tell me you're not serious."

She glared at him, and the frustration of it all came tumbling forward.

"You can't practice. No way. You can hate me, you can even break up with me, but if you intend to compete tomorrow, then you had damn well better give your shoulder a break tonight."

She pushed against his stomach and buried her face in his shirt. "You're doing it again. I can protect myself, Rush."

"Excuse the hell out of me, but you're not even using your right arm. In what fantasy world can you safely ski at fifty miles an hour in the dark?"

She tried to step away, and he set his palms on the wall on either side of her, trapping her between. She glared up at him.

"I'm only going to say this once, Jayla; then I'm going to walk out that door and go to practice. You can decide if you want to see me after practice or not while I'm gone and I'll respect your decision, but this time, it's my turn to talk and your turn to listen."

She blinked in perfect time to the nervous sinking in his gut.

"I'm just fool enough to stand behind your desire to compete tomorrow—assuming you can move your arm—because I know how goddamn stubborn you are and I respect the hell out of you as an athlete. But if being your boyfriend means kowtowing to your need to take it a step further and ski *tonight* when you can't even move your arm, much less use it to ski, then..." His chest squeezed; his throat thickened. He pushed past the awful feeling as he admitted the one thing that would slay him. "Then maybe I'm not the man for you, Jayla. I love you too damn much to keep my mouth shut and watch you cripple yourself for no reason."

Her eyes dampened, and he continued with a softer tone.

"Tonight's practice isn't going to make you faster tomorrow and you know that. At best it'll further injure you and ruin your chance to compete. At worst...hell, it's not worth discussing. I know you, and you only want to practice to prove that you can compete tomorrow, and I don't blame you. But I won't support it. I can't. Tomorrow will be hard enough." He stood up tall and ran his hand through his hair, half expecting—hoping—she'd reach for him and tell him not to go.

She didn't move.

Or make a sound.

She was on one side of the tilt, and he was about to fall off the other. He moved to the door, hardly able to breathe. He reached for the doorknob, hesitated, and glanced back. She still hadn't moved.

"You have nothing to prove, babe. Not to me, not to the coach, and not to your fans. We all know you're a star. You're risking permanent injury to prove something to yourself, so be damn sure that it's worth it." He took a bag out of his coat pocket and tossed it on the counter. "I know you're upset, and I want to give you space to think. If you want to see me, you know where I'll be."

Chapter Twenty-Eight

JAYLA COULDN'T MOVE. She'd gone completely numb with the words *then maybe I'm not the man for you.* Everything after that was one big blur. She was unable to push her voice from her lungs, and she was pretty sure the cabin walls were closing in around her. When Rush walked out the door, he'd taken the air from her lungs along with him. Now, as she gasped for air, the argument with Kelly came rushing back, the weight of Rush's hand on her shoulder—which she'd give anything to feel right now—followed by the disgusted and pained look on Suzie's face as she confronted her mother. The realization that he'd done exactly as she'd asked him to—he'd left her alone—sliced through her like a knife. The pit of her stomach burned and her body began to shake. She pressed her palms to the wall to stabilize herself, and the movement sent a shock of pain through her right side. She sank down to the floor as her legs turned to mush. Sobs rumbled from her chest. She clenched her jaw against them and was powerless to stop the desperate flood of tears that tore at all of her frayed edges.

An hour later, Jayla was still bound and determined to compete the next day, but she knew that Rush was right about tonight's practice. She should have admitted it to him when he'd said it, but she couldn't. Maybe she was in denial. Hell, of course she was, but what were her options? Walk away from the competition and *then* find out her career was over? No, she couldn't give up what might be her last race. She wasn't a quitter. If she was going out, she was doing it in a blaze of glory. Injured or not, when she stood at the top of the mountain, goggles on, poised to compete, she knew the adrenaline would carry her down the slope at racing speed. She knew in her heart she could win, even with her injury. She'd spent her whole life training to compete. It's what she did and who she was.

She also knew that after those endorphins that pushed her through the race subsided, reality would be waiting at the finish line, and she'd have to face her injury and all of the ramifications that came with it. She could face it *after* the competition. She retrieved her cell phone from her coat pocket, and sadness vibrated through her when there was no message from Rush, only one from Jace, who apparently was coming into town earlier than he'd planned. In typical Jace fashion, there was no mention of exactly when she'd see him. She debated calling Rush, but she'd already proven to be a distraction to him. She couldn't even begin to pretend that he'd be able to concentrate at practice. She'd seen the burdened, hurt look in his eyes, and she hadn't missed the truth of his words.

Was she asking him to be less of a man? Was she one of those women who pushed people away?

No. I'm a competitor. There's a difference, and of all people, Rush knows that.

Then why do I hurt so badly?

And why isn't he here?

Two hours later, darkness surrounded Jayla as she sat on the couch beneath a blanket. The silence of the cabin pressed in on her. She flicked on the light with a sigh and went into the bathroom to take Tylenol and Motrin, still unwilling to give in to the stronger pain meds. She missed Rush so much she could barely move. Practice was over, and he'd said to call if she wanted to see him. She wanted to—desperately—but she was still confused. She did the only thing she could think to do. She called her older sister Mia. Jennifer was her go-to person when she was on the fence, but Mia...Mia was the definition of decisive. She was a planner, and she was anything but a risk taker. She didn't manipulate situations, like Jennifer did with her body or her cleverness, depending on what her goal was. Mia worked in the fashion industry and she approached life as she did the fashion business. She listened, researched, contemplated, and then she planned until she was sure that no thread was stretched too thin, no corners were cut. Then she moved forward. Jayla couldn't see the forest beyond the trees. She was in too deep.

She needed Mia.

"Jayla?"

The sound of her sister's voice brought new tears.

"Are you crying? What's wrong? Where are you?"

Mia asked.

"I'm…"

"Are you still in Colorado? What's going on?"

"Yes." Jayla nodded, though her sister couldn't see her. "I'm in…Colorado."

"Okay." Mia breathed a sigh of relief. "Take a deep breath. Are you hurt? What's wrong?"

Jayla clenched her eyes shut, trying to stop the tears.

"Jay, breathe. Come on, one deep breath. Is Rush there? Can I talk to him?"

Jayla cried harder at that. Her whole family saw Jayla and Rush as a unit. A package deal during ski season. And now he was gone.

"Did something happen to him?"

Jayla shook her head.

"Jayla, you know you need to tell me what's going on or I'm calling someone there. I'm giving you three seconds, so find your voice. Please."

Taking control, another reason Jayla relied on her sister's strength.

"Okay." Jayla wiped her eyes on her sleeve and took several deep breaths.

"Okay? Are you okay?"

She pictured Mia pacing her Manhattan apartment in her spike heels like they were running shoes, tucking her straight dark hair behind her ear.

"I need your advice." Her voice was shaky at best.

"Whatever you need. Tell me."

She had no idea what she needed, only who she needed.

"Rush. I need Rush." Her pulse sped up, which was

a good thing, because even through all of her crying, she worried that when he'd walked out the door, he'd taken that part of her with him.

"Jay, is he getting married or something? Dating a woman who's jealous of your friendship? I don't get it."

"It's none of those things. We...moved beyond friendship. Way beyond."

"Oh." Her voice escalated. "Oh! Jayla."

"Don't get too excited."

"I'm...a little perplexed, I guess. I mean, there was a time when I thought you two would hook up, but that was, gosh, years ago, and he's not exactly the marrying type, you know?"

Jayla covered her face with her hands as she sank to the couch. She forgot that although she knew Rush had changed, her family didn't.

"He's not like that. At least not with me."

Mia didn't respond.

Jayla threw herself back and winced in pain.

"Mia, I know who he was. God, if anyone does, it's me." *Painfully so.* "But trust me, okay? He loves me, Mia, and I love him."

"O-kay. I'm going to try not to needle you about this, but are you one hundred percent sure that the love you both feel is true, want-to-love-and-protect-honor-and-cherish love and not I-wanna-see-how-the-sex-I've-been-missing-is kind of love?"

She imagined Mia's hazel eyes staring up at the ceiling as she asked Jayla the most painful question she could with very little emotion, because to Mia, this was a practical question, not a heart-wrenching, world-spinning,   tear-my-heart-out-and-feed-me-doubt question like it was as it landed in Jayla's ears.

"Remember when I first told you I wanted to be a skier?" Jayla smiled at the memory. She had been seven at the time, and Mia was the wise old age of ten.

Mia laughed. "How could I forget? You listed about twenty reasons why, including the well-thought-out reason that skiers got to have hot chocolate whenever they wanted."

"I do that, you know."

"I'm sure you do."

Jayla was already breathing a little easier. "Well, with Rush, it's the same thing."

"He lets you have hot chocolate whenever you want? Isn't that sweet of him."

"Ha-ha."

"I'm sorry. Okay, so you're both in love. And..."

"And I messed up. Really badly messed up." She bit her lower lip and closed her eyes with her next admission. "And I'm not ready to fix it even though I want to."

"What does that mean? How did you mess up? Give me details so I know if you're screwing yourself or Rush over, because when I hear you tell me that you messed up but you won't fix it, the first thing that goes through my mind is...then you don't really love him like you think you do."

"I knew you'd think that, and it hurts to hear you say it." She took a deep breath. "But that's why I called, to see if I'm being an idiot."

"I'm pretty sure you are, but spill it."

"Okay. Here goes." Her stomach sank like she had

taken a downhill ride on a roller coaster. She forced herself to tell the truth, and when she finally spoke, her words came fast. "I hurt my shoulder a few weeks ago, hid it from everyone. Now I can barely move, but I want to compete tomorrow. I wanted to practice tonight, but Rush basically gave me an ultimatum and walked out when I didn't agree not to practice."

"First, your injury," Mia began. "Where does that stand? How bad are we talking?"

"Bad enough for Rush to say he wouldn't sit back quietly and watch me cripple myself. But he'll support me competing." *Because that's the type of boyfriend he is. He loves me too much to see me take an extra risk when the benefits aren't important. And he also loves me enough to allow me to take an equally scary risk with the competition, because he understands how a competitive athlete's brain works.*

He's perfect.

I'm a fool.

What am I doing?

"That makes no sense at all." Mia's tone turned deadly serious. "If he thinks you can't practice because it could cripple you, then why would he let you compete? Crippled, Jay? What the hell are you thinking? This is your body, and you only get one."

"First of all, no one *lets* me do anything," Jayla said too forcefully.

"You know what I mean. If he really loves you, he wouldn't let you make a bad decision."

I forced him to step back. Her heart swelled at the reason he'd done as she asked. "He's a competitor. He knows I have to compete. He doesn't like that I'm doing it, but he'll accept it." *Because he loves me.* "But he also knows that practicing could—*could*, not definitely *would*—injure me so badly that I can't compete anymore." Fear clenched her chest again, but somehow explaining everything to Mia made her see things with Rush more clearly. What the hell was she doing? And how could she have let Rush walk out the door?

"You're both nuts."

This, she knew. Competitive athletes were all nuts when it came to competing.

"Jay, what's the issue? If he's going to stand behind you to compete, just don't practice. You said yourself it could injure you further. Why chance it? Or a better question is, why chance losing Rush over it if you love him?" Mia didn't pause long enough for Jayla to answer. "Can we back up a minute? I have to ask you again. What the hell are you thinking? Get your shoulder looked at. Get it fixed. Do whatever needs to be done." The escalation in her voice told her that Mia was on the move again, probably waving her hands as she paced. "You've already won an Olympic gold medal. Do you even know how few people can say that?"

"Yes."

"Then what the hell? Why? This isn't even a big competition. It's some rinky-dink little thing."

"So what? Mia, the minute I think that way—that one race is more important than the next—I won't train as hard. I won't push myself as hard as I should."

"You won't injure yourself so badly that you lose your career or push away the only man you've ever loved and call your sister wondering if you were being stupid or not, either."

She had a point. "I already figured out what I needed to do anyway. Just talking to you helped. Thank you."

"I didn't give you any advice other than...Wait. Does that mean you decided not to compete and to get your shoulder looked at?"

She heard hope in Mia's voice and felt hope in her heart for an entirely different reason. "Nope. It means I'm going to find Rush and apologize, because he's not only right, but he's the only thing I've ever wanted more than skiing."

"I'm so confused. Are you going to compete?"

"Yes." *Hell, yes.*

"Jayla, you are infuriating. I'm calling Jace. He's going to be there. Maybe he can talk some sense into you."

Jayla sighed. "Whatever. Thanks, Mia, and I'm sorry. I didn't mean to make you worry about me, but if I'd have called Jen, she would have focused on all the wrong things."

"Sex, sex, and more sex? You think? Jen?" Mia laughed.

"Actually, she gives me really good advice, but I needed you. You never seem to get sidetracked by anything."

"Sure I do, but I'm glad if I helped in some way."

Jayla ended the call with a promise to let Mia know what the doctor said about her shoulder after the competition. She noticed the bag that Rush had thrown on the counter. She might be willing to screw up her shoulder, but there was no way in hell she was going to screw up her relationship with Rush.

RUSH CHECKED HIS cell phone for the hundredth time, then turned back to the revolving images on his laptop. He'd seen the conviction in Jayla's eyes. She was dead set against being told what to do, and so was he. He'd been so distracted at practice that he thought the coach was going to wring his neck, but he hadn't said a word, and Rush had been thankful for it. He was nowhere near having his emotions in check and wouldn't have trusted his reaction.

He wished he could blame Jayla and her stubbornness for the way they were running head to head, but the truth was, she'd done him in—all hundred twenty pounds of her. Flattened him like road kill. It was his fault they were in this position. If he'd never kissed her, they'd still be safely immersed in the friend zone, instead of tangled up in their heartstrings.

And he'd be sitting beside her right now, talking about how she'd kick ass in the competition tomorrow injured or not, eating those damn gummy bears.

Rush slammed his laptop closed and tried to push thoughts of Jayla away. He needed to calm down so he could compete tomorrow, and he knew the minute he went into the bedroom, he'd think of nothing but Jayla, naked in his bed, whispering all those sexy little things into his ear. *More. Yes. Please. Oh God, Rush.*

There was only one thing he could do to calm this type of fervor. He grabbed a few things and headed out the cabin door.

Chapter Twenty-Nine

JAYLA STARED AT the Icy Hot and Bengay containers feeling like a complete bitch. She'd sent him away when she was confronting Kelly, and he'd gone to get her pain-relief medication? She scooped them back into the bag and eyed her coat. *Forget it.* His cabin was only a minute away, and a minute already seemed like fifty-nine seconds too long. She swung the door open. Realizing she didn't have shoes on, she pushed her foot into a boot. *Come on. Come on. Come on.* She steadied herself against the counter as she shoved her other boot on, then flew out the door and crashed right into a wall of muscle. *Rush.*

"Ow, ow, ow." She looked up at him. It wasn't just his chest she'd knocked into. He had a big bag of something hard in one arm and his computer tucked under the other.

"I'm sorry. Your shoulder. Are you okay?" He stepped back and ran his eyes up and down her. "Where are you going? Where's your coat?"

"I'm...You're here."

"Of course I'm here. You think I'm going to let you and your Raggedy Ann arm ruin this relationship? No way."

She had to laugh to keep from crying. She lifted up on her toes, and he met her halfway. When their lips met, it put pressure on her neck, sending pain to her shoulder.

"Ow, ow."

"Sorry." He opened the cabin door and they went inside. "Where were you going?"

"To your cabin. To get you." She was breathing hard, shivering with nerves and cold.

"You could have texted."

"Maybe if my brain was working, but it's been on overload. You're here. You didn't wait for me to ask you to come back."

He looked at her out of the corner of his eyes and wrinkled his forehead, like she'd said the stupidest thing she could have ever said, and maybe—just maybe—she had.

She looked at the medicated ointments on the counter. "You brought me stuff for my shoulder."

"'Cause I'm a good boyfriend." He set the bag he was carrying down on the counter. "How's your shoulder?"

"Sucky." It felt good to be completely honest. Finally.

"Did you take something?"

"Motrin. Tylenol." She watched him emptying the large bag. Protein powder, yogurt, frozen fruit, and a stack of clean clothes. Then he rifled through the kitchen cabinets.

"Fine, but the minute you're done competing, you're taking something stronger and going to the doctor. Like it or not."

They were perfectly in sync on that point.

He loaded up the blender with ingredients for a protein shake. "Want a shake?" He set his hand on the top of the blender and turned it on.

"No, thanks. Why did you bring all that over?"

He turned off the blender and poured the contents into a glass, offering it to Jayla before taking a sip himself.

"Because we're always in sync, and this stupid argument isn't going to change that. I need my stuff in the morning, and I'm not leaving you tonight. You can try to push me away, but I'm not going to budge. I might be *just* your boyfriend, but I'm a man. I'm your man. And I'm not going to put what comes as second nature away because you bitch at me or because you don't like what I say. I don't care if we argue. I can take it. I'm going to protect you, and I'm going to love you as if we were still in the friend zone, only a billion times better."

"More."

"What?"

"More. You'll love me a billion times more. And better." The thought sent a shudder through her.

"Yes. And when you say that word, with that sexy as hell look in your eyes, it's exactly what I want to do. But first I need to show you something." He took off his coat and boots and then helped her to take off her boots.

"I think it's time for more rules." Rush grabbed his

laptop and led her into the bedroom.

"They didn't work so well last time." He helped her change into her favorite pair of flannel pajama pants and one of his soft long-sleeved shirts. He drew down the comforter, and Jayla climbed in.

"Don't even think about making a move on me, either. I'm going nowhere near that shoulder. If you're gonna compete, you need all the energy you can get."

She rolled her eyes. "You ruin all my fun."

He took off his shirt and jeans and climbed in beside her in his boxer briefs, lifting his arm as she snuggled against his chest. "This whole snuggle thing where you use me as your pillow? Don't ever stop doing it."

She smiled and cuddled closer.

"You need to make a decision, Jayla. I'm going to be protective of you. I'm granting you immunity from that for this last competition, but after that, I'm going back to the badass you fell in love with who's not afraid to push you in directions you don't want to go if I think it'll help you. And I expect you to do the same for me, like you always have. Got it?"

She yawned. "I'm not sure what that means, but okay."

"It means if I see you're hurt, you respect my suggestions, or if you're in a position where I feel you're being threatened, I get to step in."

She ran her fingers along his forearm. "I don't need you to protect me in situations like the one with Kelly Baker."

"No, you sure as hell don't, but something in me needs to at least be nearby. I can't promise that I won't stand too close or say the wrong thing, but I'll respect your ability to handle the situation. One of the things I love about you is your strength, but that doesn't mean that I won't react to that kind of situation, and it's not right for you to expect me not to. You have to respect that about me."

"Okay."

"Okay?"

"Yeah. Fine." She placed her hand on his thigh, so glad that he was there with her again. "I was all messed up today. Between my arm and that woman and learning that you had tried to protect me by not telling me what she said. I couldn't think, much less process, how I was treating you. I'm sorry for all of it. And when you walked out earlier, it just about killed me. But I was still so overwhelmed that I couldn't move, much less act rationally."

"Fair enough." He opened his laptop and set it on his legs.

"Home movies?"

"Sort of. Watch."

Images of the two of them appeared on the screen, each one fading into the next. Most pictures were taken at arm's length, the two of them together, making silly faces with pink, cold cheeks. In some pictures, Jayla's eyes were sad, and in those pictures, Rush was looking at her, not at the camera, and the concern in his eyes was palpable. Seeing it warmed her from the inside out. There were pictures of Jayla wearing her flannel pajama pants and Rush's fuzzy slippers and Jayla standing on the slopes, the sun glistening in her eyes. When the picture of her wearing

Rush's clothes from the other night appeared, it tugged at her heart. The picture of the sunrise Rush had taken on the chairlift flashed on the screen, and she took his hand in hers. She'd forgotten about some of the pictures from when they were younger, like the one they took when they were in their early twenties, standing by a bonfire. Rush held up a stick with four marshmallows on it, and Jayla was looking at him. The love in her eyes was as strong as the concern she'd seen in Rush's just a few pictures earlier.

"Tell me what you see." Rush stroked her hair.

"Us."

"What else?"

"Happiness. Love." She kissed the back of his hand.

"Want to know what I see?"

More than anything. She nodded.

"Jayla Stone, a funny, caring, sometimes sad, sometimes ridiculously happy, always painfully sexy woman. I see the best friend I could ever ask for. I see a girl who likes to take walks, loves books that make her cry, and loves the way babies smell, which, by the way, I still think is weird." He smiled. "I see a woman who rolls her eyes at anything too girly and who once nursed a baby bunny back to health after she found it in the woods. I see a sister who loves her siblings enough to send them socks the week before Christmas every year because she worries that they won't buy new ones for themselves."

"Rush." She was working hard to keep her tears at bay.

"You know what I don't see?"

"What?"

"Just a competitive skier." He paused, as if letting the words sink in.

Which they did.

She turned toward him.

"I know part of pushing yourself to the point of not being able to move is that you're afraid of who you'll be if you can't compete." His voice was comforting. He pointed to the screen. "This is who you'll be. The same person. All of us have an expiration date on competing, babe. You know that. We just don't know what it is until it shows itself with injury, failure, or age."

He brushed her hair from her shoulder, and the intimate touch made her long to be closer to him.

"You may still be able to come back in a year, after you get whatever treatment you need. We won't know until you've been seen by the docs. But what we do know—what I know—is that even if you can't compete, the only thing that will change is how you spend your winters. Training until you can barely move, or enjoying life a little more and taking care of me when I can't move."

"I'm not becoming your little masseuse." She was teasing him, but she felt a sting at the thought of not competing. Just a sting. A prickle. She was surprised to realize that thinking about not competing no longer felt like Freddy Krueger was banging at the back door.

Rush touched her cheek and kissed her lips softly, lingering as only a lover would. "You're too big a part of my life to be my *little* anything. You're my everything."

Chapter Thirty

JAYLA WOKE UP the next morning to the sound of the cabin door closing and Rush talking, his footsteps crossing the hardwood floor. The digital clock read six forty-five. *He let me sleep in.*

"Jayla will be so excited to see you," Rush said as he passed the slightly ajar bedroom door. She listened, trying to figure out who he was on the phone with.

"Shouldn't she be up by now?"

Jace! Her brother's deep voice filtered into the bedroom. She pushed up from the mattress and stifled a groan against the pain in her shoulder and arm.

Rush peeked into the bedroom. "Hey. You're up." He went directly into the bathroom and brought her Tylenol, Motrin, and a glass of water. "Here, take this, babe. Pain? One to ten?"

"Six." She took the medication. "Maybe seven."

His eyes filled with concern. "Which on a normal person would be an eleven. You can still back out."

She glared at him and started for the door. Jayla found Jace standing with his back to her, looking out the window. His broad shoulders nearly filled the window frame. His dark hair touched the collar of the black leather jacket he'd worn ever since Jayla could remember. The soft leather tapered to the waist of his distressed jeans. His standard outfit. She loved the familiarity and comfort of knowing he never really changed.

"Jace."

He flashed a wide smile. His hair was brushed back from his face, highlighting his wide forehead and chiseled cheeks. He had deep-set hazel eyes that were common among the Stone men, olive skin, and thick, low brows, which gave him a perpetual brooding, mysterious look. His goatee gave him a rugged, dangerous edge.

Jace opened his arms and crossed the room. "Jay-Jay."

"You're the only one who calls me that, so don't say it in public. Got it, big brother?" She fell into his arms, and he gently engulfed her—too gently. At six five, he was more than a foot taller than Jayla, and with his black leather boots, he was more like six six. She hadn't realized how much she'd missed him until he held her.

"Yeah, yeah. I know the rules. Heard your shoulder's giving you hell." Jace kissed her cheek, tickling her face with his scraggly beard.

She ignored the comment, knowing Rush and Mia must have filled him in and wanting to avoid a lecture. She tugged the ends of his goatee. "You know you could get even more women if you trimmed that thing."

"Don't wish that on me. I need the little bit of sleep I get." He winked, then narrowed his eyes. "I hear you're competing with that bum shoulder you're trying to avoid talking about."

"I see Rush got to you." She cast a heated stare at Rush. He held his hands up in surrender. "We're not talking about it." Jayla went to the kitchen to make coffee and hopefully distract Jace from her shoulder. "How did you get here so early?"

Jace took off his leather jacket, exposing multicolored tattoos that snaked around his arms and peeked out at the top of his shirt collar. He leaned against the refrigerator, kicked one heavy boot over the other, and watched her with an assessing gaze.

"Closed the deal early." He crossed his arms and glared at her. "You really planning on competing today? You cringe every time you move your right hand."

No shit. Jayla ignored him and handed Rush a cup of coffee; then she held a cup toward Jace. "If you stop talking about my shoulder, I'll let you have this."

He lifted his thick brows. "I'm good, thanks."

Rush went to Jayla's side and kissed her cheek. "I always thought *I'm good* was a Jayla thing, but now I realize it's a Stone family trait."

Jace ran his eyes between them. "So you two really are a thing, huh? Finally." He smiled at Rush.

"Finally?" Jayla breathed a sigh of relief at his acceptance of their relationship. She touched Rush's cheek. "Yes, we're really a *thing*."

"Well, you're lucky to have him, Jay-Jay. Most men would find that attractive little outfit of yours a little homely." He eyed her flannel pants and Rush's shirt, which nearly touched her knees.

Rush gently pulled her to his chest. "I've never seen flannel look so hot."

Jayla felt her cheeks flush.

Jace shook his head. "What took you so damn long, Remington? She's been in love with you forever."

You knew I loved him?

"How do you know it was me holding out?" Rush leaned down and whispered to Jayla, "You better get ready. We have to be at practice in an hour. Do you need help in the shower?"

"Hey, she's still my little sister," Jace warned.

"He means because of my shoulder, you twerp." She turned to Rush. "I'm good, thanks. I might need help getting dressed, though."

"Whoa, hold on." Jace pushed from the fridge and held up his hands. "You need help getting dressed, but you're going to compete? I don't think so, Jayla May Stone."

"I'm twenty-eight years old, Jace, not ten. I think I know what I'm capable of." Jace kept busy with his own life, but for as long as Jayla could remember, he'd also found time to set her straight or beam with pride for her accomplishments. Even if he wasn't at most of her competitions, he usually found time to Skype or FaceTime and let her know he was proud of her. When she was growing up, he'd been more overtly protective, never allowing anyone to look at her sideways or say a harsh word. On more than one occasion when he'd come home to visit after college, he'd scared away her dates with nothing more than a piercing stare and a warning of broken fingers if they touched her.

Now, as Jace locked eyes with Rush and lifted his chin in Jayla's direction, she wondered if he'd try to play the same threatening role with Rush. He'd be in for a tough fight. Rush wasn't intimidated by anyone, including her imposing, bearded brother.

"Don't expect him to stop me, either," Jayla said as she headed into the bedroom to get ready.

Chapter Thirty-One

SPECTATORS GATHERED BEHIND the ropes on the sidelines of the slopes. Colorful sponsorship banners hung over the finish lines, and the media was everywhere. Adrenaline soared through Jayla's body, humming so loudly that it masked the din of the crowd. Pain radiated from Jayla's shoulder into her chest and back and down her arm. She thought about the pictures Rush had shown her last night and the things he'd said. She *was* more than a competitive skier; of course she was. But this was what she craved.

Rush hadn't left her side at all during the morning team meeting, the press interviews, and even now, when he should be heading over to his own competition area, he stood beside her as she headed over to the practice area for one final run. He was her rock. Her supporter. Her biggest fan and her lover.

Jace had smothered her just as much, asking every few minutes if she was sure she wanted to compete and reminding her that their family was proud of her even if she backed out. Jace might often be scattered, but he was also a voice of reason and she loved him for it. Even when she'd hated him for sticking his nose into her personal life when she was younger, she'd always known he was doing it out of love. And now, as they stood at the bottom of the practice slope, Rush hovering, pampering, protecting, doing all the things she'd asked him not to do, and Jace's hazel eyes piercing her with so much worry that he looked like he was ready to throw her over his shoulder and run her off to Younger Sisterland, where siblings were kept out of harm's way, she was rethinking her decision to compete.

Kia and Teri stood among the group waiting for the chairlift just off to the left, wearing their blue numbered racing vests proudly on their strong bodies.

Neither Rush nor Jace had pushed her not to race after Jace's initial comments back at the cabin. The pampering and peppering of *are you sure you want to race* was expected, but she'd feared another ultimatum and was glad when it hadn't come.

She realized that words were unnecessary when the man she loved more than life itself and the brother she adored were practically draped in concern.

Rush's eyes were dark and serious when he leaned in close and wished her luck. "It doesn't matter if you win this one, babe. Just come out safely on the other side." His eyes shot to Jace. "You're staying with her, right?"

"You bet." Jace wore a thick black sweater, turtleneck, and leather jacket, and Jayla had no idea why he wasn't shivering. Then again, he and Rush were the toughest guys she knew, and she imagined their blood ran hot at all times.

With them staring at her like their lives depended on her safety, Jayla took one last glance at her teammates before reaching for Rush's hand.

Her chest was so tight, she could barely breathe. She'd debated all night what she wanted to do, and now, as Rush's jaw clenched and Jace swallowed hard, exchanging a frustrated glance, she knew she was making the right decision. "I'm not competing. I'm just going to take one last easy ski down the mountain for sanity's sake."

"You're not...? You're sure?" Rush searched her eyes.

She nodded. "It's the right thing to do, even if I hate it."

"Babe." The word was laden with disbelief as he lowered his forehead to hers and cupped the back of her neck. "Thank you. God, thank you, Jayla. I love you so much."

"I love you, too, and I love that you cared enough not to force me not to compete. If you had—"

Jace interrupted her. "You would have had a rebellious Jayla on your hands, and not only would she have competed, but she would have probably added events to her schedule." He touched her hand. "I'm proud of you, sis. But that's nothing new. You always make me proud."

"I'm not doing it to make anyone proud. Rush helped me see what I was too scared to face. My what-ifs. It turns out that competing isn't everything." She smiled at Rush. "We are."

She nodded at Kia and Teri. "I made my mark. It's their turn. Besides, the last thing I need is to get hurt while competing and have you two oafs telling me you told me so. I'll tell Chad when we reach the top, and after this last run down the mountain, I'll find Coach Cunningham."

"I couldn't love you more than I do at this very second," Rush said, and she knew he was wrong. He'd love her more with every passing second. Forever.

The chairlift came around and Jayla took a deep breath. "Slow and easy. Promise. Go get ready, and I'll come watch as soon as I take my last run for the season." Her heart squeezed at the thought and she swallowed against it. "I'd say good luck, but you don't need it. You've got this one. You always do."

Chapter Thirty-Two

RUSH SKIED THROUGH the crowds to the downhill slope, where the men's competition was slated to take place. He felt lighter, stronger, and knew it was driven by Jayla's decision not to compete. He'd had to fight the urge to tell her not to take one last ski down the slope, but she'd given in on the competition, and he trusted her to take it easy.

"Rush!"

He turned at the sound of his younger brother Kurt's voice.

"You made it." Rush embraced him with one arm, holding his ski poles with the other. Kurt and Rush shared the same vivid blue eyes and at six two they stood eye to eye.

"I had a book signing a few hours from here. Glad it worked out." Kurt had written several bestselling thrillers. Although he was the most reserved of the Remington men, and Rush the most risky, they'd always had a strong relationship.

"Me too. Did everyone else make it?" He scanned

the crowd for his family.

"Yeah, except Sage, Dex, Kate, and Ellie. Jack told me about you and Jayla. You're really taking the monogamous plunge? During competition season? You sure you're not sick?"

"This thing between us is stronger than me, man. I couldn't fight it if my life depended on it."

"Great. So now I'm the last single Remington? That should be fun at family dinners."

"I don't think you have to worry about it. We all know that a woman would have to barge into your office and pry your fingers from your keyboard to get your attention."

Kurt peered around Rush. "Looks like someone's in trouble."

The emergency medical team's snowmobiles were speeding toward the slope where Jayla was skiing. An icy chill ran down Rush's back.

"You have your phone? Gimme your phone. Fast. Hurry up." He was already moving toward the slope.

Kurt thrust his cell into Rush's hand. "What's wrong?"

"I don't know, but that's where Jayla is and I have a bad feeling." Rush called Chad. *Answer the phone. Come on. Answer your goddamn ph*—"Chad. What's happening? Is it Jayla?"

"Rush? Yes. Someone clipped her, knocked her into the woods. She circumvented the trees but flipped when she hit the brush."

No. God no. "Blood?"

"Clipped her head on something, but not bad. They've got her on a stretcher. Nothing broken, but we

278

can't tell exactly what's going on with her shoulder and arm. You've got to get over to your competition." It was a command—one that Rush was not going to follow. "I'll call as soon as I know what's what."

He handed Kurt the phone. They reached the base of the slope just as the rescue team brought Jayla down the mountain. He broke out in a cold sweat at the sight of her lying still, wrapped in the stretcher. Press swarmed around them.

"Jayla!" He pushed past the cameramen and reporters and was relieved to see anger instead of pain in her eyes.

"Some bastard clipped me. I was taking it easy." She said through clenched teeth.

"Babe. Your shoulder? What else?"

The paramedic answered as they hurried toward the parking lot. "Shoulder, arm, neck. No breaks that we can detect. Shallow breathing, probably from pain. We have to get her to the hospital."

Jace kept pace on Jayla's other side. Chad moved to clear the press from coming too close.

"I'm coming with you," Rush said.

"Rush, I've got this," Chad said.

Jayla narrowed her eyes. "Don't you dare leave this competition. Stop, please," she said to the paramedics.

"I'm not letting you go alone."

"I've got Jace, and I'm fine. Go. Win your race for us." She was so damned stubborn, it tore at his heart.

"I'll go with her," Kurt said from behind him.

He'd nearly forgotten his brother was there. "Thanks, Kurt, but I'm going, too. Jayla."

She shook her head.

Chad stepped to the side and made a call. Within seconds, a host of volunteers for the race were managing the encroaching crowd and giving the paramedics and Rush and Jayla a wide berth.

"Rush, you've got a competition in twenty minutes," Chad reminded him.

"I know that." Freed from his skis, he grabbed one of the paramedic's arms. "Give us a sec?"

Jace and Kurt stepped between the paramedics and Jayla.

"One to ten?" Rush demanded.

She gritted her teeth.

"Fifteen. Got it." Rush swore under his breath. "I'd like to kill that asshole."

"Focus, Rush. It's my shoulder. I'm sure that's all it is. I'm fine."

"You're not *fine*, Jayla, and I'm not leaving your side. I don't give a rat's ass about this race."

"Shut up and listen to me. I'm injured. You're not. The team is counting on you. I'm counting on you. Now, get Jace to take our picture so we have something good from this crazy day, and then get your butt up that mountain and win. For me. And if you argue, I'll climb out of this stupid thing and get back on my skis. You know I will." She kept her eyes trained on him. "Jace, can you take our picture?"

Jace stepped forward. "Your picture?"

"It's our thing," Jayla explained.

"Damn it, Jayla."

"You two are definitely made for each other." Jace took out his cell phone, and Rush went down on his side in the snow beside Jayla's stretcher. He pressed his cheek to hers, and Jace snapped a picture.

"Go," Jayla urged. "I have Kurt and Jace. I'll be fine, and if you don't win, there will be hell to pay."

"You're going to be the death of me, Jayla Stone. I'm pulling boyfriend rank."

Jayla clenched her jaw. "If you want to still have boyfriend rank, get out of here and win that race."

"You're the most frustrating, stubborn woman I know." Rush gently cupped her cheek and pressed a soft kiss to her lips. "I hate you for sending me away."

"But you love me for so many other reasons."

Rush shifted his eyes to Jace and Kurt. "Don't leave her side."

"Like I need you to tell me that?" Jace crossed his arms over his chest.

"Like ink on paper," Kurt said with a nod.

Rush looked down at Jayla again. "When this is over and your shoulder is healed, I'm taking you away for a week of nothing but..." He eyed Jace, who shook his head and looked away. Rush lowered his voice. "Us. No competition, no stress, no teammates, no coaches, and no distractions. Just you and me with sand between our toes and a warm bed at night."

"Win this race or it'll be a long time before I'm in your bed again."

"You're a pain in the ass, but you do know how to motivate me."

Chapter Thirty-Three

LATER THAT EVENING, after having been put through a battery of tests and discussing her injury with the hospital doctors, surgeons, team doctor, and being lectured by the coach—which was more painful than any of the tests—Jayla was back in her cabin and finally able to relax. The stronger pain meds they'd given her at the hospital had helped, and knowing that Kia had won the race in her place and that Rush had crushed his competition had added some good news to the reality of her injury.

She sat on the couch in front of a roaring fire, with her arm in a sling. To her right was Rush's sister, Siena, and to her left, Jack's fiancée, Savannah. Siena's boyfriend, Cash Ryder, was a tall, muscular firefighter, as handsome as Siena was pretty, and Siena hadn't taken her eyes off of him all evening. Cash, Jack, Kurt, and Jace stood by the fireplace, talking about the new motorcycle Jace had designed, flexing their all-things-male knowledge. Testosterone brewed in every corner of the cabin. Jayla looked across the room at Rush talking with his mother and father and realized that her worst what-ifs no longer scared her. She thought she'd feel lost, empty, without competitive skiing, but with Rush by her side, she knew that no matter what happened with her career, she'd never feel anything but fulfilled in her heart.

Jayla had spent time with Rush's family on many occasions, but she'd never before noticed the way Rush drew his shoulders back when he spoke with his father and how his facial expression softened every time he looked at his mother. She knew that James Remington had always been strict, with his military background and belief that hard work was all that mattered, but now she saw something more. Despite his steely gaze and squared shoulders, when Rush spoke, his father really listened, lifting his brows with interest. And sometimes the side of his lips curved up and his face softened in a fashion similar to Rush's crooked grin, which she loved so much. She wondered if beneath all those sharp edges there was a softer side that even he didn't know existed.

Like me.

Rush's love had peeled away her hard, competitive shell, and she realized that with Rush, she didn't have to be the strong one, and she liked that. She'd taken care of herself and pushed herself in every way for so many years that she'd almost forgotten how to let herself be cared for. Rush was good at that, caring for her. Rush's tender heart and fierce determination helped her see herself, and her future, more clearly.

Savannah touched Jayla's leg, drawing her back to

their conversation. "So you definitely need surgery?"

"Yes. When we go back to New York, I'll have surgery to repair the tear in my labrum, the lining in my shoulder; then, after six weeks, I'll start rehab." The injury had seemed like the end of the world at first. But with Rush by her side and a good dose of perspective, she realized that this was just another mountain to scale. And she was good at conquering mountains.

"Will you still be able to compete?" Savannah brushed her long, auburn hair from her shoulder, and her green eyes filled with concern.

"We won't know for a long time, but she's not going to push it." Rush sat on the coffee table in front of Jayla and locked eyes with her. He flashed that sexy grin of his, and Jayla wished she wouldn't have taken that last stupid run down the mountain so she could wrap her arms around him.

Siena leaned forward. "I know you won't let her." Then she sat back and said to Jayla, "Not that you need him holding you back, but he's right. You really shouldn't push it."

Jace came to Jayla's side. "My little sister needs a reminder sometimes. Trust me on that."

Jayla rolled her eyes.

"Jayla, honey, I'm just glad you're all right. I worry about you two every time you compete." Joanie Remington, Rush's mother, put a gentle hand on Rush's shoulder. The colorful blouse she wore hung just below the waist of her wide-legged slacks. She was as laid-back as Mr. Remington was rigid in his dark slacks and starched button-down shirt.

"I can attest to that, having watched some of your competitions on television with her. She covers her eyes sometimes," Kurt added.

"Really, Mom?" Rush scoffed.

"You wait until you have children of your own. Between worrying about Jack flying all over creation in that little bush plane, you two speeding down the slopes, and now Sage and Kate going off on a different adventure every few weeks, it's amazing I get any sleep at all."

"Please don't mention me and children in the same breath," Rush said.

You don't want kids? She'd never bring it up in front of his family, and they hadn't ever talked about if they wanted children or not, but his comment made her heart squeeze a little.

"Oh, Rush, please," his mother said.

He looked at Jayla. "Thanks, Mom. Like she didn't have enough on her mind."

She had almost forgotten that he could see right through her.

"Don't worry, babe," Rush said. "I want kids. I just don't want my mother pushing me...us...to have them."

Us. Kids. She breathed a little easier, though now, with everyone's eyes on her, she was thoroughly embarrassed. She tried to laugh it off. "We're dating, not married."

Rush got a funny look on his face that Jayla couldn't read.

"Well, we'll give you grandkids for sure." Savannah reached for Jack's hand.

Cash reached for Siena's hand. "And we both want

kids someday."

Siena looked up at him and smiled. "And we're not engaged or anything yet, but we know we'll be together forever."

Kurt moved to Jace's side. "Is it getting a little thick in here?"

"Very. Think you can revise this scene?" Jace looked at the bedroom door. "Maybe wipe the sappy stuff and replace it with something dark and scary?"

Kurt glanced around the room, and Jayla could practically see him revising their conversation in his mind. Rush, on the other hand, still had her locked under a serious stare, and she was beginning to wonder why.

"Hey, no rewriting family moments," Joanie said.

"Don't worry, Mom. Nothing in this room feels the least bit dark or scary. I think we're stuck with the mushy dialogue grooving through the cabin."

"Well," his mother said, "I'm so happy Jayla and Rush have come together. I can't imagine two people being any closer. You two know more about each other than most married couples, and you still love each other. That's a testament in and of itself."

Rush reached for Jayla's hand. "Me too, Mom. In a way, we have Jack to thank." He looked at Jack, who was leaning on the arm of the couch beside Savannah.

"I'm a miracle worker. What can I say?" Jack teased.

Jayla stifled a yawn. The pain meds were definitely taking their toll. "I'm glad you guys got to see Rush compete. Kurt and Jace, I'm really sorry that you had to spend the day at the hospital with me."

Jace pulled a piece of paper from his front pocket and waved it at her. "Totally worth it, sis. I have a hot date with a nurse tomorrow night."

"Blonde?" Kurt asked, reaching into his pocket. He pulled out a piece of paper and looked at it. "Christie?"

"You've got to be kidding me," Jace said flatly.

"Nope. I couldn't get a signal on my cell and asked to borrow their phone. When I thanked her, we talked and..." He shrugged. He crumpled the paper and handed it to Jace. "I've got a publishing deadline and I'm heading to Cape Cod with absolutely no intention of spending one minute away from my keyboard, so go for it."

Jace tossed both pieces of paper in the trash. "No, thanks."

"I can't believe you guys were scoping out women when I was getting those tests done." Jayla yawned again. "Anyway, you guys should go out to dinner or something. I feel bad making you all stay in after you've come all this way."

"Family comes first, and you're family." Jack turned to Jace. "You, too, Jace, now that my brother finally got his head out of his—"

His father took a step closer to Jack and lowered his chin, cutting him off with one hot look.

"Thanks, Jack. These two were bound to get together at some point," Jace said.

"Glad you're so sure, because I thought I was going to have to live with my Rush fantasy forever."

"Fantasy? Hm. I'll have to explore that further." Rush leaned forward and kissed her.

Heat vibrated through her, flushing her cheeks.

"Rush," his mother chided him with a harsh whisper.

"It was just a kiss."

"The comment, not the kiss," she clarified.

"Sorry, Mom." Rush rose to his feet. "Do you guys want to go eat at a restaurant, or should we order in? I don't think Jayla should go into town after everything she's been through."

"I'm okay," she lied. It had been a grueling few days, and with the competition no longer hanging over their heads, her injury now professionally diagnosed, and pain meds on board, she was whipped. She couldn't wait to be wrapped in Rush's arms again.

"Oh goodness, I didn't even think about how exhausted you must be, Jayla. I'm sorry, hon," Joanie said. "James, why don't we all go eat and let Jayla get some rest? We can catch up with everyone tomorrow."

Rush's father placed a hand on his back. "I'm proud of you, son."

Jayla understood from the look in Rush's eyes, and the way he swallowed hard before responding, how much his father's statement meant to him.

"Thanks, Dad."

"I've always been proud of you, and if I don't tell you that enough, I'm sorry. I'm learning in my old age that you and your siblings can't read my mind, as I'd always thought." He slid a smile to Jack.

Savannah reached for Jack's hand. Jayla knew that Jack and his father had had a falling out right after Linda died and they'd come back together only when Jack and Savannah fell in love. Watching the love in Rush's family made her long to be part of it.

"Thanks, Dad. That means a lot to me." Rush embraced his father, and Jayla wondered if she was the only one who picked up on the way Rush's voice cracked.

His father turned his attention to Jayla. "I'm proud of you, too, Jayla. I've known you since you were twelve? Thirteen?" He shook his head. "I can't remember how old you were, but you've always been determined and very strong." He nodded. "And you've always been good to my son, and that's really all that matters in the grand scheme of things."

"Dad?" Kurt laid a hand on his father's shoulder. "Are you all right? You're not terminally ill or something, are you?"

He ran his hand down his face and glanced at Joanie, who nodded and smiled. "No, Kurt. I'm just learning to be a better man."

"Your father is just realizing that his message to his children to be better, be more, be...whatever...didn't always allow his real message to come through."

Rush smiled at Jack. "Well, we're never too old to better ourselves."

"Okay, that's enough drama for one day," Joanie said, moving toward the door. "Let's give Rush and Jayla a little peace and quiet."

Rush reached for her hand. "Mom's probably right. I can order in something for us, or run over to the lodge to pick something up. You must be tired."

She caught a hint of desire in his eyes and felt her cheeks flush. "Maybe a little," she admitted. "I'm sorry. I don't want to push you guys out."

Jace kissed Jayla's cheek. "I'm proud of you."

Savannah rose to her feet. "Sounds good to me. Jayla, I hope you aren't in too much pain with all this." She waved at Jayla's arm.

"I'll be fine, thanks."

"Rush, congrats, bro." Kurt patted Rush's back.

"Did you have any doubt I'd win?" Rush smirked.

"I meant congrats on being with Jayla."

"Ass."

"Boys." Joanie shook her head and moved to gently hug Jayla. "Feel better, Jayla. Don't let Rush keep you up too late."

"He takes good care of me." Jayla snuggled against Rush's side. "When I let him."

Jace pointed at her. "You've got a serious injury. Let Rush take care of you, or I'm coming back here and doing it myself."

"Oh God, no. You limit my gummy bears. Rush, *please* take care of me."

Chapter Thirty-Four

RUSH COULDN'T WAIT for everyone to leave. He'd been itching to talk to Jayla ever since she'd said they were *dating*. Yes, of course they were dating, but weren't they so much more?

Jayla leaned against the counter by the front door. "I feel like we just pushed everyone out."

"They know you need to rest." He placed his hands on her hips and nuzzled into her neck. "I'm glad they're gone. I missed you."

"Mm...You're kinda like gummy bears."

He drew back and looked into her eyes. "Gummy bears?"

"Yeah, never get enough." She lifted up on her tiptoes and kissed his chin.

"How's your shoulder?"

"Hurty."

"Complete and total adorable honesty. Who are you?" He ran his finger down her cheek, being extra careful to measure every movement to avoid hurting her. "Do you think a hot bath would help?"

"Only if you're in it with me. I feel like I've been away from you for a year."

He lowered his mouth to hers and kissed her softly.

"I'll get in the tub with you, but I can't promise I won't have wandering hands." Maybe a bath would ease the tension that was mounting inside him. He wasn't quite sure how to bring up the topic of their *dating*, but he knew if he didn't, he'd be sidetracked by it all night.

"I can live with that."

He filled the tub, then turned his attention to Jayla, first helping her to remove her sling, then removing her shirt and bra. He placed his hand over her heart and looked into her eyes.

"Your heart is going crazy," he whispered.

"I know. I can't help it. Every time we're close, I want to be closer."

The hunger in her eyes drew his lips to hers. She tasted so good, so sweet, so...*Jayla*.

"Love me," she whispered. "All of me."

He trailed kisses down her neck. She buried her left hand in his hair and brought his mouth to her breast. He loved when she urged him on. He kissed, licked, tasted her sweet skin before rubbing his thumb over her nipple and taking her in another greedy kiss. Rush took off his shirt, pressing his chest gently to hers, taking care to avoid putting pressure on her right side.

"I love the way you feel against me," he whispered.

Jayla was breathing hard, her eyes half closed. He kissed her sore shoulder, then kissed his way down her arm, wishing he could kiss the injury away and somehow take it on as his own. Her skin was warm and he was hard. So hard.

"Bath," he said between kisses. "Or I'm going to take you right here, and I'm afraid I'll hurt you."

"Take our pants off." She bit her lower lip. A glint of mischief sparkled in her eyes, which drove him a little crazy.

He took off her pants, then stepped from his own. She held her left palm up to his mouth.

"Lick it."

Holy hell. He dragged his tongue along her palm. The erotic, unexpectedness of it made his balls tighten.

Jayla stroked his hard length, driving him out of his mind.

"Jayla." His voice was rough, gravelly, and driven by lust that he had no intention of ignoring. Her touch was magical, tight and wet, slow, then fast. He fought against the need to come. "Jay..."

"Lift me onto the counter."

Done.

His heart beat so hard, so full of love for her that he thought he might come apart. He brought his hand to her wet center, then brought his fingers to his mouth and licked the taste of her from them. Her eyes went wide, then narrowed as she brought her lips to his and kissed along his bottom lip, then across his jaw, and nipped at his earlobe. He could barely restrain himself from driving into her. She guided him to her center and wrapped her legs around his waist. He pushed slowly into her, careful not to jostle her shoulder, until he was buried deep, and they both stilled.

Heaven.

"Are you okay?" He searched her eyes for a sign of discomfort.

"More than okay."

"Am I hurting your shoulder?"

She shook her head, then used his arm for leverage as she inched forward, taking him in deeper and drawing a moan of pleasure from deep within him. He held her hips still as he withdrew, then pushed in slowly again, hyperaware of every sensitive inch as it slid into her and she tightened around him until he was buried to the hilt again and again. They both went a little wild, their muscles tight, corded, as they panted for breath and Rush moved harder, faster, deeper. Heat coiled low in Rush's belly as Jayla began to suck in tiny breaths.

"Rush...More...Oh God."

He captured her pleas in his mouth and breathed air into her lungs as she went over the edge, taking him right along with her.

When he was finally able to breathe again, he buried his hand in her hair and kissed her lovingly. It wasn't enough. With Jayla, nothing was enough. His heart opened in a way he never imagined possible, and he wanted her in every aspect of his life. So much emotion welled within him that he was nearly driven to tears for lack of knowing how to channel it.

He carried her to the tub and placed her in the warm water, then settled in behind her. She leaned back against him with a contented sigh. Rush gathered her hair over her left shoulder and kissed the crest of her sore one. He didn't want to think about how much pain she must be in, but he'd never turn his back to appease her again—not when it meant she was in danger or hurting in any way. He also didn't want to think about her going to her own apartment just outside of New York when they left Colorado, or dating her a few nights each week. He didn't want to worry about whose place they'd stay at or where their clothes were in the morning. He didn't want to think about spending a single night without her ever again.

"Move in with me." The words came out and instantly felt right.

She turned in the tub, and he helped guide her legs around his waist. Her eyes flitted over his face, as if she were assessing his seriousness.

"Move in with me," he repeated. "You said we were dating, and I feel like we're so much more, so much bigger, than *dating*." He didn't give her time to answer. "Do you feel it, too? Or is this what it feels like to just date? Do I have it all wrong? Because I've never felt like this before."

"It's way bigger than dating. More," Jayla said with a smile.

"I don't ever want to wake up without you in my arms, and I want you snuggled against me on the couch eating gummy bears and wearing your flannel pajamas. I want to be the guy who you get mad at when I'm overprotective and the one you whisper *more* to when you come apart in my arms."

She blushed. Rush was a stoic athlete through and through, and yet he was powerless to calm his emotions for Jayla. They swept through him with the strength of a blizzard and left him craving more of her.

"I love you, Jayla."

"I..." She was shaking. "I love you so much I can barely stand it." She blinked against tears that welled in her eyes.

Her fingertips found his belly, and he lowered his forehead to hers and closed his eyes for a breath. When he opened them, a tear had slipped down her cheek and his chest tightened.

"Marry me."

"Rush..."

"I don't want to be your boyfriend. I want to be the father of your children, and I want to watch our kids fall in love like our parents have watched us. Marry me, Jayla." He couldn't stop himself from telling her how he felt. "I know it feels fast. But fifteen years isn't fast at all." He paused long enough to realize she was really shivering. He grabbed a towel from the rack and wrapped it around her. The edges dipped into the water and he held her close.

"Do you love me?" he whispered.

"I've loved you since I was thirteen," she said against his neck.

He let out a breath he hadn't realized he'd been holding.

"Look at me." She leaned back and searched his eyes. "How do you know that in six months you won't be sick of me?"

"Because in fifteen years I have never spent one hour being sick of you. And the thought of not being with you makes me sick to my stomach."

This earned him a smile.

"And how do you know that if I can't compete after the surgery and the rehab, you won't see me differently?"

"Because when I saw you on that stretcher, I knew that even if you could never move again, I wanted to be right there with you, taking care of you, every second of every day. You're my everything."

Her eyes jumped from right to left, and she smiled again. "I'm your...You are telling me the truth. Every word of it. I love that."

"Do you love me enough to want to wake up next to me every day? Do you have doubts about me or my love for you?"

"Yes. Not at all. Next question."

He smiled. "Do you want to have my babies? Eventually?"

She swallowed hard, and another tear slid down her cheek. "Yes."

"And will you share your gummy bears with me?"

"Always. Maybe. Probably."

He laughed. "And would you rather just date me?"

"I've never wanted to just date you. I've always wanted to marry you."

She touched his cheek, and he reveled in her touch and in the love in her eyes.

"Is that a yes?"

"It's most definitely a yes. Yes, Rush. God, yes."

The End

Please enjoy a preview of the next
Love in Bloom novel

Read, Write,

LOVE

The Remingtons, Book Five

Love in Bloom Series

Melissa Foster

NEW YORK TIMES BESTSELLING AUTHOR

MELISSA FOSTER

read, write,
LOVE

the remingtons

Love in Bloom: Contemporary Romance

Chapter One

THE TIDE LAPPED at the sandy shore beyond the deck of the cedar-shingled bungalow where Kurt Remington sat, fingers to keyboard, working on his latest manuscript. *Dark Times* was due to his agent at the end of the month, and Kurt came to his cottage in Wellfleet, Massachusetts, to hunker down for the summer and complete the project. He lived just outside of New York City, and he wrote daily, sometimes for ten or twelve hours straight. In the summers, he liked the change of scenery the Cape offered and was inspired by the Cape's fresh air and the sounds of the sea.

He'd bought the estate of a local painter a few years earlier with the intent of renovating the artist's studio that sat nestled among a grouping of trees on the far side of the property. Initially, Kurt thought he might use the studio as a writing retreat separate from where he lived, with the idea that leaving the cottage to work might give him a chance to actually have a life and not feel pressure to write twenty-four-seven.

What he found was that the studio was too far removed from the sights and sounds that inspired him, and it made him feel like even more of a recluse than he already was. He realized that it wasn't the location of his computer that pressured him. It was his internal drive and his love of writing that propelled his fingers to the keyboard every waking second. The idea of making the studio into a guest cottage crossed his mind, but that would indicate his desire to have guests, which would mean giving up his coveted writing time to entertain. So there it sat, awaiting...something. Though he had no idea what.

The cottage was built down a private road at the top of a dune, with a private beach below. A curtain of dense air settled around him. Kurt lifted his eyes long enough to scan the graying clouds and ponder the imminence of rain. It was 7:20 in the evening and he'd been writing since nine o'clock that morning, as was his daily habit. Right after his three-mile run, two cups of coffee, and a quick breeze through the newspaper and email. Once Kurt got into his writing zone each day, he rarely changed his surroundings. The idea of moving inside and breaking his train of thought was unsettling.

He set his hands back on the keyboard and reread the last few sentences of what would become his thirteenth thriller novel. A dog barked in the distance, and Kurt drew his thick, dark brows together without breaking the stride of his keystrokes. Kurt hadn't risen to the ranks of Patterson, King, and Grisham by being easily distracted.

"Pepper! Come on, boy!" A female voice sliced

through his concentration. "Come on, Pepper. Where are you?"

Kurt's fingers hesitated for only a moment as she hollered; then he went right back to the killer lurking outside the window in his story.

"Pepper!" the woman yelled again. "Oh God, Pepper, really?"

Kurt closed his eyes for a beat as the wind picked up. The woman's voice *was* distracting him. She was too close to ignore. *Get your mutt and move on.* He let out a breath and went back to work. Kurt craved silence. The quieter things were, the better he could hear his characters and think through their issues. He tried to ignore the sounds of splashing and continued writing.

"Pepper! No, Pepper!"

Great. He was hoping to squeeze in a few more hours of writing on the deck before taking a walk on the beach, but if that woman kept up her racket, he'd be forced to work inside—and if there was one thing Kurt hated, it was changing his surroundings while he was in the zone. Writing was an art that took total focus. He'd honed his craft with the efficiency of a drill sergeant, which was only fitting since his father was a four-star general.

More splashing.

"Oh no! Pepper? Pepper!"

The woman's panicked voice split his focus right down the center. He thought of his sister, Siena, and for a second he considered getting up to see if the woman's concern was valid. Then he remembered that his sister often overreacted. Women often overreacted.

"Pepper! Oh no!"

Being an older brother came with responsibilities that Kurt took seriously, as had been ingrained in him at a young age. That loud woman was someone's daughter. His conscience won over the battle for focus, and with a sigh, he pushed away from the table and went to the railing. He caught sight of the woman wading waist deep in the rough ocean waves.

"Pepper! Oh, God. Pepper, please come back!" she cried.

Kurt followed her gaze into deeper water, which was becoming rougher by the second as the clouds darkened and the wind picked up a notch. He didn't see a dog anywhere in the water. He scanned the empty beach—no dog there, either.

"Pepper! Please, Pep! Come on, boy!" She tumbled back with the next wave and fell on her ass, then struggled to find her footing.

Christ Almighty. Really? This, he didn't need. He watched her push through the crashing waves. She was shoulder deep. Kurt knew about the dangers of riptides and storms and wondered why the hell she didn't. She had no business being out in the water with a storm brewing.

Drops of water dampened Kurt's arms. He swatted them away with a grimace, still watching the woman.

"Please come back, Pepper!"

The rain came in a heavy drizzle now. *Damn it to hell.* Kurt spun around, gathered his computer and notes and brought them inside. He checked to see that he'd saved his file before pushing the laptop safely back from the edge of the counter, then turned back to the French doors. *I could close the doors and go right back to work.* He eyed his laptop.

"Pepper!"

She sounded farther away now. Maybe she'd moved on. He went back out on the deck to see if she'd come to her senses.

"Pep—" Another wave toppled her over. She was deeper now and seemed to be pulled by the current.

"Hey!" Kurt hollered in an effort to dissuade her from going out any deeper. She must not have heard him. He scanned the water again and saw a flash of something about thirty feet away from her. *Your damn dog.* Dogs were smelly, they shed, and they needed time and attention. All reasons why Kurt was not a fan of the creatures.

The rain picked up with the gusty wind. *Damn it.* He grabbed a towel from inside and stomped down the steps, *Dark Times* begrudgingly pushed aside.

LEANNA BRAY WAS wet, cold, and floundering. Literally. She'd been floundering for twenty-eight years, so this was nothing new, but being pummeled by rain, wind, and waves, chasing a dog that never listened? That was new.

"Pepp—" A wave knocked her off her feet and she went under the water, taking a mouthful of saltwater along with her. She tumbled head down beneath the surface.

Now Pepper and I will both drown. Freaking perfect.

Something grabbed her arm, and she reflexively

fought against it, sucking in another mouthful of salty water as she broke through the surface, arms flailing, choking, and pushing against the powerful hand that yanked her to her feet.

"You okay?" A deep, annoyed voice carried over the din of the crashing waves.

Cough. Cough. "Yeah. I—" *Cough. Cough.* "My dog." She blinked and blinked, trying to clear the saltwater and rain from her eyes. The man's mop of wet dark hair came into focus. He held tightly to her arm while scanning the water in the direction of where she'd last seen Pepper. His clothes stuck to his body like a second skin, riding the ripples of his impressive chest and arms as he held her above the surface with one arm around her ribs.

"Come on." She coughed as he plowed through the pounding surf with her clutched against his side. She slid down his body, and he lifted her easily into his arms, carrying her like he might carry a child, pressing her to his chest as he fought against the waves.

She pushed against his chest, feeling ridiculous and helpless...and maybe a little thankful, but she was ignoring that emotion in order to save Pepper.

"My dog! I need to get my dog!" she hollered.

Mr. Big, Tall, and Stoic didn't say a word. He set her on the wet sand and tossed her a rain-soaked towel. "It was dry." He pointed behind her to a wooden staircase. "Go up to the deck."

She dropped the towel and plowed past him toward the water. "I gotta get my dog."

He snagged her by the arm and glared at her with the brightest blue eyes she'd ever seen—and a stare so dark she swallowed her voice.

"Go." He pointed to those damn stairs again. "I'll get your dog." He took a step toward the water, and she pushed past him again.

"You don't have t—"

He scooped her into his arms again and carried her to the stairs. "If you fight me, your dog will drown. He won't last in this much longer."

She pushed at his chest again. "Let me go!"

He set her down on the stairs. "The waves will pull you under. I'll get your dog. Please stay here."

Her heart thundered against her ribs as she watched him stalk off and plow through the waves as if he were indestructible. She stood in the rain on the bottom stair, huddled beneath the wet towel, squinting to see him through the driving rain. She finally spotted him deep in the sea, wrapping his arms around Pepper—the dog who never let anyone carry him. He rounded his shoulders, shielding Pepper as he made his way back through the wild waves.

She ran to the edge of the water, shivering, tears in her eyes. "Thank you!" She reached for Pepper and the dog whined, pressing his trembling body closer to the guy.

"You have a leash?"

She shook her head. Her wet hair whipped across her cheek, and she turned her back to the wind. "He doesn't like them."

He took her by the arm again. "Come on." He led her up the stairs to a wooden deck, opened a French door, and leaned in close, talking over the sheeting rain.

"Go on in."

She stepped onto pristine hardwood. The warm cottage smelled of coffee and something sweet and masculine, like a campfire. She reached for Pepper. Pepper whined again and pressed against his chest.

"He..." Her teeth chattered from the cold. "He must be scared."

"I'll get you a towel." He eyed the dog in his arms and shook his head before disappearing up a stairwell.

Leanna scoped out the open floor plan of the cozy cottage, looking for signs of *crazy*. How crazy could he be? He'd just rescued her and Pepper, and Pepper already seemed to be quite attached to him. *He went into the water in a storm without an ounce of fear. Damn crazy.* It dawned on her that she'd done the same thing, but she knew *she* wasn't crazy. She'd had no choice. To her right was a small kitchen with expensive-looking light wood cabinets and fancy molding. A laptop sat open beside two neatly stacked notebooks on the shiny marble countertop. The screen was dark and she had an urge to touch a button and bring the laptop to life, but she didn't really want to know if there was something awful on there. He could have been watching porn for all she knew, although he hadn't checked her out once, even with her wet T-shirt and shorter-than-short jeans shorts. She couldn't decide if that was gentlemanly or creepy.

She shifted her thoughts away from the computer to the quaint breakfast nook to her left. Her eyes traveled past a little alcove with two closed doors and a set of stairs by the kitchen, to the white-walled living room. There was not a speck of clutter anywhere. A pair of flip-flops sat by the front door, perfectly lined up against the wall beside a pair of running shoes. She located the source of the campfire smell. A gorgeous two-story stone fireplace covered most of the wall adjacent to an oversized brown couch. There was a small stack of firewood in a metal holder beside the hearth. The cottage was surprisingly warm considering there wasn't a fire in the fireplace. Dark wood bookshelves ran the length of the far wall, from floor to ceiling, complete with a rolling ladder. The room was full of textures—a chenille blanket was folded neatly across the back of the couch, a thick, brown shag rug sat before the stone fireplace, and an intricately carved wooden table was placed before the couch. Leanna had a thing for textures, and right now she was texturing the beautiful hardwood with drops of water. She snagged a dishtowel from the kitchen counter as the man came back downstairs with Pepper cradled in his arms like a baby and wrapped in a big fluffy towel.

The possibility of him being crazy went out the door. *Crazy people don't carry dogs like babies.*

He shifted Pepper to one arm and handed her a fresh towel. "Here. I'm Kurt, by the way."

Pepper sat up in his arms, panting happily. *Show-off.*

"Thank you. I'm Leanna. That's Pepper." She tried to mop up the floor around her. Every swipe of the towel brought more drips from her sopping-wet clothing. "I'm sorry about this. For the mess. And my dog. And…" She frantically wiped the floor with the dishrag in one hand, using the fisted towel in the other

313

to scrub her clothes, trying desperately to stop the river that ran from her clothes to his no-longer-pristine floor. She lifted her gaze. He had a slightly amused smile on his very handsome face. She rose to her feet with a defeated sigh.

"I'm so sorry, and thank you for rescuing Pepper."

He glanced at his laptop, and that amused look quickly turned to one of pinched annoyance. His lips pressed into a tight line, and when he glanced at her again, it was with a brooding look, before stepping forward and closing his laptop.

"You should have"—Pepper barked in his ear; he closed his eyes and exhaled—"had the dog on a leash."

The dog.

"He hates it. He hates listening, leashes, lots of things." Pepper licked Kurt's cheek. "Except you, I guess."

Kurt winced and set Pepper on the floor. "Sit," he said in a deep, stern voice.

Pepper sat at his feet.

"How did you do that? He never listens."

He dried Pepper's feet with the towel, apparently ignoring the question.

"Labradoodle?"

You know dogs? She was intrigued by the dichotomy of him. He was sharp, brooding, and maybe even a little cold, yet Pepper followed him to the fireplace as if he were handing out doggy biscuits. Leanna couldn't help but notice the way Kurt's wet jeans hugged his ass. *His very hot ass.* He crouched before the fireplace, his shirt clinging tightly to his broad back, his sleeves hitched up above his bulging biceps, and she made out the outline of a tattoo on his upper arm.

"Yeah, Labradoodle. How'd you know? He looks like a wet mutt right now."

He shrugged, expertly fashioning a teepee of kindling, then starting a small fire. "Where's your place?" He slid an annoyed look at Pepper and shook his head.

"Um, my place?" she said, distracted as much by Pepper's obedience as by Kurt's tattoo. *What is that? A snake? Dragon?*

He looked at her with that amused glint in his eyes again. "House? Cottage? Campsite?"

"Oh, cottage. Sorry." She felt her cheeks flush. "It's about a mile and a half from here. Seaside? Do you know it? My parents own it. I'm just staying for the summer. I've known the other people in the community forever, and Pepper likes it there."

He looked back at the fireplace, the amusement in his expression replaced with seriousness. "Come over by the fire. Warm up."

She tossed the towels on the counter and joined him by the fire, shivering as she warmed her hands.

He kept his eyes trained on the fire.

"Did you drive here?" He picked up a log in one big hand and settled it on the fire.

"No. I biked."

"Biked?"

"I bike here a couple times each week with Pepper, but we usually go the other way down the beach. Pepper just took off this time. I left my bike by the public beach entrance."

315

His eyes slid to Pepper, then back to the fire. "I don't know Seaside, but let me change and I'll drive you home." He headed toward the stairs with Pepper on his heels. Kurt stopped and stared at the dog. Pepper panted for all he was worth. Kurt looked at Leanna, as if she could control the dog.

Fat chance. "He's not really an obedient pet." She shrugged.

Kurt picked up Pepper and brought him to Leanna. "Hold his collar."

Okay, then. She looped her finger in Pepper's collar and watched Kurt go into the kitchen and wipe the floor with the towel he'd given her. Then he wiped the counter with a sponge before disappearing into the alcove by the kitchen. He returned with a laundry basket, tossed the dirty towels in, and then returned the basket to where he'd found it and climbed the stairs.

"Guess he doesn't really like dirt...or dogs after all," she said to Pepper.

Pepper broke free and ran up the stairs after Kurt.

Leanna closed her eyes with a loud sigh.

Just shoot me now.

Slope of Love

(End of Sneak Peek)
To continue reading, be sure to pick up the next
LOVE IN BLOOM release:

READ, WRITE, LOVE, *The Remingtons*, Book Five
Love in Bloom series, Book Fourteen

317

LOVE IN BLOOM
A contemporary romance series
featuring several close-knit families
Check online retailers for availability

SNOW SISTERS

Sisters in Love
Sisters in Bloom
Sisters in White

THE BRADENS

Lovers at Heart
Destined for Love
Friendship on Fire
Sea of Love
Bursting with Love
Hearts at Play

THE REMINGTONS

Game of Love
Stroke of Love
Flames of Love
Slope of Love
Read, Write, Love

THE BRADENS (II)

Taken by Love
Fated for Love
Romancing my Love
Flirting with Love
Dreaming of Love
Crashing into Love

Acknowledgments

While researching this novel, I was blown away by the reality of competitive sports and how far athletes will push themselves. The courage and determination it takes to succeed among top athletes is far beyond what I ever imagined, and I don't think I'll ever look at competitive sports the same way again. A big thank you to Marlene Engel for her research efforts. You saved me oodles of time (yes, oodles).

I'd like to thank my readers for their support. I am inspired by your emails and social media messages, and I hope you will continue to reach out to me. I'd also like to thank the members of Team PIF and the staff of the World Literary Café—my friends, my comrades, and my sisters.

Tremendous gratitude goes to my editorial team, Kristen Weber, Penina Lopez, Jenna Bagnini, Juliette Hill, and Marlene Engel. Thank you for making my writing stronger and putting up with my million questions. Many thanks to my talented cover artist Natasha Brown, and Clare Ayala, a formatting genius.

My family encourages and supports me on a daily basis. I love you guys. Thank you.

Melissa Foster is a *New York Times* and *USA Today* bestselling and award-winning author. Her books have been recommended by *USA Today's* book blog, *Hagerstown* magazine, *The Patriot*, and several other print venues. She is the founder of the Women's Nest, a social and support community for women, and the World Literary Café. When she's not writing, Melissa helps authors navigate the publishing industry through her author training programs on Fostering Success. Melissa also hosts Aspiring Authors contests for children, and has painted and donated several murals to the Hospital for Sick Children in Washington, DC.

Visit Melissa on her website or chat with her on The Women's Nest or social media. Melissa enjoys discussing her books with book clubs and reader groups and welcomes an invitation to your event.

www.MelissaFoster.com

73182463R00198

Made in the USA
Middletown, DE
11 May 2018